HERO'S
TRIBUTE

HERO'S TRIBUTE

A Novel

GRAHAM GARRISON

Kregel
Publications

Hero's Tribute: A Novel

© 2009 by Graham Garrison

Published by Kregel Publications, a division of Kregel, Inc., P.O. Box 2607, Grand Rapids, MI 49501.

ISBN 978-0-8254-2685-8

Printed in the United States of America

09 10 11 12 13 / 5 4 3 2 1

To Katie,
for your inspiration,
encouragement, and love.

Prologue

There were no famous last words from Michael Gavin. Nothing like George Washington's "I die hard, but am not afraid to go," or General Lee's "Strike the tent." When Michael stopped talking late in the night, he simply held Lynn's hand. When he was too weak for even that, she took the weight of his pale left arm in hers and gently rubbed his palm. She watched his chest as it registered, however faintly, the struggle for each final breath, until she could barely tell if the battle was still joined. Finally, his eyes, once steely and strong, faded to a dull, dark black. Thirty-nine short years after his arrival, Michael Gavin, American hero, was gone.

It was a Monday.

Lynn Gavin sat by the bedside for fifteen minutes, with Michael's lifeless hand still in hers, before reaching for the phone to call his parents. She felt selfish for taking that time to mourn alone while the rest of the family was unaware of his passing, but she had lost this fight with cancer as much as he had.

That horrible day when Michael was diagnosed.

The trips to chemo.

The sleepless nights as Michael shivered against the disease.

The day-by-day erosion of the strongest man she'd ever known.

Lynn dampened her sobs to a persistent, ragged groan that seemed to settle deep in her chest, and she started thinking as a parent instead of simply a wife. Addy, their six-year-old, had slept over at Michael's parents' house last night, at Lynn's request. She hadn't wanted to expose Addy to the final throes of death, or to anything more than she had already experienced in the last few months. During Michael's cancer, Addy had seen more from this world than any child should have to. A six-year-old should be singing along to *Veggie Tales* and laughing at *Sesame Street*, not tiptoeing around IV lines and smelling of disinfectant after hugging her daddy.

Guilt crept in. Shouldn't everyone be here? Why did I want this time with him to myself? What kind of person am I?

She felt an impulse to ask forgiveness, as if Michael had died in the early morning hours only because there was an empty household for the first time in three weeks. She reached for the telephone on the nightstand and dialed Michael's parents.

Chapter 1

Betty Gavin answered on the second ring. Only one person would be calling this early.

"Mom, Michael's gone."

Betty had braced herself for those words, but they still struck like a hammer to the ribs. She stifled a reflexive sob. "Oh dear," she said, dropping the spoon she had been using to stir her tea. "I'll be right over."

"What should I do?" Lynn asked.

"You just sit tight, honey. I'll be right there." There was no correct protocol for times like these. Lynn had been so good about making the tough decisions during Michael's illness. When friends or family stopped by to offer prayers or a kind word, Lynn would be consoling and encouraging them by the time they left. Now it was time for others to lift Lynn up.

Betty had just enough presence of mind to tell Lynn not to worry; that they would figure out what to do next, together. Then she found herself at the front hall closet, fumbling with the buttons on her coat.

If things took a little longer with arrangements, then that'd be fine. Addy would be fine at their place until they sorted things out. There was always someone around the neighborhood to help in a pinch, and this was one of those pinches the entire town would come around for.

She covered her face with her hands, her body convulsing. "Oh Lord, oh Lord."

★ ★ ★

Paul Gavin didn't have the best hearing in the world after sixty-seven years, but he had a sixth sense about when his wife needed him. At the crack of dawn on Monday, he was where he always was, sitting on the front porch, sipping coffee and tying his shoes for a morning jog down the same street where he'd beaten the pavement for years. He was religious about his morning constitutional: five days a week, rain or shine, he'd circle the neighborhood cul-de-sacs and wave to the commuters embarking on their forty-five-minute commute from town to city. He didn't need to be at work at the local college until nine, the reward of tenure from teaching graduate-level business courses for more than a decade, following his service in the Army. This morning, instead of going for his jog, Paul opted to enjoy the sunrise and read the city paper. He'd make it up this evening, he told himself.

Paul didn't hear the phone ring, or see Betty collapse onto the sofa, but he had a feeling he was needed inside.

As Paul stood to his feet and folded the paper under his arm, the front door opened and Betty stepped out onto the porch, ashen faced, the key to the Volvo dangling absently from her hand. Paul instantly knew what had happened.

Tossing the paper onto the rocker, he reached for Betty, wrapped her in his arms, and hugged her for all he was worth.

"Could you—" Betty's words dissolved into a sob, and she tried to catch her breath.

"Don't worry, sweetie, I'll take care of Addy. You go."

After Betty drove away, Paul returned to the front porch and sat in his rocking chair to sort through his thoughts and make sense of everything that would now be required.

Phone calls to relatives and friends. A call to the newspaper to have an obit made so out-of-towners would know the details of the funeral. The family had made some of the arrangements in advance but still needed to finalize a few things with the funeral home.

Then there was the package he promised Michael he'd deliver.

A promise was a promise.

Analyzing decisions was Paul's way of getting through tough times. Like Michael, he had a knack for remaining calm under duress, making snap decisions that others found too difficult or too emotional. But even now, as he sat in his rocking chair ticking off the preparations to make before saying good-bye to his son, his eyes retreated to a certain spot on the front lawn. The clearer the green became, the less he thought about the arrangements, and the more he walked through memories of Michael's childhood.

He envisioned a ten-year-old boy with dirty knees, a Braves cap, and a big, broad grin on his face, winding up to toss the baseball back. Or sprinting for all he was worth toward the far corner, football helmet askew and arms outstretched for "just one more pass, Dad, before we head in."

Paul stopped his mental checklist and just stared at the grass.

Word traveled fast in a town like Talking Creek, with or without cell phones. Granted, cell phone towers had popped up in this corner of northwest Georgia like in every other part of the country, and a cell phone company had put a store over on Main Street five years ago, but it's not like the residents needed all that. You could shout from one end of Main Street to the other and someone could easily hear you, it was so small. And with a population of just under six thousand, everybody knew everybody, and probably knew everybody's relatives, too. Only about a thousand of those folks came and went, those being out-of-town students of Tributary University, the local liberal arts college.

The west end of Main started with a hamburger joint and a pizza place, then proceeded through town, passing two banks, the grocery store, a busy café, the drug store, a combination book and coffee shop, the barber shop, hair stylist, and post office. On the east side, the town's two big churches, United Methodist and First Baptist, sat on opposite sides of the street, close enough for parishioners to wave to one another before walking into their respective Sunday services.

Talking Creek's claim to fame was the annual fall firemen's parade. As home to one of the finest volunteer fire departments in the state—and possibly the entire Southeast—the town rolled out its big red engines every year and invited towns near and far to bring theirs too.

Gene Woods, one of Talking Creek's volunteer firemen, lived three streets down from Paul and Betty in the town's lone subdivision. Like Paul, he was a creature of habit. Up at the same time every morning, he showered, put on a dress shirt and tie, brewed a cup of black coffee, read the paper, and hit the road at 6:30 sharp for his job at the local power plant. Gene's routine coincided with Paul's run, and the two usually exchanged waves halfway between their two homes. Today, however, Gene noticed that Paul wasn't running.

Gene knew Michael, and about his fight with cancer. Well, everybody in Talking Creek knew Michael. Many remembered him as the kid who'd broken all the state passing records in high school. Others still half-expected to see him hiking the Georgia mountain trails with those kids from the foster care retreat. Everyone knew what he'd done in the war; about the big, shiny medal he'd earned, and how quiet he'd been about it when he returned.

Gene's wife, Mary, was in Betty's prayer group at the Methodist church, and she had relayed Betty's prayer concerns as Michael's cancer had worsened. Each time Mary brought bad news, Gene would just shake his head. How could a strong kid like that get beat by something that starts so small? The power and frailty of the human body never ceased to amaze Gene. How in the world could a person live on pizza, beer, and cigarettes all their life and make it to eighty, while some middle-aged marathon runner has a heart attack at fifty? Or what about some stupid kid who drives drunk as a skunk and crashes head-on into a Suburban. He survives, with a few scratches and a bump on his head, but the family in the SUV doesn't? And how can something no bigger than a speck when it starts cut down a tree trunk like Michael? It just didn't make any sense.

Gene slowed as he neared the Gavins' property. To most folks, spotting Paul on the front porch wouldn't be cause for concern, but Gene's heart sank. He knew his friend should be getting his laps in before work. Guys like Paul and Gene didn't mess with their routine just for the heck of it. Maybe the polite thing to do would have been to keep on driving and let Paul be; but that didn't sit right with Gene, and he was in the business of doing the right thing. He pulled his Dodge Ram into the driveway and hopped out.

Paul and Gene were part of a close-knit fraternity. Both were combat veterans: Paul in the Army, Gene as a Marine sergeant. Their rival service loyalties elicited jabs and good-natured jokes between the two, but not today.

Paul stood and nodded as Gene got out of his truck. Gene took three steps down the walkway and paused. What should he say? He was always at a loss for words at times like these. He clenched his right fist, frustrated at his lack of words. Then it hit him. He pivoted slightly toward Paul and in a crisp, forward motion, lifted his right hand to his temple.

Paul returned the salute.

"This town won't ever forget your boy," he said.

Ten minutes later, Gene was doing what he always did in a crisis: taking charge. He walked into the fire station storage room and grabbed Big Glory, the biggest American flag you've ever seen. Then, climbing the steps of the tallest landmark in Talking Creek, the fire tower they used for drills, he unfurled the flag and attached it to the brass hooks along the edge of the parapet. It seemed the right thing to do.

"Hey Gene, what in the world are you doing?" It was one of the paramedics on shift, looking up from the ground below. "Parade ain't for another two weeks."

Gene mulled over what to say. "You're needed at the younger Gavins."

"Oh."

Gene watched as his words sank in.

"Okay, we're on our way."

After securing the flag at half mast, Gene went down to the dispatch room and called the chief of police.

"What's up, Gene, is there a fire?" a groggy Heath Jackson muttered into the phone. He wasn't due at the police station until three cups of coffee from now.

"No, no fire," Gene said. "Paul's son passed away this morning."

"Oh, I hate to hear that, Gene."

"Yeah, listen, you think you should send some of your boys down to the house to make sure everything's all right?"

"Consider it done. Thanks for letting me know."

★   ★   ★

A few miles away, Betty and Lynn tried to collect themselves. The shock was wearing off, but numbness crept in. That's when Betty decided to call the funeral home to come and take Michael, and they received the first of many surprises from the town of Talking Creek.

"Yes, ma'am, the police department asked permission to handle your request," the funeral home receptionist said. "And we're really very, very sorry."

She probably shouldn't have been, but Betty was taken aback at how fast word had traveled. "Thank you," she managed. "When do you think they will get here?"

"Ma'am, they should be there already."

Skeptically, Betty looked out the window. Sure enough, parked by the fence was an ambulance, flanked by two squad cars. By the time Betty and Lynn walked out the front door, two more police cars had arrived. Police Sergeant Mark Lovejoy met them halfway, head slightly bowed. Betty didn't bother asking him how they knew.

"We're here to escort Michael," Lovejoy said.

★   ★   ★

The ambulance and police procession through downtown to the funeral home proved more effective than any newspaper headline. One glance at the convoy set off a firestorm of discussion up and down Main Street.

Once the people who knew—mainly Gene walking into Reese's Café for his second morning coffee—gave the news to a few of the town's movers and shakers, word spread quickly to shops like Smith's Pharmacy, into the faculty offices of the university, and among parents in the carpool lane at the elementary and middle schools.

Talking Creek High School assistant principal Gus Hilliard caught wind of Michael's passing from the front office workers. As Sue Holton was about to press the talk button on the school microphone for the daily announcements, Gus gently tapped her shoulder.

"I'll take this one," he said.

Gus never did the announcements. He hated public speaking. He did most of his talking behind closed doors, lecturing kids busted for chewing gum in class or running amok on school property. He was good at cracking skulls without touching them; just forcing the fear of God into misfits with his deep voice, broad shoulders, and harsh scowl.

The front office folks immediately hushed their conversations when Gus wrapped his knuckles around the microphone.

"This is Assistant Principal Hilliard," he began. "We'll be doing announcements differently today. Before we say the Pledge of Allegiance, I want to have a . . . a . . . moment of silence."

The front office ladies let out a sigh, thankful he hadn't said "moment of prayer." Someone no doubt would have raised a fuss at the next school board meeting.

"And if you want to pray," Gus continued, "well go ahead and do that too. And if anyone is offended by that . . . well, they can come and talk to me about it."

Eyes rolled behind his back.

"A former Talking Creek High student died this morning. Michael Gavin. If you didn't know him—and that's probably just one or two of you—you missed out on knowing a good man and a true hero. He did a lot for this community, and a lot for this country, and we here at Talking Creek High are all going to miss him. Please take a moment or two now to remember him."

★   ★   ★

Ralph Frink, owner of Southern Décor, got the news around lunchtime from one of his production managers. Southern Décor, a manufacturer of outdoor decorations, was Talking Creek's largest employer, outside of Tributary University. Yesterday, the company had put the finishing touches on some Christmas decorations for a central Alabama town, and the production line was up and running. Frink didn't have to think too hard about this one. He called a company-wide meeting in the plant, asked for a vote, and it was unanimous. The next day, Southern Décor would shift the line over to making large yellow ribbons and American flag decorations to wrap around every sign and streetlight from here to the county line. He'd foot the bill.

The churches geared up early. Mondays were Bible study days at both the Methodist and Baptist churches, and two group leaders who did their grocery shopping in the morning before class bumped into each other in the produce section, like they always did. Joanne Reed, a lifelong Methodist and friend of Lynn's and Michael's, was noticeably shaken.

Naturally, Liz Montgomery was concerned. She gave Joanne a warm hug and asked her what was wrong. When Joanne told her about Michael and Lynn, Liz's eyes welled with tears. Then she got determined.

"Call your group leaders, and I'll call mine, and we'll figure out what to do." By the afternoon, there wasn't a cold oven in the city limits.

Smith's Pharmacy ran out of Hallmark cards by 3 p.m. The first to go were condolences. Then encouragement. Then thank you cards; because by that point the only other cards in the racks said "Happy Birthday" or "It's a girl."

Mondays were also soccer days at Glenn Park. Kids walked out of the elementary school with their cleats and shin guards in hand, down the hill to Glenn Park and over to the soccer fields. The parents pulled up a few minutes before game time, helped their kids into uniforms, and then plopped lawn chairs on the sidelines to catch up on the latest news while cheering on a mass of children circling a ball for an hour.

The games couldn't start without the national anthem. A Boy Scout or Cub Scout from one team would be in charge of raising the flag up the pole at the edge of the field while everyone saluted. Jesse Blackmon, a Tenderfoot, and by far the smallest kid on his team, got the assignment this time. His coach whispered something in his ear, and although he was a little confused by the request, Jesse dashed to the flagpole and, as everyone began singing, did exactly what his coach had told him to do. He raised it to half-staff.

★   ★   ★

Talking Creek football coach Bud Lawler didn't let the news pass his team by. The current Eagles were a far cry from the glory days of Michael's run at quarterback. Coach Lawler would know that better than anyone else; he'd been a tight end on those teams. He'd been back at his alma mater for seven years now, and was trying to rekindle some of the old magic. His resume included five winning seasons and two playoff berths, largely because of the Summers boys: Tripp, Taylor, and Travis. None of the three was very big, or had an arm like Michael's, but man, could those kids run. A few brave souls in town had even suggested—whispered is more like it—that they were as fast, if not faster, than Michael. During their respective senior years, Tripp, Taylor, and Travis had each led the county in rushing. Times had been good again for the Eagles with the Summers boys in school. During Taylor's senior year, they'd even found themselves in the Georgia Dome for a semifinal game against powerhouse Buford. But that was three years ago, and now, in order to get the "Summers over" tag off his back, Coach Lawler needed to do something with this latest crop of boys.

The Eagles were 3–1 and preparing for their first regional game, against archrival Calhoun, which was ranked fifth in the state and had a three-game winning streak going against Talking Creek. A win against Calhoun and the Eagles would be in the driver's seat of Region 5-A. A loss, and they'd be right back in the middle of the pack, where they'd been since the Summers boys graduated.

Fifty teenagers in blue and gold trotted out of the fieldhouse and onto the practice field across from Grady Stadium. It used to be that Talking Creek squads practiced on the stadium field, but seeing as how everybody else had a practice field for practice and a playing field for playing, Talking Creek boosters had chipped in to pay for some nearby brush to be cleared and a field to be readied. The team broke off into offensive and defensive squads. Coach Lawler limped out of the fieldhouse a minute later, game plan in hand and a scowl on his face.

"Boys, hats off and huddle up," he said. The Eagles squeezed together amid sounds of chinstraps unsnapping and helmets coming off. "You know this week's a big week with Calhoun. Well, it just got a lot bigger."

He paused, checking to make sure he had everyone's attention. "Michael Gavin died this morning. He put all those trophies in our gym. He brought a lot of great memories to this town, and now it's our turn to make some more memories."

"On Friday, that place"—he pointed behind his shoulder to Grady Stadium—"is going to be packed tighter than a can of sardines. And it ain't just 'cuz we're playing big, bad Calhoun. It ain't 'cuz they've whipped us the last three years and their blood is up; and it ain't 'cuz they want to shut you seniors out a fourth and final time." He pointed to his two team captains.

"It's 'cuz a lot of people are going to come to the game to remember what Michael Gavin did on that field years ago. And you know what? We're gonna give them something to remember him by! So, you ain't just playin' for yourselves or for this team this week. It's bigger than that. We need to do him proud."

Chapter 2

Wes Watkins hated vending machines.

He walked into the break room late Monday afternoon with spare change and a Snickers craving, and five minutes later he was still there with both. First off, his two quarters and a nickel didn't work. One quarter kept funneling back out the change slot. So he switched the quarter for two dimes and a nickel from the company change jar, which was on the microwave for just such an emergency. Well, it worked, but instead of the Snickers spiraling off the rack and into the chute, the wrapper got pinned to the side.

One would think, after decades of perfecting vending machine technology, that someone would have been smart enough to develop a system that eliminated these kinds of mishaps. Maybe they have. But Wes's workplace was years behind those innovations, and this was a vending machine that other snack machines would probably call Old Timer.

The *North Georgia News* was not a beacon of ingenuity. The *News* published daily to a circulation of just under thirty thousand. The *News* covered Talking Creek and a good chunk of the North Georgia mountain communities. The editorial content was similar to any other small paper: school board meetings, wedding announcements, Rotary club briefs, obits, and a classifieds section that could get you a John Deere tractor and a talking parrot in one phone call.

What the *News* covered best, and the reason why Wes was doing time there, was local sports. The sports department was bloated compared to the rest of the staff. They had three—count 'em, three—reporters. Nester Jacobs covered Tributary U. athletics and some general assignment stuff. Scott Friedman's beat was the surrounding county schools. Wes had the so-called plum assignment of the group, not because of his résumé, but mainly because no one else wanted it. When the previous reporter had quit for a job in Pensacola, and Scott and Nester had said no thanks, they needed a warm body to cover the mighty Talking Creek Eagles.

Wes had joined the sports desk last June with the ink still wet on his college diploma. Because school was already out, he had zilch to cover, aside from the occasional fishing tournament at Carter's Lake or a kids' basketball camp. So he sat around writing about how little Anne Williams had won the free throw shooting contest at the twelve-and-under basketball camp. They called it "community journalism." Wes called it a waste of time.

Working at a community paper like the *News* wasn't all bad. Talking Creek was a fifty-minute drive from the Atlanta Braves, and an hour and a half from the University of Georgia in Athens, his alma mater. Wes often wished he'd stayed there and slept in class long enough to earn a master's in history or political science; but he was already up to his neck in student loans, so he'd taken the small town reporting job.

Whenever Lewis Banner, the sports editor, was in a generous mood and offered press passes to the Braves, Wes jumped at the chance to get out of town. Clips of bigger stories were what got reporters out of podunks like Talking Creek to places like Birmingham or Nashville, or beyond. When he would eventually take a book full of his clips for a job interview at a bigger paper, little Anne's basketball camp story wouldn't be in there.

Wes negotiated the vending machine into giving him the Snickers bar. "Come on!" He kicked its side twice, because he didn't have the biceps to shake it. Finally, the Snickers dropped. Wes needed the spike in blood sugar to keep his levels between 80 and 120, but he still eyed the candy bar warily, knowing it wouldn't help with the extra pounds that were showing up around his waist, or the slight double chin that had started in college but was lately making some serious gains. Staying on track with his diet was a more serious matter for him than for most people, but he

still struggled with it. Healthy snacks hadn't made their way to the *News'*
break room, so he'd have to make do with what little protein there was in
peanuts and chocolate.

"Defacing *News* property, Watkins?" Keith Starks's voice reverber-
ated off the tile floor. A killer whale blowing water out of its airhole, Wes
thought. Starks looked the part, too, with a shiny bald head and a ring of
blubber bulging beneath his unpressed dress shirt and over his belt. He
wasn't exactly the spitting image of respectability, but he was the boss.

"It wouldn't give me my Snickers bar," Wes said sheepishly, tucking his
shirt back in and pressing down on the stubborn shock of brown hair at
the back of his head. He suddenly felt the need to get his wavy hair cut for
professional appearances.

"Well then, instead of destroying the machine and ruining it for the
entire office, why not leave a note and let Roy take care of it." Roy was the
janitor. He usually just shook the machine, took the note off, and kept
the snacks for himself.

"I'll remember that next time, sorry."

Starks stood, arms folded, looking at Wes like he was judging the sincerity of the answer. He seemed to smell it: Wes didn't want to be here.

"How's Coach Lawler these days?" Starks asked, checking up on Wes's
beat.

Coach Lawler loved to rile his players by using articles from the *News*.
He would say disparaging things about his players and then turn around
and say that Wes had misquoted him. The first time he'd pulled that trick,
Wes had had to answer to Starks. As the managing editor, Starks ran
interference for the publisher, who spent his time at his lake house instead
of at his newspaper or his tire factory in the next town.

Starks seemed to enjoy the double duty of being the de facto publisher—with all the local politics that went with that role—coupled with
having authority over what was said in the local newspaper. When he'd
called Wes into his office to discuss the article, Wes had pulled out his digital recorder and began to search for the Coach Lawler interview in question, only to be waved off.

"I don't want to get into pointing any fingers," Starks had said. When Wes held up the recorder again, Starks had shaken his head, as if he didn't want to hear it. "Just be a little careful with what he says, no matter what he says."

So Wes had taken to paraphrasing Lawler, which kept Starks off his back for directly quoting the coach when he poor-mouthed his team, and which continued to give Coach Lawler fodder to motivate his team. Wes would see his stories pinned up on Lawler's "Board of Doubters."

"Nothing new to report," Wes said. "He's been pretty good with interviews, I just have to be at his office at a certain time or he's in the weight room lifting."

"That's a sight now isn't it? Bud, the old tight end, pumping iron like a senior trying to impress the girls in gym class." Starks chuckled. He enjoyed reminding the news staff that he knew everyone of importance in town on a first-name basis. "Bud lives for adrenaline. He'll sit up for hours at night trying to come up with the next great speech to fire up the troops."

"Yeah, he can get into it," Wes said. "He really focuses on the off-season conditioning, I hear."

"Well, he's reined it in, like every other coach. Too many kids today playing video games in air conditioning; not enough time outside. If they had practice like we did back in our day, they'd be dropping like flies." It took all of Wes's willpower not to glance at Starks's midsection.

"I guess they would."

Starks checked his watch. It was a few minutes past five o'clock, about thirty minutes later than Starks usually stayed in the office. "What do your assignments look like?"

"I called the Calhoun coach for quotes, and I'll have a story on that. I was planning on going out to Talking Creek's practice tomorrow to do a player feature for Wednesday."

"Good, good," Starks said impatiently. "Always look for the stories about people's kids. That's what we do."

Wes nodded.

"Got a few minutes? Let's go to my office."

Only the publisher and managing editor had an office at the *News*. Everyone else was assigned workstations in cubicles. Starks probably liked it that way, because it cut down on closed doors and gossip rings while he was there. Most of the reporters, and especially the editors, hated it. It didn't really bother Wes, who was out doing interviews and usually back in the office around the time that Starks and the publisher left.

Starks's office was a case study in organized chaos. Half his desk was immaculate, showing off pictures of himself and the mayor of Talking Creek, the president of Tributary University, and a congressman. The other half of his desk was a mountain of assorted paperwork and files. A huge, outdated computer monitor took up a side table, and the keyboard was piled under more papers inside the pullout shelf. A bookshelf in the left corner displayed pictures of his kids and a wife who had seen better years. Wes wondered what kind of father he was, then let the thought pass with a shiver.

Starks had two seats in his office—a plush black leather chair, well worn on the bottom, that he called home eight hours a day, and a small maroon-colored chair that he'd probably stolen from a local church. On the maroon seat was an envelope.

"Take a seat," he said, closing the door. "You heard the news?"

"About?" They were a newspaper, there was a lot of news, even in Talking Creek.

"Michael Gavin died this morning."

Wes gave a quizzical look, as if the name was supposed to mean something. Apparently it did to Starks. "Did you know him?"

Wes shook his head no.

"Great guy," he said. "Played ball at TCHS with Coach Lawler, was an All-American his senior year, and then played at the University of Georgia. Could have been great there if he'd gotten the chance. Won the Medal of Honor, came back and started a weekend retreat for foster kids. He spoke at a lot of the town's Memorial Day celebrations. Knew him well."

There he went again, name dropping.

"Michael's father, Paul, stopped by today and gave this to me, along with some information for Michael's obit." He pointed to the envelope.

"Is this for a sports story?" Wes asked.

"Not exactly."

"I thought Gary did obits."

"He does," Starks said. "And he'll be doing the obit on Michael for Tuesday's edition. This is something different." He handed Wes an envelope cutter. "I've already talked with Lewis, and he's okay with it."

"With what?" Wes asked.

"Go ahead and open it. For the next week, you're going to have a new assignment."

"New assignment?" Wes didn't like the sound of that.

"Yeah," Starks said. "Something wrong?"

"No, it's just that it's the Talking Creek–Calhoun game."

"Yep, and we're going to have Scott cover it."

"Oh."

There went covering the only game worth a lick on his beat. Wes took that as a cue to open the envelope. Inside was a single sheet of paper with names and numbers. Taped to it was a smaller white envelope. Surprisingly, his own name was written on it.

Wes sliced the envelope and took out a handwritten letter addressed to him.

Wes:

Before I write anything else, I want to apologize. You're probably going to hate me for what I'm about to request, but there wasn't anyone else that I could have asked, and I think you'll figure out why.

My name is Michael Gavin, and a few short months after I write this, I'm probably going to die. I've got a type of cancer that won't quit, and after extensive chemotherapy and other treatments, it's only grown worse. So I guess you could consider this one of my last requests.

Everyone in Talking Creek knows me. Growing up here and then returning to work and live, it's hard not to be known in a town like this. I'm fine with that, but something I can't have is everyone going around during my funeral saying how great a person I was.

That's where you come in. I've read your articles in the News and I like your style. Bet you'll go far. I also know from talking with Keith that you went to Georgia.

Wes looked at Starks. "What's this all about?"
"Keep reading."

As a reporter, I know it's your job to ask questions that other folks wouldn't, and the journalists who seem to go far are the ones who ask the toughest questions. You'll get your shot here. Enclosed is a starter for contacting people who knew me. Some liked me. Some didn't. And I think that's the point.

I don't want this town going up to the pulpit and spitting out pleasantries about my life. That seems standard practice, like somehow when you croak you all of a sudden become an unblemished person. Well, as you'll find out, I was anything but. I want you to have an open door to the people in my life, the good and the bad, the successes and the mistakes. If my life was worth what I hope it was, then it will probably show as much through the people I hurt as the people I loved. They were often the same folks.

Wes, I want you to give my eulogy. You, and only you.
Sincerely,
Michael Gavin

Wes folded the paper and put it back in the envelope. "I can't do this."
"Sure you can," Starks said, quick to his pitch. "Look, like I said, for the next week you have a new assignment. You're also going to get to write

the story on Michael for Sunday's paper. Front page and a special section. I don't have to tell you that's pretty big apples. You can make your own hours, talk to whoever you want. Just don't embarrass me, all right?"

"Mr. Starks, will all due respect, you've got to be kidding."

Starks didn't even blush. Ordinarily a remark like that would have gotten Wes a tongue-lashing, but Starks seemed to expect the remark. He nodded for Wes to continue.

"Write the story on Gavin, fine, but give his eulogy? That's—"

"Crazy?"

"Well, yeah."

"I thought so too. When Mike came in here and talked to me about this at the beginning of the fall, I tried to talk him out of it. If he wanted to have one big sit-down interview, I was all for that. But some publicity stunt just for his funeral? No way. We'd be teetering the line between making news and becoming it. We're not the *New York Times*, though, Wes. We're the *North Georgia News*. If handled correctly, and I'm counting on you to handle this correctly, it'll be a big boost for us. The ball is moving on that special section for Sunday's paper. A lot of local merchants want a part in it."

"Who else knows about this?" Wes asked.

"Mike assured me he had already talked to his family about it and they agreed . . . albeit somewhat reluctantly."

"So I don't have a choice in this?"

Starks shifted in his chair. "Not really, no."

"Okay then, I guess I'm in," Wes said as diplomatically as he could.

"That's good to hear. So here's your 'catch' on this assignment."

Wes sat back in his chair, arms folded, ready to receive the bad news. "This is going to be a sensitive subject. Blessed by Michael Gavin or not, I want to be updated on your progress. Constantly."

"So what if I find something embarrassing? Like what if he was part of some scandal and that's why he wanted me to do this?"

"You run it by me, of course," Starks said evenly. "I'm your editor after all."

"So I have free rein to do the reporting?"

"Yes, as long as you run it by me."

"But what if I get some lead and you're not in the office? For what you're asking, I don't have a lot of time to work with here."

Starks's face soured. "I doubt that'll be the case, but if it'll make you feel any better, then fine. Do your job and report back to me once a day, unless you've got something juicy."

By the smallest of margins, the leash had slackened.

"Why don't you get with Lewis and talk about where to start. Make sure Scott knows who to talk to for TCHS–Calhoun," Starks said.

★   ★   ★

Lewis Banner was hunched over his desk eyeballing a layout on his computer when Wes interrupted him. "Starks has me on a special assignment for this week," Wes said, handing Lewis the one-page sheet with names.

Lewis nodded. "He told me earlier about pulling you off your beat." His thick drawl, coupled with his shabby appearance, probably classified him as a hick to outside observers. But he was college-scholarship sharp, just not real-world motivated to climb the career ladder out of his local paper's sports desk. "I think I can still get you at the game writin' a column or something. We'll see."

"So help me out then," Wes said. "Have you heard of Michael Gavin?"

"Of course," Lewis said. "Think we did an article on some run or walk in his honor at the high school track beginning of summer. Was a heck of a blocker in college for a conference championship team at UGA, back when I was entering middle school. Guy sounds like he was Chuck Norris on steroids after he graduated college."

"That's what I've been gathering," Wes said. "Problem is, nobody is that good."

"Well, first of all, he's a Bulldog, so I like him already. And I heard them special forces guys can nail a terrorist at four hundred yards with three bullets to the pupil before ya can say aim!"

"So where should I start?" Wes asked.

"Well, you know a coupla names on the list already."

Included on the list were Coach Lawler, and former UGA coach Earl Bishop, whom Wes had interviewed once or twice in Athens for the school paper.

Lewis slid a pile of printouts across his desk. "Copied these from what we're using for the obit. For more, check the archives," Lewis said, pointing to a Post-it note with specific dates. "And for interviews, try Reese's Café tomorrow at noon. Coach Lawler will be there. Bunch of old timers tellin' war stories—football, I mean. They'll happily give you everything you need to know about his playing days, I'd betcha."

Wes took the notes, but hesitated.

"So, you think you'll get me a column for the game then, at least?"

"I'll see what I can do," Lewis said. Wes knew that meant to just leave it be. "Maybe this Gavin profile will be something the AP can pick up. I'll make a call or two and see if someone catches it on the AP newswire."

Chapter 3

The archives had a microfiche and every copy of the *News* from 1958 to the present. Wes took a deep breath, stretched his arms, and inched his chair up to the table.

Michael's sheet from the envelope provided sources, but as Wes glanced at a few of the names, he realized they weren't a good starting point. There were only names and numbers, no descriptions. He frowned. Cold calls were for salesmen, not reporters. Wes opted instead to try his luck with the newspaper clippings, in hopes of matching sources with the names on the sheet. He also planned to use previous articles about Michael as the framework for his piece.

Michael's high school exploits were first on the list, so Wes pulled up the fall editions. The number of stories teetered on obscene. It took a good half hour to sift through Michael's freshman and sophomore years. His junior and senior clips would take all night if Wes wanted to hit every story. He skimmed through them and scribbled notes.

"Hey, Wes." Scott Friedman's head craned into the archive room, the rest of his lean body masked by the wall. His face looked like a vulture's, long and jagged at the chin and nose. Folks around the office called him Big Bird, but not to his face. He'd probably cry if he found out that was his nickname, or that he had a nickname.

"Hey Scott, what's up?" Wes said.

"Busy with a new beat I see." His inflection was like a poke to the ribs. Scott took things way too personally. He lived for his beat, but any time he had to do an assignment that in his mind someone else should be covering, watch out. Scott liked his universe tidy and his work predictable. Covering two beats for one week? That was chaos. And judging from his rigid jaw, he blamed Wes.

Not that Wes minded Scott's scorn this time. If anything, this assignment restructuring was payback for a stunt Scott had pulled during Wes's first few months at the paper. One day, he'd pleaded for Wes, cub reporter and new guy at the sports desk, to join him for a double byline on a monumental series for the sports section.

"Steroids," he said.

Wes wasn't that naive. "Here? In Talking Creek?"

"Yeah," he said in that irritating, raspy voice. "We talk to all of the coaches about performance enhancing drugs. I'm sure they know players who have done them. It'll be great."

And it'd be a great way for Wes to introduce himself to his new beat. "Hello, I'm Wes Watkins, new beat writer for the *News*. You got kids on 'roids?" Unfortunately, Lewis gave Scott the green light on the project, with Wes reluctantly attached. Two weeks later, Scott dumped it all on Wes.

"It's just not working out," Scott said. "My coaches won't talk to me. I kind of feel uncomfortable talking to them about it."

Your idea, you moron, Wes wanted to say.

"I just don't have the time to do it, with all the schools I have to cover. Why don't you finish it up for me?"

Wes had about punched him. He'd about punched Lewis too, when he made him finish Scott's stupid story. Wes crafted it into the most boring, nonconfrontational story about steroids in the history of muckraking. It didn't even get a grunt from Starks. Scott's grand idea faded into obscurity, and Wes vowed never to help the guy out again. Now, the tables had turned.

"Yeah, thanks for taking Talking Creek," Wes said, all smiles. "Looks like they're going to have me busy with this funeral thing."

"Well, you already missed a fire-and-brimstone speech from Bud," he said.

"Oh, yeah?"

"I went by their practice real quick. Coach Lawler put it into 'em. Said they were playing for the town and for Michael Gavin as much as they were playing just to beat Calhoun. Then he made 'em go full pads and knock the snot out of each other. He installed the Oklahoma drill. I think two of his linemen are out for the game already—one of which Coach Lawler himself got down in a three-point stance and drove into the ground after the poor guy missed a block. There may not be a player left by the time he's done with his kamikaze act. He watches too many war movies."

"I wouldn't disagree with that."

"I just got too much to do," Scott said. "Had a story I was gonna write and now I can't even get quotes for it. Gotta write this Talking Creek thing, then hope the Jasper coach returns my calls and isn't mad I didn't make his practice. There's just too much to do, you know?"

"I know," Wes said. He envisioned Lewis taking bets on what day Scott would cry. Scott barely made deadlines in Talking Creek. The man averaged one mental breakdown per sporting season, calling Lewis ten minutes till deadline and crying like a baby because he couldn't think of a lead.

"Well, good luck with that," Wes clucked.

"Thanks."

Wes spent another hour in the archive room, scribbling notes on Michael's life in print. His press clippings dried up considerably in college. As Wes trudged through AP stories about Georgia football, maybe there'd be a brief update at the bottom of the article. The *News* staff had highlighted Michael's name, in an effort to make the report more local, but he didn't show up much until his senior year.

Apparently, Michael had signed with Georgia as one of the top prospects in the state, but he didn't play until his sophomore year, and then he suffered a season-ending injury. Somehow, he resurfaced as a fullback. How does a top prep quarterback reinvent himself as a fullback? And why? Why would a coach convert a quarterback into a fullback; a passer into a blocker? Wes filed those away as questions to ask.

The *News* had done a feature on Michael's going to war in the First Gulf War. But it chronicled more about his football days than his Army duty. Considering they'd squeezed a mere two quotes out of Michael for the article, Wes was surprised they made it as long as they did. Michael wasn't much of a talker after college.

His Medal of Honor ceremony came next chronologically. Wes noticed that they had used a *News* reporter's byline instead of the AP for the story about the ceremony. That must have been a huge deal for the reporter, to go up all the way to Washington, D.C., and attend a press conference at the White House. Must have felt like a small fish in a big pond. It was a front-page article for almost any paper in the country; in Talking Creek, it was inflated into two full-blown articles on Michael Gavin and the ceremony, along with a rather dull opinion column, Wes thought, on how people should be more respectful to military vets.

Wes sped through the article, but paused at Michael's photo from the ceremony. His eyes were distant, impassive. His body may have been in the room, but his mind wasn't. Was he having some kind of flashback? Regret?

Included in the archived edition of the *News* was the full medal citation. Wes skimmed the highlights.

> For conspicuous gallantry and intrepidity at the risk of his life above and beyond the call of duty:
>
> Captain Michael Gavin distinguished himself by acts of gallantry and intrepidity above and beyond the call of duty in action with an armed enemy in southern Baghdad . . . On that day, Captain Gavin's company was part of a battalion-wide sweep of the southern portion of the city to locate and engage insurgents firing on forward operating base McDonald . . . Captain Gavin's front detachment was ambushed with IEDs on the road into the city. Four men were killed, including two in Captain Gavin's transport vehicle. Captain Gavin and one other soldier were wounded from the blast, and pinned down . . . The enemy held key positions to slow a counterattack from Captain Gavin's supporting platoons . . .

Captain Gavin, with the use of hand grenades, an M16 and a handgun,
rushed the enemy stronghold single-handedly . . .

Wes zoomed in on Michael's face again. Sadness. Infinite sadness. His
cheeks were taut. His eyes, Wes was convinced, were swollen from crying,
but had been powdered with makeup for the bright lights of the White
House ceremony. Had no one else seen this? Michael said the right things.
He praised the National Guard, his president, and especially the men in
his company. He said heartfelt things about the men who had died during
the attack. He said nothing of himself. He made no reference to besting
his enemies—or to the country that was honoring him, for that matter.
Perhaps he understood the lightning rod he possessed.

For Michael's civilian life, Wes moved from the cumbersome microfiche
to a computer. Michael Gavin's name showed up thirty-three times in the
search engine, mostly in community service, Memorial Day speeches, or
other local functions. His fight with cancer was chronicled in a syrup-
laden article about a charity race he and his family had run over the summer. He was diagnosed more than a year ago, went through an extremely
aggressive treatment program, and thought he'd beaten it into remission
as of press time for the article. Obviously, that hadn't been the case.

Wes scanned the reports of Michael's charity work. Why hadn't he ever
gone into politics, even locally? Football star, war hero, community ser-
vant. It seemed like as good a résumé as any. Instead, he had wasted that
clout on entertaining foster kids during weekends and hosting Georgia
legislators who needed a photo op with someone other than a lobbyist.
Michael didn't need a political party or a stump speech; he probably could
have just shown up and won. But he hadn't.

Wes made a note to visit the courthouse to see if Michael had a criminal record. It didn't add up with the clips he was collecting; but then
again, neither did having a stranger give your eulogy.

The articles pieced together at least an outline of the man. Wes didn't
need much to start a good story, really. He'd taken a college course on
investigative reporting, in which the professor had told a story about a

big-shot reporter, who, after covering the White House for years, was recalled to his paper's New York City office and told he'd be writing about the city's trash problems as his new beat. Apparently, the new managing editor didn't like him very much. Undeterred, the reporter spent months snooping around every square inch of waste in the city, and reemerged with an award-winning series. Pulitzer Prize–winning stuff out of garbage.

Michael's story wasn't Pulitzer material, but it was the biggest story in Talking Creek. At worst, Wes would have a front-page clip and—if he worked it right—an AP article. But there were no guarantees the AP would pick up his story or that Starks would allow it to happen. And there were no guarantees he'd get to write the story he wanted to write anyway, judging from Starks's reaction and oversight. It dampened the potential, but only somewhat. There were newsworthy angles from a feature perspective: star QB, war hero, philanthropist. A man revered for having the golden touch. In today's society, if you could throw a perfect spiral or a 100-mph fastball, make deals under the table or star in a few movies, people were apt to ignore your flaws. But Michael apparently didn't want his flaws ignored. He had invited Wes to dig. Open season on his life. Easy for him to ask; he wouldn't be around to face the music. But was this town ready for its hero's secrets?

★   ★   ★

By dinnertime, Paul, Betty, Addy and Lynn had all settled in at Lynn and Michael's. The younger Gavins lived on a country road that you wouldn't take unless you had business being there; but today the otherwise quiet road mirrored a busy Atlanta freeway. The driveway went a good fifty yards from the front porch to the road, and by lunchtime three quarters of it had been filled with parked cars. The white fence lining the property was swamped with yellow ribbons, cards, and signs made by grade-school classes earlier in the day.

Lynn's best friend, Holly Nichols, guarded the front porch, taking a collection of pastas, salads, and dinner dishes. Even with a dozen relatives staying at the Gavins', they wouldn't run out of food for a month. Holly had so many plates that she finally started making a list of which dish belonged to whom so they could return the dinnerware to the proper person.

Inside, the Gavins were busying themselves to keep the sadness at bay. These first few days, even weeks, would be when family members near and far would come together, so the last thing Lynn, Betty, and Paul would feel was lonely. It wouldn't be until everyone had paid their respects and had gone home that they would really begin to feel the void. Lynn sat cross-legged on the floor with Addy and a handful of nieces and nephews and read them all a story. Betty was in the kitchen warming a beef stew the neighbors had delivered. Paul was in Michael's study, looking through the collection of books his son had accumulated over the years. Holly's husband, Matt, had just come in from the back yard after spending an hour raking leaves.

The crowd arrived at dusk. Holly noticed a number of vehicles parked down the road, and expected it to be people who didn't know which house the Gavins lived in. But they got out of their cars and milled about, waiting for more cars to arrive. Holly could make out some of the faces—a lot of folks from church and a few she didn't recognize. When the crowd had swelled to fifty or more, they all marched silently up to the Gavins' fence.

"Hey, y'all, there's something I think you should see out here." Holly rallied the family from throughout the house.

One by one, they stopped what they were doing and shuffled out to the front porch. The crowd didn't enter the property; they just occupied the fence line at a respectful distance from the grieving family. As the sun set, someone in the crowd passed around a candle, and soon dozens of little lights flickered on the country road. After a few more moments passed, Anita Maxwell took two steps around the fence at the edge of the yard and walked to a spot about halfway between the fence and the house. Anita had the most beautiful voice. Everyone had been glad when the music department at Tributary University offered her a scholarship to stay in town and earn a degree. It guaranteed that the best vocalist from recent high school plays and church choirs would be in town for a while longer.

While most of the town did what they could that day to honor Michael through cards, cakes, and moments of silence, Anita offered her voice.

"Amazing grace, how sweet the sound, that saved a wretch like me," she sang.

The crowd joined in. "I once was lost, but now am found, was blind, but now I see."

Holly kept a protective eye on the Gavins, who stood on the porch in stunned silence. For some of the adults, the outpouring of community support was too much, and they broke down in tears. Lynn tried to hold it together, but soon was reduced to uncontrollable sobs. Addy listened attentively.

"Momma?" said Addy, tugging Lynn's arm.

"Yes?"

"We sing this in big church," she said.

"Yes, we do."

"Why are they singing it here?"

"They're singing it for your daddy."

"Why are they singing it for him?"

"Because," Lynn said, "your daddy is a hero."

At that, Holly gave in to her own tears.

★   ★   ★

There would be more tears, and more tributes during the week. Some said it would be the biggest memorial service the town had ever seen. There were rumors an ex-president was going to make the trip, and that meant for sure the governor would be here. They'd no doubt do something special at the Talking Creek–Calhoun game. Maybe even UGA, Michael's alma mater, would pay tribute this weekend.

As the crowd found a rhythm through "Amazing Grace," it appeared that the town of Talking Creek was beginning to find its way in mourning one of its finest sons. That is, until they discovered that Michael had his own ideas.

★ ★ ★

Besides Lewis Banner, Wes didn't have many people he would call friends in Talking Creek. Acquaintances, yes. Friends, no. He hung out with a couple of the copy editors from work, but that was because they were all the same age and living in the same town. His sports department colleagues were aging and ornery. Most of his college friends were living in Atlanta, starting their careers in flashy new sky-rise offices, and blowing through their higher salaries. Wes drove down to the city when he found the time, and joined his friends in the posh spots for the young working class like Buckhead or the trendy Vinings area. But even then, he was disconnected. He lived too far away to be an official part of the social circle, and his low salary, chain store wardrobe, and Chevy Cavalier placed him firmly on the fringe.

As a creative outlet, and to help him stay in touch with his Atlanta friends and school paper colleagues, Wes had created a blog. He called it "Back Words" and kept his profile information close to the vest. All he divulged was that he was a sports reporter for a small-town paper in the South. He asked his friends not to include any personal information in their comments, and they obliged him by coming up with distinctive screen names for their posts: Moonpie, Lucky Dog, and Red Clay Redneck. Through his journalism buddies, the blog filtered out to a ring of like-minded beat writers from other papers, some of whom blogged on behalf of their employers, who had discovered that blogs drove Web traffic to their newspaper sites. Other bloggers in the group were more like Wes—undercover, for a variety of reasons, but mostly to allow complete candor without consequences. Wes enjoyed the mystery of it all, never revealing names, but only personalities or other vague identifiers.

No one in Talking Creek—except Big Bird Friedman—knew about the blog, and that was only because he was nosy. Once when he and Wes were covering a game together, Wes had made the mistake of going to the concession stand without taking his laptop with him. When he'd returned to the press box, he'd found Big Bird's nose smudging the laptop screen,

Wes's blog page open. Friedman had never mentioned the blog after that, and Wes hoped he'd forgotten about it.

Surprisingly, the blog elicited a fair amount of response. Each entry averaged a few dozen comments, and Wes enjoyed seeing the progress of the blog and the readership it was gaining. There was an occasional snarky comment, but for the most part, the people who read the blog were similar in ideals. A trio of reporters from some larger suburban papers would occasionally comment about how much they liked Wes's writing. He archived their remarks, in case one of them would be able to give him a referral when the time came to look for another reporting job beyond the *News*. From time to time, a few other small-town reporters would share a war story with him; but for the most part, Wes maintained the blog for himself. It allowed him to set aside the journalistic conventions he had to follow when writing for the *News*, and it was good therapy—it kept him from pulling his hair out sometimes. Tonight was no exception.

Back Words

More than 8 million people live in New York City. That means millions of story ideas. Thousands of news events each day. Hundreds of sources per writer, and those writers have to get juicy, unique assignments. Today, however, the big city writers got nothin' on me.

The assignment: write a eulogy. Not an obit; not a personality profile; a eulogy. Capture the essence of a man's life, laud him to family and friends at his funeral, and then write about it for Sunday's paper.

Oh, and I've never met him.

Work is already underway behind the scenes to cash in on my perilous situation. My boss is working feverishly to rake in advertising dollars for a special section. Nothing like an advertorial for a funeral. He has likewise taken a personal interest in my prose, and will no doubt have a speech coach in before the weekend.

And what of the deceased? What was he after?

He was a small-town hero—one of those athletes a town remembers for decades. He was also a genuine war hero, and a general do-gooder. Not a crack to be seen in his chivalrous armor. Well, there is one thing: At possibly the biggest memorial this town has ever seen, he wants me to deliver the keynote address. I don't know anything about the man except for the press clippings. What possible reason(s) could he have for wanting me to speak on his behalf when there are a thousand people better suited? What was he hiding?

Chapter 4

The online map services were worthless in Talking Creek. Despite living less than ten miles from the Gavins' ranch, Wes nearly got lost. Main Street became some other road once out of town, and on that new-name road was a turn for Wiley Drive, where the Gavins lived. Unfortunately, Internet directions can't help it when a sign is bent away from the road. Bullets and BBs will do that. That was one of Talking Creek's biggest crimes, defacing of government property . . . by means of buckshot. The hunters must have cleaned out the deer population and turned to road signs.

The Gavins' place was a mile down Wiley Drive on the right. A white fence—littered with yellow ribbons, American flags, and cards—led up to the driveway. Americana offerings were piled on both sides of the drive-way entrance. The house—a lot bigger than Wes had imagined—was about fifty yards from the road, behind a well-kept field in front, with the driveway winding around it and into a large carport. It had a cottage feel, complete with a large porch sporting two gliders and four rocking chairs. Opposite the main house was a cabin, which Wes took to be an area for the foster kids the ranch hosted on the weekends. How Michael had paid for all this, he didn't know; but he made a note to check out the real estate val-ues. A few of the houses on Wiley Drive leading up to the Gavins' were on the expensive side. Land didn't seem cheap in this corner of Talking Creek.

Despite the map snafu, Wes pulled up to the house at 9:00 a.m. sharp. He had called the Gavins last night, and though he hadn't talked to a member of the family, the person on the other end had confirmed that Lynn Gavin would be available to talk this morning. Before Wes could close his car door, a tall, dark-haired woman stepped outside to greet him.

"I'm Holly Nichols, Lynn's friend," she said, extending her hand and eyeing him critically. "You must be Wes."

The voice on the phone, Wes surmised. He nodded, took her hand, and ignored the look. "Seems like this is a pretty busy place," he said, noting the tire marks on the gravel.

"You're lucky you came when you did or you would have been parking all the way up at the fence. We had a full house last night and probably will again this afternoon."

"Any other reporters stop by?" he inquired.

"No," Holly said. "Although we've been getting calls. From what Lynn told me, you are the only one the family will talk to this week." She locked on his eyes. "I hope you take that seriously."

Her "hope" was more like a demand. "Yes ma'am," Wes stammered, shoving his hands into the pockets of his khakis.

"She's out back."

He obediently followed Holly around the side of the house. It was eerily quiet outside, as if his ears were sensing the atmosphere after a big rainstorm had passed by. Behind the house, there was a spacious deck with another half dozen rocking chairs. A staircase from the deck led to a garden, and a pathway from the garden connected to the driveway. The little trail split into two to the left of the house and ran straight to the cabin and a pond about fifty yards back. The backdrop to everything was a green covered mountain.

When Lynn, who had been sitting in one of the rocking chairs, saw Wes, she smiled like she might when a neighbor visited. He'd seen that kind of smile from interviewees before—usually faked—but in this case the smile was genuinely disarming.

"Did you have any trouble finding the place?" Lynn asked.

"Well, I think someone in town has declared war on the county road signs, but other than that, no," Wes said.

She chuckled, and he could tell she hadn't done that for a few days by the way she patted her throat, which was probably hoarse. She couldn't hide the remorse in her eyes, the dry tear ducts and puffy edges; but she hadn't tried, either. She wasn't wearing any makeup. She had on blue jeans and a T-shirt, and her strawberry blond hair was pulled back in a ponytail, as if she were about to do some yard work.

"Would you like a tour of the ranch?" she asked.

Wes accepted. Tours were great for stalling, and he wasn't sure yet which direction the interview should take.

"Basically, we started the ranch about ten years ago with a few acres of land and a large playroom. I was working as a social worker at the time, and saw a need for the county foster care kids to get out of town and have some fun without all the restrictions they typically endured. Regular kids can ride their bikes over to a friend's and spend the night. Kids in foster care need permission from their foster parents and a lot of paperwork from the county DFCS. The restrictions are for safety reasons, but it still stinks. How fair is it for a child to have all those restrictions just because they were put in that position one way or another? The ranch was a loophole from the protocol, a way for the foster parents to get the weekend off and for the kids to run around in a supervised area without feeling handcuffed by policies they couldn't understand and didn't deserve."

They walked into an open field between the house and the cabin.

"It's gotten a lot bigger than a playroom," Wes said.

Lynn nodded. "As our attendance grew, so did the acreage. About 120 acres were purchased, we built the cabin and added more activities as we went along. By then, the ranch was more than a married couple like us could handle. We ran the administrative stuff during the week, but thankfully we had the help of about a dozen volunteers, including some of my fellow social workers from the county, who saw the ranch as a good investment of their free time, because it often kept problem kids from getting into trouble and having to be placed somewhere else. All told on the 120 acres, we have two ponds to fish and canoe, a winding trail, woods for fort building—one of Michael's favorite activities—an area for riding horses that were brought in each weekend from a local equestrian center, a basketball court, and a large field for games. The only things we don't have are video games and a TV. We might show a movie every now and again, but we'd rather the kids be doing activities that are more fellow-ship focused."

"Did having a child of your own make it even more complicated, run-ning the facility?"

"Well, Addy *was* a surprise," she said, stopping to brush a few stray strands of hair from her face and pull her ponytail tighter. "After trying for a while, we didn't think we'd be able to have children of our own, and we went the foster care retreat route rather than adopt.

"Then—*surprise*—we had Addy, right around the time Michael was gearing up for his deployment. He missed her first birthday being over-seas, but then came home earlier than his unit because of his wounds. But yes, to answer your question, it became more complicated. But sometimes that's a good thing."

"That must have been hard, not having him around for that."

"It was," Lynn said matter-of-factly. "Deployment was hard as an Army wife, and it was just as hard as a National Guardsman's wife. But you get through it with family and friends—fellowship. We like that word around here. The county helped staff the administration stuff full-time, which helped me out; and Michael's mom, Betty, was over here practically 24/7 to help with Addy. She adores her grandchildren."

As they walked the property, Wes noticed smooth black rocks outlin-ing the path from the kids' cabin to the pond and woods. In some places, such as beside the cabin, they were in a neat row, about a foot wide, and traced the trail toward the pond. Farther out, they came in small sections, maybe one or two rocks for every foot.

"Are you still building?" Wes asked.

"No," she said.

"Oh. Well, I'm just curious about the rocks. It looks like they are fol-lowing the trail you have here, but they're not all along the way."

"Those are prayer rocks," Lynn said. "Each child that comes here has the opportunity to place a rock along the trail for a specific prayer request. It was an idea we got from a church service a few years back. The kids kind of took it and ran with it. And they're all pretty individualized. A group of girls that comes here regularly has a large section by the cabin. Then there are the occasional ones leading to the mountain trail. Those are usually left by the boys."

"I've never heard of prayer rocks," Wes admitted. "I'm surprised with some of the kids who visit here that you don't get any broken windows."

Lynn chuckled. "Rocks through windows, no. Wrestling matches and temper tantrums, yes. The prayer rocks are a way of visualizing something intangible. You can say a prayer and have it symbolized by these rocks, and when the kids come back, they can see that it's still there. Like God never forgot about it, and they won't either, as long as they're reminded about it when they visit."

Wes kicked some dirt with his left shoe and watched the dust float in the air. He took a slight gamble with his next question. "How often do you put down prayer rocks for yourself?"

Lynn stopped and looked him in the eye. "This morning, actually."

"For your husband?" he said as softly as possible.

"I was praying because I may lose this ranch."

"B—but I thought it was a nonprofit, funded charitably?"

Lynn continued along the trail, and he followed a step behind.

"Michael and I built this retreat together, Wes, but our skills complemented each other. We each had our share of duties and did them without involving the other person. Michael was a people person; he was so good at raising support. He made a lot of friends in college, the Army, and in this community, people who eventually helped out in raising support for the retreat. But now that he's gone, I'm not sure I have the skills, or the energy, to do it."

A screen door slammed shut and a woman's voice called out, "Lynn, where are you?"

It sounded more like an echo, because Lynn and Wes had wandered a hundred yards or so from the back porch.

"Momma!" a child's voice screeched.

"We're coming!" Lynn lengthened her stride, and Wes had to jog a few paces to catch up with her as she returned to the house along one of the trails.

An elderly lady and a little girl scurried from the porch as they approached. "Well hello, hello," the woman said. "You must be Wes. I'm Betty Gavin, Michael's mother."

Before Wes could respond, the little girl took hold of his arm and began dragging him toward the house.

"You have to eat something first, sir!" she said with a stubborn determination. Wes looked at Lynn and Betty, who nodded for him to follow the leader. He sighed and tried his best to play along.

"Here, sit down please, sir," the girl said, leading him into the dining room. She and Wes still weren't at eye level even with him sitting down, but she looked him straight in the eye. "I am Addy Grace Gavin, pleased to meet you. And you are?"

"Wes Watkins, ma'am," he said. Betty and Lynn watched from the kitchen with amusement.

Addy proceeded to put her palm on his forehead. Though surprised, Wes held still.

"Yep, it's what I thought."

"Uh, what's that?"

"You have no personality," she said. "And you're hungry. Momma, can we feed him?"

"I am sure that you have some questions for us," Betty said, pulling out a chair at the dining room table. "We've got plenty of time to do plenty of talking; but for starters, Addy is right, would you like some brunch?"

"Well, I'll have to pay you for it, as a reporter," he said. "Standard policy."

Betty looked horrified. "You wouldn't dare."

"We didn't make it," Lynn said. "It's all this food that people have dropped by. Perhaps that might lighten the restriction?"

"Fair enough," Wes said, smiling.

He entered the kitchen and took in the smells of baked foods and roasts. On the nearest counter was a clutter of cleaned dishes, each decorated with a sticky note bearing a name. Scattered along another kitchen counter were half-eaten casseroles. Betty waved her hand frantically at the countertops.

"Please excuse the mess; it's just a disaster. We've got more to eat than we know what to do with."

Lynn opened the fridge to even more dishes. She pulled out a large baked ham. "You're welcome to any of these casseroles here, or I could make you a ham and cheese bagel, if you want to keep it simple."

"Simple sounds fine," Wes said.

Betty called for Holly, who came in from the front porch, still eyeballing Wes with a look he couldn't quite read. Two minutes later, with the food prepared, Wes sat down with Lynn, Betty, Addy, and Holly to bagels and orange juice. Before he took a bite, he pulled out his Accu-Chek from a small black bag and did a quick reading of his blood sugar. The women politely busied themselves with placing napkins and silverware. Wes excused himself with the bag in hand and went to the bathroom to give himself a shot of insulin. When he returned, the women were occupied passing food around the table.

Addy, however, cupped her hands to her mouth.

"What in the world were you doing to yourself, sir?" she exclaimed.

"I checked my blood sugar, then gave myself an insulin shot."

"Are you some kind of vampire or something?"

"No. I'm diabetic."

"What's that?"

Wes paused, searching for a way to explain diabetes to a first grader.

"It's when your body doesn't produce the things that break down your food when you eat," he said. "I have to monitor it."

"By stabbing yourself? Ick!"

Lynn patted Addy on the shoulder. "All right now, Addy, we need to pause and say a prayer, okay?"

Wes politely bowed his head as they said grace, then Betty surprised him by asking where he was from and how he liked the paper. Wes answered between bites, trying to give answers that wouldn't require follow-ups. Lived in Roswell. Went to school at UGA, like Michael, but after his time there. Enjoyed writing for the *News*. All dull descriptions.

"Well, that's great," Betty enthused.

Lynn took the paper plates they had eaten from and ferried them into the kitchen.

"Addy, honey, why don't you go in the living room with Aunt Holly and put together one of your puzzles."

Addy glared at Wes, as if he were to blame for her banishment, and walked away. It was obvious she possessed the energy and innocence of a child. Holly chuckled, giving Lynn a knowing look, and followed Addy out of the room. The little girl was probably running circles around all of them. Had they told her about her dad yet?

"She doesn't know yet; not completely," Lynn said, apparently sensing his question.

"Oh," Wes said.

"She knows that he was really sick, but she thinks he's just away for a while, visiting with Jesus. I'm not sure how we're . . . how I'm going to tell her that he's not coming back."

Betty squeezed her hand. The women glanced at each other in silence, and Lynn straightened in her chair.

"Who have you talked to so far?" she asked.

"You're the first," Wes said. "I'm heading downtown to meet Coach Lawler and a few other guys who played with Michael."

"Oh, Coach Lawler," Betty said, with a knowing look. "I'm guessing Bud will give you an earful. Lynn here was behind him and Michael in high school. They left quite a legacy. Bud was always into trouble. I believe he was suspended Michael's senior year."

"Really?" Wes said with a raised eyebrow. "Never told me that story."

"Of course he didn't," Lynn said. "Not exactly a good thing to be remembered for, and not something his mother was fond of retelling, the poor woman. The week before they were supposed to play the Paulding

County Chiefs, Bud conjured up a wonderful idea to have a bonfire at his parents' farm, to rally some of the team. Instead of using regular firewood, though, he decided to sneak into the state park after dark and chop down a wooden statue of a Native American that's there to honor the local tribe. He and a few players chopped it down and burned it at the bonfire—and they would have gotten away with it, too, if Bud's mother hadn't seen one of the leftover pieces of the Chief. She asked Bud what it was, and he broke down and told her everything. He was such a mama's boy."

"Now, that's not a bad thing, Lynn," Betty said, grinning.

"His mom gave him a lecture and then she told the police," Lynn continued. "It was all over the news. 'Eagles players act out hate crime against Native Americans.' Bud, for all of his stupidity, didn't hate the local tribe. He was too dumb to put two and two together until his mom explained things to him. He and the other players were sentenced by a local juvenile court to sensitivity training and ten hours of community service, and they were required to meet and apologize to the local tribe."

"Michael wasn't one of those players, was he?" Wes asked.

"Oh, heavens no!" Betty said. "I would have had a heart attack. Paul would have whipped him raw."

Wes received a brief explanation of how they'd disciplined Michael and their children and what was cause for discipline. The Gavins ran a tight—but fair—ship, Wes observed. Once Betty finished her parenting history, there was a lull in the conversation.

"So what questions do you have for us?" Lynn finally asked.

Wes sat up straight. "If you could give me any leads as to who I should be talking to, that would help me out a lot. Honestly, the biggest question I have is why Michael chose me to give his eulogy."

Lynn and Betty stole a quick glance at each other. He couldn't read what it meant.

"He didn't want a big funeral," Lynn offered, "but I think he's going to be getting one anyway. We're having the service at our church, but the preacher has already called and asked if we'd be okay with a video and audio feed of the service to the Talking Creek gymnasium. We're fine with that. I think Michael knew in a way he couldn't control how people wanted to remember him, except for one thing . . . his eulogy."

"But why me? Why a reporter?"

"Wes, dear, the only answer we can offer is that you would have to have known him," Betty said. "And that's why you're here, which we appreciate very much."

"Fair enough," Wes said.

He pulled out his tape recorder, which made Lynn take a noticeable deep breath. Betty had a motherly look on her face, as if what Wes was doing were cute. He decided to start the formal interview off light.

"So Lynn, how did you meet Michael?" Wes asked. "Did you start dating in high school?"

"No," Lynn said. "I wouldn't have dated him then. He was a little too into football."

Betty agreed. "All boys at that age believe in themselves more than is healthy. You just hope they snap out of it."

"Michael did what any successful teenage athlete did; he fed off the admirers," Lynn said. "We'd talk afterward about how silly it was. The high school hierarchy is so warped compared to the real world that you wonder how it even created itself. I had to suppress a laugh sometimes, walking through the hallways and seeing the athletes puff up their chests wearing their letterman's jackets. Michael was no different, but I didn't hold it against him. How else would you react to being famous in a town like Talking Creek at that age?"

Betty waved a finger in the air. "If there was one thing Paul and I taught him, it was not to treat women badly," she said forcefully. "Some of those boys took their status as an excuse to fling the girls by the wayside like it was a sport. Michael could make a fool of himself however he saw fit, but if he ever said one cross word about a young lady in front of us, or if we found out about it, then Paul was going to set him straight."

"Actually, Mom, I believe Michael's high school sweetheart broke up with him," Lynn said, smiling. "She was a year ahead of him and went to Tennessee, and that was the end of that."

"So how did you two get together?" Wes asked Lynn.

Lynn tilted her head. "We had mutual friends in college, a few people from Talking Creek and then friends at Georgia. Still, we didn't really bump into each other until his junior year. Michael was into the football thing. It's very time consuming. They work out at 6:00 a.m., go to class, practice, and then come home to more studying, or they blow it off and mess around. Of course, Michael never did anything like that." She flashed a knowing glance at Betty, who played along with a mock sulk.

"My Michael? No, no of course not."

"And if he did," Lynn said, "then he quit most of it by his junior year—when he was benched. We started seeing each other then, actually. He was much more . . . realistic . . . when we talked."

"What do you mean?" Wes said.

Lynn pursed her lips, and fiddled with her napkin. "Michael was dealing with adversity in an area of his life where he had only known success, being bumped down to second string quarterback. That would shake anybody, you know? I can't imagine what it was like for an athlete. At the time, I didn't feel bad for him, though. It's no secret football players get their perks. Free food, a free ride with the scholarship, and thousands of adoring fans. When that goes away, or dwindles, it's a shock, I'm sure. That's why he had a knee-jerk reaction after losing out, and almost transferred."

"He did?"

Lynn looked up, acknowledging Wes's interest in the subject.

"He talked with his coach about transferring, but the coach let him sleep on it, and he decided to stay."

Wes surmised that this had to be a sore spot for Talking Creek—their beloved never panning out as a quarterback, opting instead to become a fullback and playing a supporting role on a championship team. It would explain the lack of coverage the paper gave to Georgia football Michael's junior year. Because fullbacks didn't receive many carries and were no-shows on the stat sheet, Wes hadn't been surprised that Michael's name wasn't around much in the archived articles his senior year. He made a mental note to ask Coach Lawler about it, and let any grudges surface.

"It was the best thing to happen to him, if you want to ask me," Betty said matter-of-factly. "Look at that poor soul who took his spot. He got all that money from the NFL and then ended up wasting away on drugs and alcohol. It's so sad, really, to see anyone do that. His life fell apart once he left for the NFL; and though Michael would never say it, I'm sure that young man wasn't a perfect angel in college, either. At a certain point as a parent, you have to let your kids go, and pray that they learn their lessons on their own. This was one of the first Michael would get without us—that there was someone out there better at what he did, and he had to adjust accordingly. I was so worried how he'd take it."

"Seems like he handled it pretty well," Wes offered.

"Oh, I think we can give credit to Lynn for that," Betty said, beaming. Lynn blushed. "It's always a woman who sets a man straight."

"Let's just say he went from a person I'd never give the time of day to, to a man I could consider dating," Lynn said. "And we did, for two years, before he proposed at the end of his senior year, well, his fifth year with football. He was much more unassuming. I wouldn't say he was unsure, but instead of adamantly sticking with every word that came out of his mouth, if someone challenged him on an idea, he'd try and find an answer for it. He became curious. Instead of conquering the world, he wanted to know more about it."

"Why did he decide on the Army? Weren't there other options after college?"

"He had a lot to choose from. Too much, really."

"Like what?"

"There was still football. He thought about declaring for the NFL draft, but he would have most likely signed as a free agent with no guaranteed spot on a team. There was still money in that, though. I remember him saying that scout team players, who don't even dress out for games, made a salary comparable to a CEO. He wasn't enthusiastic about pro football, though. There were oodles of opportunities in business. His degree was in business, but he never really used it. I think he went into the Army because it had what he was looking for in a career: a calling."

"Mrs. Gavin," Wes said, turning the recorder toward Betty, "do you think it had anything to do with your husband being in the military?"

Betty shook her head. "Paul rarely flaunted his military service. As much as we raised Michael in a military family's discipline, Paul never encouraged Michael to join. That was his decision."

"Do either of you have anything from Michael's military service?"

They both smiled. "You want to see his medals, don't you?" Betty said.

Wes followed Lynn and Betty into the study. It had a typical wooden desk, with a black leather chair behind it and a reading chair in the right corner. Two large shelves behind the desk housed what had to be hundreds of books. And not just the hardbacks that people buy to fill up their shelves. A good chunk of space was devoted to paperbacks. Along the walls were framed pictures of the Gavin clan, the kids, mostly Lynn's and Michael's nephews and nieces, and what Wes took to be kids from the foster care retreat. The Gavins, and Michael especially, were lean, chiseled. A fit family for sure. Wes couldn't help but feel self-conscious. He'd never been much of an athlete. He noticed that the pictures were all about family. Another difference. They had family. Wes shook his head and studied the room more closely. There were no football photos or trophies. Michael's college diploma hung beside Lynn's, but in a much smaller frame.

Betty pointed to the far wall beside the diplomas while Lynn sat in the black chair to open a drawer and thumb through some files.

"There they are," Betty said.

Wes walked over and examined the casing. It was just one small, framed case with maybe a dozen items in it.

"You seem disappointed," Betty said.

"Oh, no, I'm sorry, just a little confused. I see a lot of patches, not very many medals. I recognize the Purple Heart. Which one is the Medal of Honor?"

Lynn walked over to the case. "None of them."

"Oh," Wes said again. "Where did he put that one then?"

Lynn paused. She tapped the glass casing with her fingers.

"I think I pinned every medal he ever received, and sewed on every tab he earned," she said. "There are some good stories in those citations . . . in those years. So you'd think I'd know where his biggest medal was. But we don't know. We don't know where it is."

Chapter 5

Shaky hands. Whenever Lynn Key visualized the unity candles at her upcoming wedding, it triggered shaky hands. She'd heard horror stories about candles popping out of holders and starting a fire. She wanted a perfect wedding, but beyond the months of planning she and Michael had done, the ceremony's execution was beyond her control. It didn't stop her from visualizing it, worrying over it.

Lynn liked things neat and predictable. It was a compulsion born from living in the same house in Talking Creek all her life, and having Holly as her roommate in college all four years. She'd spent hours sifting through wedding magazines for the right type of dress and floral arrangements— and way too much time cataloging CD lists for wedding songs.

It was ironic, considering the man she was marrying. Whereas Lynn lived through a leather-bound daily planner, Michael lived by the seat of his pants. Lynn loved strolls through the park; Michael wanted to hike into a gorge. Lynn enjoyed a good book on a rainy day. Michael was out muddin, getting his beat-up Jeep stuck in the woods. Michael was gung ho about everything he did, and yet there was a softness to him as well. The puffed up ego often associated with jocks didn't fit his profile. He was just full of life, and Lynn fell in love with that, enough to accept his marriage proposal on the grassy knoll of North Campus.

She first realized her life was changing as Michael was being commissioned into the Army as an officer. She had been so consumed in the wedding preparation process and finishing up school that she hadn't stopped to think about how his induction ceremony was every bit as important to their future together as their impending wedding would be.

That thought made her hands shake. She reproached herself for feeling anxious now, and not earlier when Michael had told her of his intentions to join the Army out of college. It didn't mesh with her plans of a house and kids and soccer camps and easy living, but neither did Michael himself.

The seriousness of the decision hadn't struck her until she and Betty were standing side by side, putting Michael's "butter bars" on him in front of family, friends, and God at the commissioning ceremony. Before she was even married to the man, the two gold bars, designating Michael as a lieutenant, meant that Lynn, too, was marrying the U.S. Army.

★ ★ ★

The Ranger tab signified that their honeymoon was over. Lynn was grateful that she and Michael had survived their first long stint away from each other, and that Michael had survived the ordeal, period.

Lynn had heard the Ranger School horror stories, of how the men would suffer through drills like the "cockroach," in which the men were instructed to lie down on their backs and keep their legs, arms, and heads elevated until a certain number of soldiers quit. Then there were the marches, where if a soldier was out of step, he'd be flunked by an unsympathetic drill sergeant and sent home. Secretly, Lynn wouldn't have minded if Michael had been one of those men—but she knew Michael did. She loved him for that—how he'd fight for whatever goals he'd set for himself until he succeeded; but she was also not used to the negative effects of that tenacity. How beat down Michael could get, how much he'd push himself to the limits to succeed.

She realized that they established some sort of status quo while Michael was in the Ranger training rotation. They were married, but they couldn't enjoy all of the social engagements and perks of being married. She was at home and he was in a dusty field or a swamp or on a mountaintop, enduring one of the toughest ordeals of his life, without his wife, and with contact limited to a rushed letter or a one-minute phone call. She still had the wedding ring, of course.

She was more aware of it when she went to the grocery store and saw other couples shopping together and enjoying each other's company. That wasn't her life just yet; she was on pause. But she wasn't a girl who was rolling the dice on a man at a bar, or launching a career of her own in Atlanta or some other big city.

When Lynn saw Michael walk through the Fort Benning auditorium for his Ranger graduation ceremony, she'd never felt prouder as a wife. He had lost a good deal of weight, his eyes were bloodshot and he limped on his right leg, but Lynn swore she saw him walk taller. She beamed as she pinned his Ranger patch on his shoulder. It was a badge of honor for husband and wife, their first test as a military family.

★   ★   ★

When Michael was assigned to the 82nd Airborne, Lynn sewed the AA tab on his uniform. That was when the Army experience became day-to-day.

Lynn was pleasantly surprised by her first house on base at Fort Bragg, North Carolina, a quaint little duplex. Another family lived on the other side of the living room wall, but she didn't mind. She had a house to decorate, and she loved the neighborhood. There were families everywhere, bikes and basketballs dotting the driveways, and games of tag along the streets in the afternoon. Some of the neighborhood kids were little entrepreneurs, knocking on doors on the weekends with a rake in hand, asking if they could do yard work.

The house itself was cozy. They had a kitchen with wiggle room. Most of the appliances worked, but the stove had broken twice now; and considering the Army never used the highest bidder, getting maintenance done was a chore. There was storage space in the laundry room and guest bedroom, which Michael and Lynn took advantage of, storing all their wedding gifts to relieve their parents' basements.

The duplex floors were tile, part of a housing system created for quick transitions. Lynn countered with rugs and sections of carpeting. She decorated the walls with framed pictures of Southern landscapes and sunsets and family. She learned how to stretch a dollar. They made the most of their hand-me-downs and bought multi-functioning items at department stores for the rest—like a coffee table doubling as the dinner table.

As the wife of an officer in the 82nd, Lynn learned acronyms such SOP, NCO, and CNN. Not much for the nightly news before she got married, she was now a devoted follower of the cable news broadcasts, which provided the best source for international stories. An incident in Sudan or Venezuela held more relevance because of deployment in this small corner of North Carolina than anywhere else in America.

In the mornings, she heard the sounds of the Army. The echoes of the Airborne creed as the men ran early-morning PT; or the sound of helicopters and transport planes flying to nearby Pope Air Force Base. Whatever threshold there was, she had crossed it. She was an Army wife. It was surreal.

The reality check came in the form of a phone call. The ringing startled Lynn. Michael's arm flew across her body to the phone, almost a subconscious reaction. She tried to piece reality from dreams. "Who is it?" she said, looking at the clock.

It was 2:00 a.m.

"Uh-huh," Michael said. "Okay." He hung up, wiped the sleep from his eyes, and sprang out of bed.

"What's going on?" Lynn asked. The world was racing past her.

"I got the call."

A thousand emotions swept through her as she watched Michael scramble to get dressed. They'd planned for The Call, but she never knew how she was going to feel. Panicked? Hurried? She couldn't pinpoint it. This was so much harder to deal with now that it was happening. The moment was sweeping Michael away, and there was nothing to do but watch.

Michael finished tying his boots and looked up at Lynn. "Do you know where the insurance papers are?"

She nodded. He stood, and Lynn rushed into his arms, tears forming. She suspected there would be more of them in the next few days. Michael returned her embrace, pulling back only long enough to look into her eyes before he kissed her.

"I've got to go," he said.

Lynn nodded. "I know," she said weakly.

"I love you." Michael kissed her forehead.

Lynn heard the sound of the door closing, an engine revving, then silence.

★ ★ ★

When Michael received the Combat Infantry Badge during the First Gulf War, Lynn didn't know what to feel. She realized his life and their marriage could be wiped out with one wrong turn into an ambush or firefight. It sent shivers down her spine. There were people around Michael who tried to kill him. She couldn't get that out of her mind. It surprised her that she felt anger that Michael would want to put himself in danger.

"To lead men in combat," he had said, was one of his goals, but what made him so brave? What gave him the right to put both of them on the line? She resented it. Michael at least could see the danger. Her only warning would come in a knock at the door and a solemn chaplain delivering the news that her husband had been killed or wounded.

When he returned from combat, Lynn had hoped for a big parade, loud celebratory music, and she and Michael embracing as the credits rolled. Then they'd resume their life together. But it couldn't be that way. Investing a large chunk of their early adult lives in a war had changed both of them. Michael was leaner and more focused, his body a taut economy of sinew and resolve. Lynn was quieter and less prone to getting upset over little things that thwarted her daily planning.

In their premarital counseling, their hometown pastor had warned them of these kinds of times, that couples are often divided by unshared experiences. Most of the lessons and wisdom from those sessions faded into obscurity, but one item stuck with them, and they clung to it as they adjusted to life after war: they were not the same people they'd been on their wedding day. They weren't the same when Michael walked out the door into unknown danger. They weren't the same when he returned. The challenge was working through that reality, improving their relationship regardless of the circumstances.

★　★　★

Following his Army service, Michael decided to stay active part-time by joining the National Guard. Lynn sewed on that patch too, a thunderbolt streaking down the middle of a red shield. She attached it and accepted it, despite reservations. At the time, there was no war to worry about. The First Gulf War had ended, and the Guard commitment took only a weekend out of each month and the possibility of activation during floods or other natural disasters. But she didn't worry about natural disasters anymore.

One particular Tuesday, she stifled a yawn after pouring skim milk over her corn flakes. Tuesdays were low-key. Working a weekend foster care retreat meant having weird downtimes. Wednesdays and Thursdays were administrative days, matching volunteers with the foster children and figuring out who was coming and who to room with whom in what cabins. Friday through Sunday were jam-packed, with the pitter-patter and stomping of kids of varying ages playing, running, and discovering around their property. One minute she'd be fishing with a ten-year-old, and the next playing basketball with a gaggle of teenagers. That left Mondays and Tuesdays relatively free.

Lynn slid her bowl of cereal closer and flipped on the TV. She dutifully turned to the *Today* show, and her mind drifted to the day's chores.

"We have breaking news for you: apparently a plane has just crashed into the World Trade Center," the TV anchor said, jolting Lynn back to the present. She looked up in time to see images of a large building in New York City with smoke spewing out of the upper stories. The cohosts began discussing what caused the freak accident and how many people were in the building.

"Honey!" Lynn said as Michael shuffled into the kitchen, sipping his coffee, the smell of sweat still all over him from his run.

"Yeah, babe?"

"Have you seen this?" They watched the screen, drawn in by the breaking news, but not seriously alarmed.

"These kinds of things happen all the time, right? Plane crashes?" Lynn said, her heart sinking with each passing moment.

"No," Michael said, "not like that." He set his coffee down and grasped Lynn's shoulder.

"Another one just hit!" An eye-witness screamed over the phone to the news anchors.

Michael and Lynn watched with mounting horror and confusion as the footage replayed. Like a dart coming out of nowhere, a plane cut across the camera angle, and in one lightning quick moment, disintegrated into the side of the building, causing a large puff of smoke. Now both towers were on fire.

"That wasn't an accident," Michael remarked, his grip firmer on Lynn's shoulder.

Lynn knew the answer, but asked it anyway. "What's going on?" Tears formed on the edge of her eyes.

"We're under attack," Michael said.

A correspondent from the news station was reporting via telephone from Washington. "I don't want to alarm anyone, but it felt like there was an explosion of some kind at the Pentagon," the reporter said.

"No!" Michael punched a cabinet door, startling Lynn.

It was one of the few times she had seen her husband angry—really, truly angry. He was like a big oak tree—arms crossed, legs entrenched, pupils transfixed, his mind already a thousand miles away, a cold, quiet rage swelling.

As the events of 9/11 unfolded, the Gavins had their eyes glued to the TV and their ears pinned to the phone. Michael pondered calling one or two of his buddies who were still in the military, but they were probably busy with more important things today. Lynn checked on her friend Holly, whom she knew was supposed to be flying back from a business trip. By mid-afternoon, they finally connected. Holly said she was stuck in Chicago after they had canceled all flights; but she was fine. She said she'd rent a car and drive home if she had to. Lynn shuddered as she thought about the families in New York who would have a mother, father, daughter, or son not make it home tonight.

Michael's dad stopped by around 11:00 and the two men spent a good hour outside on the porch rehashing the events like two old war birds.

As the day went on, word spread through prayer circles that the churches were having services that night. By 7:00 p.m., sanctuaries were packed. At the Methodist church, where the Gavins were, the minister allowed members of the congregation to rise and say their own prayers. The adults did their best to put on a strong front, but when the children rose to pray, to talk about the burning buildings and the death and suffering that were now images they'd never forget, there wasn't a dry eye in the sanctuary.

Back home, Michael resumed his vigil on the porch, slowly rocking back and forth in his favorite rocking chair. Lynn put on a sweater and joined him. They didn't say anything. They didn't need to. The wind brushed lightly around them, a slight rustling of leaves along the edge of their property. The Gavins listened to the trees swaying. Such an odd sound for a world gone mad, Lynn thought. It was peaceful here, and yet their cocoon of normalcy was disintegrating.

She heard an unfamiliar sound from Michael. Sobbing. She turned to him and saw he had one hand covering his eyes. She let him have the moment, to let the emotions and sense of helplessness rush in. Finally, it was too much, and his pain gushed out like blood from a wound. She held him.

Time had slowed when the planes struck the buildings. Then it sped up. The next few years became a blur of unfolding events around the world and training for Michael's unit. When they were eventually called for deployment to Iraq, Lynn felt the quiet panic rise again. There was so much to do in so little time. They needed powers of attorney for paychecks, titles on the car, the estate. Michael revised his will. They reviewed the life insurance policy. Lynn renewed her passport. Almost everything she did in the days leading up to his departure was paperwork in case he was killed or wounded.

And then, in the middle of it all, came the wonderful, beautiful news of a baby. They'd wanted and prayed for that moment for so long, but had finally given up hope and moved on to helping children in need rather than rearing their own. Now, in the midst of a national crisis, as Michael was headed overseas again, they were given a blessing. It was almost too much to take in.

★ ★ ★

Michael's first and only Purple Heart resulted in Lynn's first and only trip overseas. One minute she was on the phone, listening to an officer explain that Michael had been wounded in a major firefight, and that he was being flown to an Army hospital in Landstuhl, Germany, in stable condition. The next minute she was on a flight to Germany, having dropped off Addy at Paul and Betty's and receiving assurances that everything would be okay. An officer with the National Guard told her that Michael probably wouldn't be in Germany for long; they'd fly him to a medical center in the States as soon as he could travel safely, but Lynn insisted on being at his side immediately. A phone call from Michael before her flight was the only thing that had kept her from a complete breakdown. He was heavily medicated and groggy, but Lynn got the gist: a gunshot wound to his right shoulder. He was expected to make a full recovery.

It still didn't prepare her for the reunion. The medical center was a little slice of America; an Army base in the middle of Europe, with PX commissaries and fast food joints. Lynn watched the green landscape rush by as her transport made its way to Landstuhl from Ramstein Air Base. Nothing was like she had imagined it in her worst thoughts. After months of separation, she finally saw Michael propped up in a hospital bed, wearing

Adidas sweat pants, not combat fatigues, and a red Georgia ball cap. The right side of his body was wrapped in gauze, and he had an IV in his arm.

Michael smiled, but not without a cringe. He clutched a piece of paper in his left hand. "I'm sorry," he said.

"Don't," Lynn said, her hand covering her lips to ward off crying. "You have nothing to be sorry about."

Michael looked down, Lynn's supportive words failing to make an impact. "This says I'm getting a Purple Heart. They should make these things for the wives," he said, holding up the paper. "I can't imagine what it was like for you, Lynn. Not just here, today, but before. When we were first in, all those days you had no idea what was going on, and then you get a message that—"

"It's okay, honey," she said. "I already have a medal. A trophy. My trophy husband." She smiled, folding Michael's fingers around the paper. "You keep this like all of the other ones, and be proud."

Michael turned to look out the window. "They said they're nominating me for the Medal of Honor."

☆   ☆   ☆

Over the next few months, Michael told her bits and pieces about that day. About the men he'd lost and how he could have tried harder, done something different. Lynn understood, after more than a decade as an Army wife, that to Michael this was healing, or attempts at it. That he talked about his experience at all, even though it was sporadically, was something for which she was extremely grateful. Every soldier had his or her own way of reacting to the pain, and many times it was a destructive kind of reaction—drinking, fighting, nightmares. For Michael, it was like shrapnel from a wound; there was still pain lodged in his body that he might never get out.

If there was a bright side, from Lynn's perspective, it was that there would be no more deployments; no more calls in the middle of the night sending him halfway around the world and into danger—in Iraq, or in any other theater. His Medal of Honor signified the highest act of bravery a soldier could attain, and the last military action he'd ever see. His shoulder was fine for civilian life, but it would keep him out of the military. Lynn detected regret and remorse from Michael. He still felt obligated to the men who had been under his command.

Because of Michael's stature as one of the "Bravest of the Brave," Talking Creek asked him to give speeches for Memorial Day and Veteran's Day. It was the only time Michael would don his uniform and medal, and each year his speeches became shorter. The people in the crowd couldn't know, and Michael didn't blame them for it, but he told Lynn after one of the town's parades how miserable he was.

"I put on this uniform and they cheer me like I did something heroic."

"But you did, honey," Lynn said.

"The true heroes are the ones who gave their lives in defense of freedom. They aren't the ones that come back."

"But Michael, we can't understand that like you. The town needs someone to whom they can express their gratitude. Just be thankful that they're expressing gratitude toward you and the other veterans, and not something else. You are their symbol."

Lynn wanted him to remember. At least in a positive light. The military service had been an integral part of their marriage, and they had met wonderful people. So one day she decided to organize. She brought three boxes full of Michael's medals, patches, awards, and citations, and spread them out in the study. She read through his deeds, and thought of the times at Forts Benning and Bragg, and when he was deployed to Iraq. She thought about all of the tears shed and nights she spent worrying. The care packages sent and the get-togethers of Guard families while loved ones were deployed. It was all in the past now, but she refused to let the memories go away. It was good to remember.

She decided to frame his medals and unit insignias. While she was sorting through the materials, Michael caught her in the act, walking quietly into the study and seeing his accomplishments on the desk. His eyes took in the medals and patches, just like Lynn's had, going back in time as he scanned each one. He looked at Lynn and offered a humble smile and a nod.

"Can you do me a favor; can you leave the Medal of Honor out of the case?" he asked.

"Sure, honey," Lynn said. "You'd still like to wear it for functions?"

"No," he said. "I'm not going to wear it."

"Why not?"

Michael paused, as if he ached to answer her, but he didn't, not fully. He took the Medal of Honor and put it back into its box.

"I'll put it in our safe deposit box at the bank or something," he said. "If you could, I'd just like the ones you are putting up to be unit patches or ones like the Ranger tab. That's all."

Lynn watched as Michael shut the lid on the Medal of Honor and walked out of the study with it.

Chapter 6

Reese's Café sat on the corner of Main and Emory, across from a bank and a dry cleaners. There were no fancy neon lights at the entrance, just a big white billboard with *Reese's* painted in bold red. Inside, Wes knew, the smells varied from hour to hour. Mornings had the aroma of strong coffee, pastries, and bacon. Lunchtime smelled like BLTs, grilled cheese, and hamburgers. At suppertime, you'd smell fried chicken and barbeque. It was more like a diner than a café, but considering it was the only real eatery downtown, Reese could call it whatever he wanted.

Reese's success was a rarity in Talking Creek. Most people seemed to prefer staying home for meals instead of going out. Wes thought that was odd. When he was a kid, his mother wasn't the cooking type. It was either mac and cheese or a very limited selection of fast food that he could eat, because he had to monitor his blood sugar. Places like Olive Garden and Applebee's had been a way for mother and son to get out of their various dingy two-bedroom apartments.

Reese's, though, was a mainstay in the community. It had its share of regulars. Construction crews and policemen, high school athletes and plant workers, depending on the time of day; but every Monday through Friday at noon, according to Lewis, the big oval table in the far left corner was reserved for a group no larger than twelve but rarely smaller than six. They called themselves the Nooners, and for an hour straight they talked nothing but football.

Wes arrived at the diner at 11:50 a.m., per Lewis's suggestion, to meet with the Nooners. Lynn and Betty had answered all of his questions thoroughly, but they hadn't been able to shed any light on the whereabouts of Michael's missing medal. Lynn had suggested that Wes talk to one of Michael's officers in the National Guard, and had even offered to set up the interview; but it would probably take a day to arrange, and in the meantime, Wes planned to see if there was anything underneath the surface of Michael's football career, both at Talking Creek High and in Athens.

Reese was the first to greet Wes, because Reese greeted everybody at the front door. He scoffed openly and often at the suburban franchise restaurants that employed bright-eyed teenage girls to do the greeting. Reese employed himself, sporting an immaculate white apron that complemented the snowy white mustache bristling on his otherwise soggy, old face. It was his way of keeping in touch with the regulars and of dissuading any teenagers with a notion to dine and dash. He'd long since stopped cooking, but he still wobbled around the café with the help of a burnished wood walking stick.

"Howdy son," he said, his big, toothy grin widening.

"Good morning," Wes said.

"Only got about ten more minutes of it left," he said, glancing at a large watch on his right wrist. "Linda's got the burgers working on the grill, so I hope you're thinking lunch more than you are breakfast."

Wes nodded and walked in. He pulled up a seat at the counter and ordered an unsweetened tea. At 11:55, the first Nooner marched in. Although the crowd inside numbered less than ten, all eyes turned toward this Nooner, because all eyes at this time of year would do so—it being Coach Lawler. He had a commanding presence, Wes would give him that, and he knew how to work a room. It no doubt helped to have that kind of personality in influencing a booster club, Wes thought, and the recent upgrades to the Eagles' weight room and video equipment spoke volumes of Coach Lawler's fundraising talents. The coach waved his hand to every individual in his line of view and nodded to the waitress, who put on another pot of coffee in response. Wes shoved off of his seat and went over.

"Hey Coach," he said, offering his hand. Coach Lawler looked confused at first, and then shook it.

"You weren't at practice yesterday," Lawler said. "A fidgety fellow showed up; nearly wet his pants trying to do an interview with me. Something is wrong with that boy."

"Sorry I wasn't there," Wes said, which he meant. He would have enjoyed seeing Big Bird stumble through an interview with Coach Lawler. "They've got me on a new assignment."

"Is that so?" Lawler sat down. He wore a blue T-shirt with a white Eagle painted in the middle, tight around his thick chest and thicker stomach. As head coach of the local football team, Lawler had his pick of when to schedule his weight lifting classes, his only responsibility to the school for teaching. And even then, the classes were more for the football players than for anyone else. He wanted as much of their time as possible, which was typical of football programs in the South. He used the open scheduling to circle in lunches with old football buddies, apparently. The coincidence of his being a Nooner worked in Wes's favor. To uncover an odd tidbit on Michael Gavin or score an in-depth interview, he needed to win the crowd. Coach Lawler would be his best shot.

"So who is covering my game then?" Lawler said with a grumpy humph.

"Same guy who visited you yesterday . . . Scott," Wes said. "He should have told you."

"Oh my," Lawler said. "I might have a talking to with Keith then. It's the biggest game of the year. Don't take this for nothing but an honest assessment, but old Scotty couldn't write his way out of a paper bag. You at least get the names of my players right."

Just then, two more Nooners arrived: one a slim, short man in khaki pants and a red polo shirt, and the other a large black man with a button-up shirt, tie, brown pants, and polished dress shoes. Lawler's demeanor lightened considerably.

"Hey fellas, we got the *News* right here in our very own corner of the world!" Lawler said, slapping Wes so hard on the back that he nearly lurched face-first onto the table.

"Well, tell him I canceled a year ago," the smaller man screeched. The two men took their seats cautiously, as if Wes might bite.

"Gents, this here is"—Lawler looked over at Wes before introducing him—"this here is Wes Watkins, *News* reporter. Wes, that big feller you see is Bruce Foster, one of the meanest, baddest defensive ends ever to suit up for Talking Creek. Now he's the best production manager at Southern Décor. This little weasel here is Clay Stoddard, but we call him Par. Takes care of Mountain Crest Country Club, which his pops started. Finished as the most efficient backup quarterback in Talking Creek history, mostly 'cause he never had to play. Man's never worked a hard day in his life."

Wes shook both men's hands. Par kept his hold until he had the chance to say something.

"I got a bone to pick with you then, Mr. *News*," he said.

"You do?"

"Here we go," said Bruce as he took a seat. Lawler folded his arms and grinned, apparently about to enjoy what Par was going to say.

"You bet," Par began. "See, we sit here and talk Eagle football. Least in the fall. Spring and summer it's the Braves and maybe some two-a-days, you understand; but because we have jobs and can't go to every practice, we rely on the *News* to get us our much-needed Eagles info. And I tell ya, I've never seen so much bias in my life. Are you covering the Eagles or covering them other schools?"

Bias. The most hated word in journalism. Reporters and editors work within the constraints of time, balanced coverage, and allotted page space to produce an objective product. For Wes, it meant Talking Creek notebooks—reports on TCHS football, complete with injury reports and Coach Lawler's words of wisdom—every other day, by far the most of any local high school. But because readers were left to their own devices, if they consistently picked up a copy of the paper on the wrong day, such as when the paper had only a blurb on Talking Creek but a feature on Jasper High football, then they play "connect-the-conspiracy dots" and bam, there's the bias.

Wes's eyes met Coach Lawler's. He didn't show Wes which way he was leaning. "We give Talking Creek the same coverage, if not more, than the rest of the area," Wes said to Par.

Par frowned. He obviously wanted to continue to grill Wes in front of his buddies. "Then why do all of the practice reports sound so depressing? You don't like our team or something?"

"I don't 'like' or 'dislike' any team," Wes said. "I try to cover everybody fairly."

"Then why are your stories so negative? We got a winning record, don't we? You'da thought the sky was falling by your tellin' it."

Wes was tempted to pull out his recorder and play back the last interview from Coach Lawler, which had the phrase "sky is falling" somewhere in the middle.

"I'm not negative about anyone," Wes pleaded.

"You're right; you're just biased against Talking Creek."

Coach Lawler and Bruce remained quiet, save for whispering to the waitress that they wanted "the usual."

This was stupid. Wes was debating a country club golfer on the merits of journalism. "You're right, Mr. Stoddard, I'm biased. I sit in my office eight hours a day trying to think of ways to avoid coverage."

Wes immediately regretted the outburst, which left his heart beating fast enough to burst out of his chest. But it got their attention. Coach Lawler and Bruce looked at each other, then glanced at Par, who was staring up at Wes, eyes wide. This probably wasn't a man used to getting called on something, outside of his circle of friends. He must have been used to debating politics and winning. For as much joy as that small outburst gave Wes, his stomach cringed. This was going nowhere, and in the grand scheme of things, maybe it was just a waste of time. As if these old football players were really going to tell him anything useful. He'd only come in to get quotes, and he could probably write what they were going to say before they even said it. These guys were easy to read, easy to direct in interviews, and getting grief was not on the list of things to do. Or worse, maybe Wes had just ruined his relationship with his lead source.

"Shoot dawgy!" Lawler said, coming to life. "Thatta boy! Now that's what I'm talking about. I like a man who will draw a line in the sand for what he does."

Bruce rolled his eyes. Par grunted. Lawler slapped Wes's back again, but not without a slight flash in the eye that implied he was saving his hide rather than agreeing with him.

"Not just any man can come in here and go toe-to-toe with the Nooners. Took some guts. You'll have to forgive ol' Par here. One of your local columnists done put a hit job on one of his daddy's construction projects for the country club; ended up losing a plan to put another nine holes in. Par's been writing rebuttals to the paper ever since, and you don't want to be anywhere near the man when the cable news shows come on at night. So, fellas, let's go ahead and get into it; what'd you come here to ask me, Wes?"

"Ask all of you, actually," Wes said, eager to change the subject. They nodded for him to continue. "It's about Michael Gavin's funeral."

"We heard yesterday," Par scoffed. "That's old news."

"Yes sir," Wes said, trying to gauge how much ground he'd already lost. His temper may have cost him some information. "I need help for something I'm working on from the folks who knew him best."

"It's a shame," Lawler said, "Whole town is rallying around the family, though. Not a house within twenty miles that doesn't have an American flag flying. In fact, Bruce here told his boss at Décor, and they're coming up with some huge ribbons and whatnot to line the streets. I rallied the boys this week for Calhoun, not that they need the extra lift. They're rip-roaring and ready to go."

"Not if your running back keeps fumbling the way he has," Par said.

"You worry about your golf game, Par," Lawler said. "I'll worry about Calhoun."

"You were saying, Wes?" Bruce interjected.

"Michael requested that I give his eulogy. I'm talking to folks who knew him to prepare for it."

"Huh?" said Lawler and Par simultaneously.

"Well, why would Michael want you to do that?" Lawler said. He sounded hurt, like he was supposed to be the one leading the community in song and prayer. Wes shrugged.

"Beats me," Par said, eyeing Wes warily.

"I mean, if anyone deserves a big funeral, it's Mike. He should have a sold-out stadium full of people praising him. Talking Creek guys; Georgia guys. Even an ex–vice president is supposed to be coming. Heard it from the police chief himself, who heard it from a state fella."

"I'm just as confused about the decision as you are, Coach," Wes said. "Michael spoke with Keith Starks about this a few months ago."

"Well Par, maybe you're on to something," Coach Lawler said, shaking his head. "New guy covering the Calhoun game, and Wes giving Mike's eulogy. Keith is gonna hear about this from just about everyone at the booster meeting."

Just then, four more Nooners walked in. Coach Lawler stopped his speech and waved to his buddies, who waved back and walked over. Three were old timers who appeared well within their retirement pensions. Another was a younger man as tall as Bruce, with lean, sculpted arms and stilts for legs. He immediately noticed Wes.

"Boys," Coach Lawler said, turning to the arrivals, "this is Wes Watkins, works with me on the football beat, and he's going to be speaking at Mike Gavin's funeral. If you can believe that."

"You knew him, then?" one of the old timers asked.

"No, not exactly," Wes said. Everyone raised their eyebrows, except for the taller man who had just walked in. He sat down in the seat farthest away and didn't make eye contact. "I'm trying to interview a lot of folks who did know him before the funeral. I was hoping y'all could help me out with his playing days."

"Wes, my boy," Lawler said, wrapping his arm around Wes's shoulder, "you came to the right place. Hey Linda! Bring over the Book of Ball. And some coffee."

The Book of Ball, located behind the cashier's counter, chronicled every playoff season of Talking Creek football. Along with having a successful café, Reese happened to have an affinity for Talking Creek athletics. The walls of the café were plastered with programs from past seasons and cal-endars for both Talking Creek and Tributary athletics. The actual book consisted of laminated newspaper clippings and photos. Lawler made space on the table for the book. An order of cheese fries also came out. Some of the Nooners dug in.

"Why don't you take a look at these, see what you think of Gavin the Great?" Lawler said.

Wes had already read plenty of these stories. The great Michael Gavin could do no wrong. At least that was the theme from his press clippings. But Wes flipped through the book to play nice and earn quotes. This gave the Nooners ample opportunity to point to their favorite games and reminisce a little more. Wes sat back and soaked it all in as the headlines rushed past him.

Eagles pound Cedartown 43–14, Gavin Throws for 300 yds.

TCH Remains Unbeaten, Gavin Scores 4 TDs.

Gavin Golden in State Final.

The list went on and on. By Gavin's junior year, the sports depart-ment at the *News* had run out of phrases to use for the boy wonder's exploits. What more could be said? Over sodas and cheese fries, the Nooners recapped Gavin's career. He had played a supporting role as a freshman at Talking Creek. No surprise there. Most freshmen are too small physically and too wide-eyed mentally to make much of a dif-ference against older and more physically endowed teenagers. Michael backed up an average quarterback during a 5–5 campaign. Mostly sit-ting on the sidelines when the offense was on the field, Michael spent most of his time flying around on special teams, and on defense as a free safety. By the end of his freshman campaign, the future star had four interceptions, eighty-five tackles, five fumble recoveries, and an All-County nod.

Michael's star shined even brighter his sophomore year. Leading Talk-ing Creek under center, the phenom passed for 2,900 yards and eleven touchdowns, and rushed for 1,400 more yards. The Eagles rode his back to their first-ever state title. During his junior and senior years, he threw for a total of 5,643 yards and 49 scores. The Eagles won another state title in Michael's senior season.

"I gotta tell ya, I ain't never seen an arm like that," Lawler said. "And I should know. I was his favorite target. Broke almost every finger catching his stuff."

"You played with him?" Wes asked, knowing the answer, but hoping for more.

"Sure did," Lawler said, pride in his voice. "All-County tight end. Par was Mike's backup and personal water boy. Bruce here was a grade behind us but lettered all four years in school and anchored the D-line our second state title run. And Wayne Griffin, that tall, quiet fella over there, he was our leading wide receiver, senior year."

Wayne said nothing, preferring to sip his coffee while everyone huddled around the scrapbook. The conversation returned to comments on the newspaper clippings.

"Michael got offers from near every school in the universe," Lawler continued. "'Bama, Auburn, both UTs, Ohio State, Michigan, USC, Tech, and UGA. Everyone wanted him."

"And he knew it," Par said.

"Yeah buddy, he knew it," Coach Lawler said. "Just like you knew you could go anywhere on your daddy's dime. Mike, bless his poor misguided soul, already had his heart set on Georgia—figured he'd have the best shot of playing there—but he took his recruiting visits to other schools. The process was one big tourist trip. School A would show up with a plane and fly him to their campus. He'd come back fat and happy, with steak sauce all over his shirt. Picked Southern Cal as one visit, 'cause he'd never been to California and wanted to try surfing. Auburn and Florida just to spy on the co-eds there. Michigan 'cause he always wanted to watch a game at the Big Show."

"Didn't he play fullback at Georgia?" Wes asked. That elicited a table-wide groan.

"What a waste of talent. That coach didn't have no sense," Coach Lawler said. "I woulda built my offense around Mike, and won twice as many bowl games, and another conference crown to boot. If Mike wasn't such a good guy, ol' Bishop woulda never won that championship Mike's senior year. Earl Bishop redshirts Mike the first year to learn the system, backs up a senior the next, and comes out guns blazing as a redshirt sophomore. Lit up a cupcake opener for three hundred yards, two touchdowns. If he hadn't torn an ACL second game against Carolina . . ."

"But he still had a few years of eligibility remaining, right?" Wes said, scribbling notes furiously so he could remember this for the trip to Athens.

"Two words: Brock Sellers," Par said. "Just as much a blue chipper as Michael. Five-star recruit out of Daytona Beach, Florida. Not even a Georgia boy. Takes over when Michael's hurt and never looks back."

"Bishop never gave Mike a real shot," Coach Lawler said.

"Michael had a chance to earn it in spring ball," Bruce said.

"Chance my hiney," Coach Lawler grunted. "First year back from a bum leg injury is a wash; everybody knows that. Bishop didn't like Mike, so he buried him so far down the depth chart our boy didn't have a chance to earn it back. That coach was stubborn, didn't want his quarterback scrambling out of the pocket like Michael loved to do. Bishop signs one quarterback too many in the next class, runs out of fullbacks and decides he'll order Michael to beef up and take a few for the team his senior year."

"He made All-SEC, right?" Bruce said.

"Proof enough they shoulda kept him at QB," Coach Lawler said. "He coulda played defensive tackle and made All-Conference. He should have been an All-American, but fullbacks don't get that kind of recognition. Ever heard of a blocker being in the running for the Heisman? That Sellers kid could throw a mile, but he was dumber than a bag of rocks. And a jerk to boot, just like his coach. Wouldn't have lost to LSU that year if it wasn't for him. Woulda won more than the SEC title with Michael taking snaps at QB. I tell you what: Georgia's lucky Bishop ain't coaching no more. I wouldn't have given his assistant coaches the time of day to recruit any of our boys. No way, no how."

Wes looked at his watch and cringed. If he was going to make it to Athens in time, he had to leave. "Guys, if I have any more questions, can I call you later?"

"Ten-four, Wes," Coach Lawler said. "We're here same time, same station. Where ya headed?"

"Funny you should ask. If I had time, I was going to head to Athens."

What Wes didn't tell Coach Lawler was that it wasn't so much to interview Michael's former college coach as it was to get a few player interviews in for a story in tomorrow's paper on the Georgia–Tennessee game—if Lewis would sneak it in. He'd penciled in this game for weeks to try to get some decent clips, and he thought with the Michael Gavin connection he still might have a shot. Wes was counting on Starks to approve of the trip because he was doing interviews with Michael's acquaintances too.

"Great!" Coach Lawler said, hands flapping in the air. "You tell that Bishop if I see him at the funeral, I'll drop-kick him."

"Hey Lawler, show him the 'Motor game,'" one of the old-timers said.

"What was the 'motor' game?" Wes asked, playing along. He hoped whatever it was it wouldn't take too long.

"Sophomore year, when we won our first state title," Lawler began. "We lost a non-region game second week of the season and a region game the fifth week, so we were 7–2 heading into the season finale. We win, we're in the playoffs for the first time since God knows when. If we lose, we're out, and our big turnaround is all for naught. Well, that's when Carrollton rolls into town."

"Big team," Par said. "Got the biggest band in the state, biggest line we'd face that whole year."

"I remember them, whew!" Bruce said. "My head rang after that game. Hadn't grown into my shoes yet."

"They were big, and they were fast," Lawler said. "They were 7–2, too. Same deal for them. They lose, and their season's over. Well, seeing as it was the tenth game of the year, secret's out on our offense. Carrollton knows we got this hotshot at quarterback. At this point in his career, Mike is running out of the option. He could throw it a mile, but we didn't have a wide receiver who could run that far."

"We had Wayne," Par said. Wayne pretended not to hear the comment.

"Yeah, but Wayne didn't break out until senior year," Lawler continued.

"So, like I was saying, Mike'd hit me on third and longs, but that was about it. So we'd line up in the 'I' and work our little option game. Carrollton knew that, and schemed their D to put a world of hurt on Mike. You shoulda seen 'em. Big uglies hootin' and hollerin' during the pregame. 'We're gonna nail ya!' 'You gonna be eatin' grass all day long.' 'Your butt is mine, MG.'"

"That was the G-rated version," Bruce said.

"Well Mike doesn't say a lick to them, but they weren't kidding. First quarter, they must have blitzed every down. We'd throw a pitch, and they'd drill Mike to the ground, ball or not. We'd try a quick dump to our tailback, or a screen, and they'd use that as an excuse to pick Mike up off the ground and plant him into the Bermuda. By halftime, we were down 7–3, despite about a hundred yards on late-hit penalties on them, and Mike had half the field sodded to his jersey. They were out for blood."

"You'd've never thought he was getting the beating of his life though," Par pointed out.

"Nope," Lawler said. "What choice did we have, put you in the game, Par? You'd have messed your pants."

"Just tell the story," Par said.

"So our coach starts laying it on thick to the offensive line; but how were we supposed to cover ten guys on a blitz with six guys, including me? Meanwhile, Mike is off to the side of the team huddle, stretching and keeping to himself. He wasn't trying to be some fuming big shot. Not a peep out of him, one way or another. I walk over there after Coach has chewed my ear off. Coach thought I wasn't checking my guy, but he'd send me on pass plays half the time, the running back wouldn't pick up my man, what was I supposed to do? Anyway, I go over and pat Mike on the shoulder to let him know we'll hold the line second half. He says, 'Let 'em come, Bud.'"

"You should have seen the look in his eye," Bruce said. "Fire and brimstone. Even the guys on D noticed. It gave me the shivers. Madman. He'd just gotten killed for a half, and he had this easygoing smile but the devil dancing around in his eyes."

"Second half, Carrollton brought much of the same," Lawler continued. "Safety blitz. Corner blitz. All out blitz. We'd make a few first downs, but every yard Mike or Mason, our tailback, gained, they'd pay for it in pain. Thing was, Carrollton was wearing down. All that headhuntin' took a toll, 'cause we were getting our hits in too. I was cut blocking over on the buck end. By the middle of the third quarter, they were huffing and puffing. Hands on their hips, then their knees. Then they'd take a knee till we lined up. They were smoked, but they thought it was worth it with the punishment they delivered to our QB."

"They thought differently, end of the third," Par said.

"You better believe they did," Lawler said, pounding the table with his fist. "With all of their blitzing, they were still only up 7–6. Our D kept dialing in three-and-outs, so the fourth quarter looked like it was going to be a battle of attrition."

"We were knocking their heads without having to blitz all the time," Par said. "Bruce would just get low and plow his guy over. Our linebackers would come in and nail the fullback, mess up their blocking assignments, and get the ball carrier in the backfield."

"End of the third, it all changed," Lawler said. "Mike bolts out to the right on a keeper, gains maybe four, and is launched into the Carrollton sideline by the weakside linebacker. He lands right at the feet of their coach, who looks down expecting to see a quarterback begging for mercy. Well, Mike looks him straight in the eye, slaps him on the thigh, and with a big toothy grin says, 'How you doin', coach?' Jumps right up and runs to the huddle. That's when they knew."

"We owned them in the fourth," Par said.

"Mike must have rushed for a hundred yards that quarter alone. Throws one score, to me, and runs one in on his own. Mason hits paydirt once too, and by the end we've won 27–7. No one tried that stupid tactic on us again."

"So you said that you didn't really have wide receivers the year you won state for the first time," Wes said. "From what I've read, Michael was recruited as a dual-threat quarterback. Did a bunch of young guys come in?"

"Not exactly," Lawler said. "Wayne over there, but he didn't come on until his senior year."

"He just about quit end of junior year," Bruce said. Wayne glanced up from his meal.

"I woulda quit under the circumstances," Par said.

"Which were . . . ?" Wes asked Wayne.

"Dropped a pass," Lawler interrupted.

Wayne's eyes met Lawler, who then looked away. "Not a pass; I dropped *passes*," Wayne said evenly. "I had butterfingers in the biggest game of the year."

"Quarterfinals against Bremen," Lawler said, filling Wes in. "Mike has his worst game as an Eagle. Throws eight of twenty for ninety-nine yards and two picks; but five of those balls hit Wayne square in the numbers. We stalled on two sure-fire scoring drives because he doesn't make the third-down catch. We're still in it at the end, down four with about a minute to go. Gavin gets us down to the 9 yard line with time for one more play. Well, Wayne is the tallest kid on the field, so Gavin throws a fade to him."

"Right through his hands," Par shook his head. He glanced over nervously at Wayne, who offered no response.

"Right through his hands," Lawler said. "We lose our shot at a second straight title. Get it back our senior year, but man."

"Thanks for reminding me," Wayne said.

"We were livid," Lawler said. "Everyone thought Wayne lost us the game. Wayne thought he lost us the game, and Mike was the most upset of all. Chewed Wayne a new one in the locker room. Some guys gave him the evil eye at school for the rest of the year. I don't even know why you came back senior year, we all hated your guts, Wayne. Blamed you for the loss."

There's a rush Wes got as a reporter when someone he interviewed unintentionally gave him a scoop. They're usually firing away clichés and memories that paint their story in a positive light; but every now and then they'd slip and give a new lead to pursue. Wes got this all the time from coaches, but the slicker ones would catch themselves and give a "Don't print that" request. Wes could print it, the coach had said it after all, but out of maintaining the relationship, he consented. Here he was talking to a bunch of ex–football players who he'd probably never see after this week, and they'd just given him his first real insight to Michael Gavin the man.

Was this a chink in the armor, perhaps? Wes went for it. "So you said Michael blamed Wayne for the loss?"

The question floated in the air. He watched Wayne's expression. No warning signs there. To Wes's disappointment, though, Coach Lawler snatched the question.

"We all blamed him, truth be told," Coach Lawler shrugged. "All he had to do was pull that ball down with both hands, touch his toes on the grass, and call it a day. The corner didn't have an angle on him. Man oh man."

"Why did you come back then, Wayne?" Wes asked.

"It took a lot of convincing," Wayne said. "I worked hard over the whole summer on my ball catching skills, but Michael still put it into me the first snap of two-a-days. I just couldn't do right by him. He was relentless, called me every name in the book. He could be ruthless sometimes."

"How so?" Wes asked. He realized he'd thrown in too much. The question immediately cooled the conversation, as he watched each face tighten. Everyone had forgotten for a minute that Wes was the outsider here to listen to their stories about their fallen hero. Now they were a little more careful on how to paint Michael's story.

"Well, you see, he was just a very competitive person," Lawler said. "We all were, but Mike took it to a new level. He had to be the best at everything. Often he was. Ticked when he wasn't. He was like that in pee wees, yelling at people if they dropped a pass or didn't lunge for an extra yard. Here we were worrying about getting home for cartoons and little Patton is marching us through Germany."

"Must have been like his father," Par said.

"If the younger Gavin weren't so dang good, we'd have probably all thought he was just some jerk," Lawler continued. "But the kid could play. He took out most of his aggression on would-be tacklers, and that was a sight to behold. He'd have set the state record for passing yardage if he wasn't as ticked at the world as he was back then. So, we'd take his jawing, most of us. Wayne took it the wrong way."

"Up until the second game, that was how it went," Bruce said. "Then it seemed like everything changed."

"Why, what happened?" Wes asked.

The old teammates looked around the table. All eyes set on Wayne. He took one last cheese fry, wiped his mouth, and sighed.

"He asked me to forgive him."

Chapter 7

The spiral was perfect, the laces a white blur as the football raced across the clear blue sky. There was no wind to worry about, though it wouldn't matter. By sheer velocity, the ball had at least sixty yards on it. It hit its peak at the 50 yard line, dipping down en route to a certain completion. On its final seconds in flight, it arced in just such a way that made a receiver's job easier. All the receiver had to do was lay his hands out and cradle the ball.

It hit the receiver's fingertips and fell to the ground.

"Oh come on!"

Michael Gavin grabbed his facemask in frustration. Another perfect pass. Another dropped pass.

"Griffin, front and center!" Wayne Griffin, head held low, reversed course and trotted back to the huddle, where the Eagles offensive coordinator waited impatiently.

"Son, I can't run those routes for you," the coach said, spitting out a wad of sunflower seed shells. "Gavin couldn't have thrown a better ball. If we're going to win region, you gotta make those catches."

The words hit Wayne like concussion blasts. He had seven months to shake off the misery of last season's playoff game, but the memory was still lodged firmly in the front of his mind. He had joined the football team as a way to stay in shape for basketball season. At six-foot-four, Wayne was a slick and crafty power forward, able to dish a no-look pass or turn for a beautiful low post move with ease. He relished the fast pace of basketball, how if you made a mistake on one end of the court you could immediately make amends on the other. Football was different. If you screwed up, you could stall an entire drive and kill your team's momentum. If you screwed up a lot, you were in Michael Gavin's doghouse, the worst spot to be—and if you screwed up on the biggest stage of the season, you had crossed into something else. Wayne was in Talking Creek purgatory.

He toyed with the idea of not playing his senior year. Basketball was his main sport, and he enjoyed it. Plus, he juggled a part-time job on the weekends with school and sports. But the competitor in him wouldn't quit. He needed to prove himself; always had. Most of the team was a collection of good ol' boys and the prep crowd. Their parents lavished them with new clothes, sporty rides, and spare change for a movie or night out on the town. The popular kids. Guys like Wayne didn't run with those crowds. The only bridge between him and their world was in strapping on a helmet—and even then he wasn't guaranteed an ounce of respect. Still, if he could take anything away from last season, it was that he could bounce back.

Wayne collected himself following the season and had made an effort to show for some summer workouts. It wasn't all bad. He had a handful of friends on the team—guys like Bruce Foster, who worked as a stock clerk with Wayne at the grocery store in between lifting sessions; but Bruce was on defense, and those guys ran their summer drills separately.

Michael wasn't impressed with Wayne's attendance record or his skills. He barked at him during the volunteer weight lifting sessions. He put extra zip on passes to Wayne, jamming his fingers and bruising his chest. He just about drove Wayne to tears for not taking time off work to attend the volunteer football camp.

"I can't take time off," Wayne said. "I've got to work."

"Why?" Michael said, fuming in front of the rest of the team in the humid, sweaty fieldhouse. "So you can have a few extra bucks to blow at Waffle House? Do you want to be part of this team or not? 'Cause you're not showing me jack right now."

Wayne resented Michael from that point on. He was the most imposing person at Talking Creek. He could be your best friend or your worst enemy; unfortunately, nothing Wayne did got on his good side. Wayne didn't resent him for that, though. He resented him for his free time. For all the guys' free time. While he was riding his bike on the hot Georgia asphalt between home, work, and the fieldhouse, they were sleeping in, playing games, dragging their butts into two-hour workouts before heading home to do nothing. Michael may have spent the most time at the fieldhouse, using his will power to force an extra lift out of a teammate, but even then, what did he go home to? How could he judge Wayne so easily?

Wayne took the hit. He took more hits in two-a-days, both physically and emotionally. He was shaky, hurt, but surviving. Even after the latest barrage. He nodded weakly once the coach had finished his rant, telling him to catch the ball, like he didn't already know that. The coordinator moved on to the offensive linemen.

"Wayne."

It was Michael.

"Wayne!"

He looked up.

"What's your problem?"

"No problem," Wayne said.

"Then why do you keep dropping passes? I can't put them out there any better than that."

"I know, Mike."

"So, you going to start carrying your load or what?"

Wayne was silent.

Michael shook his head. "Whatever man."

"Huddle up!" It was the head coach, Stew Pickens. Offense and defense met in the center of the field and took a knee. "Boys, congratulations, two-a-days are over."

Hoots rang out from a handful of players. The coach flashed them a stern look, and the team was silent again. "We made some progress in some areas. In other areas," he looked directly at Wayne, "we need to get better. Period. Now you've got a couple of days to rest up before school starts and we practice for the opener. Seniors, you think long and hard about what you want this season to be."

The team disbanded. Wayne was the first one into the locker room, dressed, and ready to leave. As he walked across the locker room to the exit, he heard the other players cracking jokes, teammates humming tunes together, and camaraderie being built for another run at a state championship.

No one said a word to Wayne.

★   ★   ★

Why am I here? Wayne thought as he ran onto the field. It was the first game of the season, third quarter, with the Eagles cruising through a blowout, 24–3. Coach had called his number, so Wayne, somewhat reluctantly, trotted off to the midfield huddle. He'd already dropped the only pass thrown his way, a slant route, thrown perfectly by Michael. He had stuck his arms out the way he was taught, but seeing the perfect spiral sizzling toward him, he hesitated.

Maybe I'll have a better chance using my body.

He tucked his arms in at the last minute, and that lack of confidence cost him a reception. The ball bounced off his jersey. Michael cursed, stared at him with a look of death. The coach caught on and pulled Wayne to the bench. For two quarters, Talking Creek ran strictly option plays.

Wayne nudged into an unwelcoming huddle. No one so much as glanced at him. They were the region's top offense with the state's best quarterback, and Wayne was just a broken part. He may have had the best speed and a tremendous height advantage, but he couldn't catch the ball. And production was all that mattered tonight.

Michael took the play in from the sidelines. "Take-off 86, left," he said.

Bud Lawler grumbled. "Ah, come on," he said.

"Take-off 86, left," Michael repeated, looking Wayne square in the eyes. The huddle broke and Wayne split wide to the left, running his route. His heart pumped. His hands turned clammy. His eyes darted to the secondary. They were playing him soft, one-on-one, daring Michael to throw with eight in the box. It was the right call to make, even Wayne saw that, but as Michael received the snap, Wayne felt a sense of dread.

Catch it, catch it, catch it . . .

Another drop.

Wayne's helmet was all that separated him from Michael's wrath on the sidelines. The Eagles' fearless leader had decided to make an example out of Wayne, in front of a sold-out stadium. He yelled and screamed and nearly pushed Wayne before he was restrained by a teammate. This was new. Usually, Michael chewed people out during practice, not games. Game days they were all part of the team. Apparently Wayne's welcome was worn out. He didn't care. He had joined the football team as a diversion, maybe even to make more friends. Now he was out, completely. The team's star player hated him. Who would want to side with him? Bruce had been the lone support in two-a-days, but there was only so much he could say to the team. This was Michael's show.

Wayne took his tongue-lashing with a detached acceptance. What else could Michael possibly say? Let Mr. All-America yell. Football wasn't about the game anymore. Forget the game. Forget the team. No, it was about beating Michael.

Following the postgame team meeting at the 50 yard line, Wayne clenched his teeth and watched Michael trot to the fence. His eyes narrowed on No. 7, like the jersey was the focus for all his pain of the last year. He released a breath, and felt the anger settle in his stomach. Let Michael hate him. Let the whole team hate him. Let them blame him for all of their problems. If that's what they needed, then fine. He still had a life away from football. He'd have his dream season in basketball. But Wayne Griffin wouldn't be called a quitter. He would finish the season, whether it was on the bench, on the field, or on a stretcher.

★　★　★

Wayne pinched himself before he rang the doorbell. Was he really here? At Michael Gavin's place? Michael, of all people, had invited Wayne over to dinner. The very same night when he humiliated Wayne in front of the entire Talking Creek community, Michael had trotted over to Wayne following the game and asked him to come over for dinner the next night.

Wayne wasn't stupid. He knew why. Michael's dad, the major, had intervened. After the game, Paul Gavin had motioned for his son to meet him at the fence separating the field from the stands. No one came within ten feet of them. Paul's scowl deterred any would-be well-wishers from interrupting the conversation. When it was over, Michael, the blood flushed from his face, walked over to Wayne and did the unthinkable, asking him to dinner. Wayne wanted with every fiber of his being to say no, but if he was going to beat Michael at his game, then he needed to keep up his own front.

"I'll be there."

The Gavins' house was on the opposite side of town. The nice side. The lawn was well kept and a garden sprouted with flowers. No cleaning and scrubbing would ever make Wayne's place as nice as this. But he'd long since stopped envying kids who had better living arrangements than his. He just lived with it. But that didn't mean he didn't notice.

When Michael opened the door, Wayne was outside, wiping a bead of sweat off his head, his bike leaning on the steps of the front porch. He had just finished an early afternoon shift at the grocery store, and had ridden the final three miles to the Gavins'. He didn't have a car, and his mom couldn't afford one for him, so he made do using a bike.

"Hey, Wayne," Michael said coolly.

"Hey, Mike," Wayne said, making brief eye contact.

"Thanks for coming." Wayne knew Michael didn't mean it.

"Wayne Griffin!" Mrs. Gavin came stomping to the front door. "It is so good to see you! Oh my goodness, you have been out in the heat too long, dear. Do you need something to drink?"

"Yes ma'am, that'd be great."

"Water? Iced tea? OJ?"

"I guess I could use some water. Thanks, ma'am."

"Well, don't just stand outside and get even more sweaty; why don't you come on in?"

Wayne let Mrs. Gavin escort him into the kitchen where she poured him a glass of ice water from a pitcher. He had taken his first gulp by the time Mr. Gavin popped inside from the screen door with a plate of pork chops. "Perfect timing," he said.

They put the salad, mashed potatoes, and salt and pepper on the table and sat. Mr. Gavin said a prayer and they passed around the food dishes. Michael's parents immediately took the smallest chops and left the two bigger ones for Michael and Wayne. Michael got the hint and left the biggest one for Wayne, who forked the remaining pork chop onto his plate and used it as his focal point. Everyone ate in silence for the first few bites.

"So Wayne, are you looking forward to the season?" Mrs. Gavin asked.

"Yes ma'am," he said.

"Now, we know you are so good on the basketball court. Which is your favorite sport?"

"Probably be basketball, I guess."

"And why is that?"

"Don't get beat up as much." He wanted so badly for that to sink in with Michael.

"Well, I sure do hope none of you boys end up hobbling off the field! Good gracious, football can be hard for a mother to watch. I bet your mom tells you the same thing."

"Yes ma'am."

"Where does she sit for the games?"

"Oh, she don't come to the games," Wayne said.

Mrs. Gavin scooped another helping of mashed potatoes and put it on Wayne's plate, which was nearly empty. "She doesn't?"

"No ma'am, she's got to work."

"What about your father?" Mr. Gavin asked.

"Dad died when we were young. Just have Mom and three sisters." Wayne left out the part where his two younger sisters were half-sisters from a failed marriage following his father's death. He didn't enjoy speaking about his family dynamics to people he barely knew, or liked.

"Sounds like a close-knit family. How is it living with all those women?"

Wayne sipped his water before speaking again. "It's okay, I guess. Gets kinda annoying after school. My older sister looks after the younger ones. She's got a part-time job in the morning."

"Where do ya'll live?"

"Cross the train tracks. In the Livingston homes."

"You mean you rode your bike all that way?" Mrs. Gavin said.

Wayne nodded. "Went to work first, then here," he said.

"But that's at least nine miles! Michael, you put that bike in the back of your truck and drive him home after dinner. If I had known you were going to ride a bike all that way, I would've had Michael come pick you up, too." Michael glared at his half-eaten pork chop.

The ride home couldn't have been any more awkward. Wayne sat silently in the passenger seat, looking out the window. At one point, he stole a glance at Michael, saw the straightness in his back, and the cold gaze in his eye.

So, he's angry. What else is new? Come to think of it, Wayne couldn't remember a single moment when Michael had ever looked happy. Possibly on the football field. But even then, his celebrations looked more like relief than joy. He pitied the road, how Michael's eyes dug into it with the fierceness that stung Wayne at practice. How could anyone as successful as Michael be this angry with the world?

But as a tinge of pity rose, it vanished just as fast. They approached the Livingston homes, a spruced-up name for what the place really was. Wayne sat up straighter. "You can drop me off here."

"My father told me to drop you off at your house."

"That's okay, Mike," Wayne said, his hand on the door as they pulled up to the entrance gate. "You can let me out here. I need to get the mail anyway."

"My father wants me to drop you off, and call from your house."

Wayne sat, stunned. What could he say?

"Fine."

"Which way?" Michael asked.

"Second left, first place on the right."

The Livingston homes weren't a suburban retreat or an apartment complex. They were single-wide and double-wide trailers, stretched out along ten acres. The blue-collar crowd of Talking Creek made their homes in the muddy, poorly kept property. Michael and Wayne drove past an assortment of trailers. Some new and well kept; others in decay, with who knows what lying around the yard.

I hate you for seeing this, Wayne thought. I hate you.

Michael pulled up to the Griffins' trailer. The sides were stained with mud, the deck outside worn with unvarnished wood. A string of laundry flapped loosely on a wire in the yard. Underneath the trailer, a rusted bicycle lay idle, its yellow seat and handlebars faded. Wayne didn't bother looking at Michael. He hopped out of the truck and made a beeline for the door.

Michael followed. Wayne hurried to the small kitchen for the phone. Plates were strewn everywhere. The sound of children laughing came from one of the rooms at the other end of the trailer. Four kids in a trailer this size made it impossible to keep clean. Wayne and his older sister did their best, but the result was the same. Now his mess—his dirty little secret, which most of the Talking Creek Eagles didn't know or care about, was on display for the team's top player and captain. Wayne handed the phone to Michael. He looked at Wayne, his expression blank, before dialing the number.

So this is it, Wayne thought. Michael Gavin's seen everything, done everything, been everywhere that could possibly humiliate me.

He watched Michael as he talked to his dad on the phone. He wanted to see a scoff, a hint of condescension. It would make him hate his teammate more; make it easier to build a wall. He was out in the open for Michael to see, all the shame that comes from a large family being raised by a mom who was just trying to get by. Living in a trailer park because rent was too expensive anywhere else.

Do you see this, Mike? Do you see why I have to have a part-time job? Do you see why I don't hang with your crowd? Do you see where I come from?

Michael hung up the phone. "Thanks," he said. Then he walked out the door without so much as a good-bye.

★   ★   ★

He wasn't sure what to expect the week after eating at Michael's, but it wasn't this. On Monday, not only was Michael not in his ear and all over his case, he wasn't around at all. He didn't show for school; didn't show for practice; nothing. Tuesday, likewise, came and went with no sign of Michael. Wednesday was the cutoff day for athletes to attend school or get sidelined for that week's athletic events. Michael showed up late, but the principal and coach let it slide. Of course they would. He was the star. He could do whatever he wanted.

Michael, though, wasn't himself. He suited up and ran the plays at practice, but without barking orders, without getting in anyone's face. He had a blank stare half the time and refused to make eye contact with anyone. A few of his buddies tried to shake whatever was irking him, but to no avail.

"I'm fine," was all he said.

But he wasn't. Wayne was as stunned as anyone. He had been the last person to see Michael before his disappearance, so naturally the questioning came his way.

"Why's he like this? What's going on?" his teammates asked. But Wayne could only shrug.

"You do something to him, Griffin?" Bud Lawler asked accusingly.

"Yeah, right, Bud," Bruce Foster said, defending Wayne. "Michael's got something on his mind, but it ain't any of us. He's barely acknowledged we even exist."

"As long as we beat Union County, I don't give a squat," Lawler said. "But if I find out you messed up our QB in any way, Griffin, your butt is mine."

★ ★ ★

Talking Creek's locker room was designed with lockers on two walls facing each other. The offense took one side and the defense took the other. On the offensive side, the linemen claimed the middle of the row, with running backs to their left and wide receivers, kickers, and assorted special teams guys to their right. Michael Gavin's locker was squarely in the middle of the linemen's, a general in the trenches with his troops. Wayne's locker, one he claimed immediately with the only privilege he had on the team—his senior status—was the furthest to the corner, far enough from the center of the action to be left alone.

In the locker room on Friday night, Wayne looked over at Lawler. He was joking with Shane Rogers, the starting left tackle, about some girl he'd dumped last weekend at the movies. Bruce, on the opposite side, could hear the conversation, and obviously wasn't pleased. As Wayne scanned the room, he observed everyone in their pregame rituals. Listening to music. Slamming hands into palms, riling themselves.

Michael sat stoically, eyes fixed on the ceiling, unconcerned with the events around him. Wayne watched him, curious about what he was thinking. He remembered the Michael of last week, and let the feeling pass.

I've got my own problems, Wayne thought. Like a sprained ankle. He'd pivoted the wrong way on a route in practice on Wednesday and paid for it. He'd winced the rest of the week, but was determined to play. He leaned to his left to grab a roll of tape.

"How's the ankle?"

Wayne startled. It was Michael, standing beside him.

"It'll be fine," Wayne said, eager to be left alone, especially by Michael. "Good to go."

"I saw you roll it Wednesday," Michael said.

How did you see anything Wednesday? Wayne wanted to say. You were out in la-la land.

"Hold on a sec," Michael said. He skipped to his locker and pulled out an ankle guard.

"I keep a couple of these around just in case," he said. By now a handful of players were eyeing the interaction. Michael did most of the pregame talks, patted his teammates on the shoulder, that sort of stuff. The fact that he was talking to Wayne, though, garnered interest.

Michael kneeled and pointed to Wayne's left ankle. "Let me take a look," he said.

"Trainer already said it's just a minor sprain, I'd be okay," Wayne said.

"Sure, but can I take a look?" Wayne nodded reluctantly, and Michael pulled off his sock. The ankle was swollen, black and blue.

"It ain't nothin' that anybody else doesn't have from camp," Wayne said dismissively.

Michael ignored him, took his foot and slipped the ankle brace on. Wayne's face flushed. By now they had a number of onlookers. Some stole chuckles, but most were quiet, waiting to see how this played out.

"Can I see the tape?" Michael asked. Wayne, still embarrassed but just as curious as his teammates, handed Michael the roll. Michael began to apply the tape. After going around the foot the first time, he drew it back to make the fit tighter. By the time he was finished, the entire team was watching.

"Can I see your shoe?" Michael said. Wayne handed him the shoe. Michael loosened the laces, slipped the shoe onto Wayne's foot, and then paused. He looked around the room, took in the audience, the full attention of the locker room, and then turned back to Wayne. He started to speak so that everyone could hear him, but the words were directed at Wayne.

"I don't think I've ever had a worse feeling than last year," he said. "When we walked off that field, losers, in a game we clearly could have won, I had never felt more angry in my life. I was angry we lost; angry at the way I played; angry at the way the team played. And I was angry at you, Wayne."

Michael tied the shoelaces, slowly, pulling each row tighter.

"So I used that anger. I enjoyed it, actually. I made it last through the spring and into summer. I breathed it in lifting weights, punishing my body with early morning runs. I fed off it."

He tied the laces.

"I fed off of hating you, Wayne. I convinced myself that you were the problem. That I had done everything I possibly could, and that you hadn't. So I used that against you. I made life horrible for you over the summer and during the last few weeks; but I came to understand something this week. I was wrong. I cost us that game."

Heads were turning now, left to right, searching for validation, as if to say "Are we really hearing this?" Michael, unfazed, finished tying Wayne's shoe.

"I've spent the last year trying to break you down. I was convinced that would solve all of our problems, make this team the best in the region, and state. And I'm still convinced we can be that, but we can't do it without you."

Michael stood, put his hand on Wayne's shoulder pad. There was now a shocked silence in the room.

"Wayne, I was wrong. I was about as wrong as I could have been. You weren't the problem. You never have been. It was me, okay? I want to ask you something, and you don't have to answer now, but I want to ask you now so that everybody hears it. I want to ask you, Wayne . . . I want to ask you to forgive me. Will you forgive me?"

Chapter 8

If your parents say they love you, check it out."

Words of wisdom from one of Wes's journalism professors. It was meant as a shock to the system and as a standard. Whenever reporting a story, always look for two sources. Three is even better. Four is a masterpiece. Five . . . well, five means some kind of award.

There were always a handful of students who never grasped the concept; they were still stuck on the whole parent thing. How could someone suggest that their parents might not love them?

Wes had no trouble with the adage. The world had long since unraveled before his eyes into the unpleasant display of what it was. His family dynamic proved another point in journalism: sensationalism trumps virtue. His mom, a divorced, single mom, who worked as a secretary for a franchising company, had done the rearing, with occasional spot help from her own parents. She poured Wes a bowl of Cheerios every morning and helped him with his homework at night while sipping on coffee, while his absentee father drank his child support away. Wes's mother, exhausted at the end of the day, would still tuck him in and make sandwiches for school. His father was somewhere at a bar, no doubt, or occasionally in a jail cell. He made the police blotters. Wes learned this in middle school, when classroom bullies somehow learned to read the police blotter in the newspaper for a school project. Coincidentally, on what had to be the one day they read that part of the newspaper and not the sports or funnies, they spotted a familiar name: Watkins.

"That yer dad, Watkins?" the biggest bully had asked.

Wes could have lied and said no. Instead, he said nothing—and the silence spoke for him. From then on, Wes read the paper every day, especially the police blotter, making sure that if his dad was ever in the news again for drunken or disorderly conduct, he would at least be prepared for it. Perhaps Wes owed his dad for encouraging him into journalism.

Young Wes knew that other kids had dads who were there all the time, and he watched how his friends reacted to their dads; but after a while, he couldn't fathom having a dad in his apartment. The few times his father did visit, it was just awkward. His father would sit on the far end of the couch wiping his brow as he watched Wes play with Matchbox cars on the living room floor. His dad perspired a lot. He smelled like smoke and sweat and breath mints, and that was an unpleasant variation from the sweet perfumes and soaps his mom used.

As Wes grew older, he learned that his father stunk in other ways as well. He found out that his dad had left the family for a younger woman in a fling that lasted less than a month. Kids sometimes take emotions overboard as they start to experience them. Once Wes had learned to hate, he attributed everything bad to his absentee father. For a while, Wes even blamed his dad for his diabetes. Every time he was stuck with a needle or felt lightheaded or went to the doctor for a checkup, it was his dad's fault.

But Wes learned something about self-reliance that two-parent kids would never understand. Self-reliance often leads to skepticism. That's not a dirty word. One has to be skeptical to be a good reporter. Everyone has a secret. There is always something under the surface, and it's almost always dirty. Look at Watergate; look at almost every president; look at any celebrity, the professor would say. They've all got something to hide. It's the media's job to uncover it, shine some light in the dark corners. Michael Gavin may have been a decent guy, but he'd handed Wes a flashlight when he asked him to write the eulogy, and Wes would be a fool not to shine the light around to see what he could see.

Wes called Lewis Banner and told him he was scrapping his initial plan to interview Earl Bishop in Athens. Instead, he was heading to the courthouse. There wasn't enough time to travel back and forth to Athens for the press conference, so he'd just have to try to set up a phone interview with Coach Bishop later. It was a downer, in the sense that he wouldn't get player profiles in for the Georgia–Tennessee game, and thus erased his chances of getting a decent clip; on the other hand, Michael Gavin's story was shaping up to be a juicy one.

"The county courthouse?" Lewis said over the phone, furiously clicking his mouse on the other end, probably working the stats page for tomorrow's paper. "What for?"

"Isn't it obvious?" Wes said.

"I'd just like you to lay it out for me, that's all," he said.

"Well, we've got a missing Medal of Honor, for starters," he said. "I think the Nooners inadvertently gave me a starting point on something else, too. This guy Wayne gave me a piece of information about how during their high school days, Michael became apologetic over a dustup and out of the blue asked Wayne to forgive him. Michael must have done something. Perhaps illegal. Nothing shakes up a high school quarterback like threats of having it all taken away, right? I want to check to see if Michael had a criminal record, for that incident or otherwise. If official records don't materialize, I'll check the archives again at the newspaper, story by story, if I have to."

"Go back to the medal," Lewis said. "What's the story there?"

"Lynn doesn't know where it is," Wes said. "And why would Michael have hidden it, especially after he found out he had cancer? Wouldn't he donate it or give it to his family? Was he ashamed of the medal somehow? I've got an interview set up with an officer who served under Michael in Iraq."

"That's good," Lewis said.

"I can't get past the invitation," Wes continued. "Who wants a stranger, a reporter, to give their eulogy? I've never heard of that, unless he had a secret he wanted off his chest. He's either an egomaniac, a man with a dark past, or something worse. I don't know."

"It could be something better."

"Sure, it could, but right now these are the only leads I have to work with."

"You cleared this with Starks?"

"Do I have to?"

A long pause.

"I'll brief him once I have something," Wes offered.

"Well . . ."

"Come on, Lewis, I'm not doing anything shady here. This is standard procedure."

"All right, all right," Lewis said. "But if he comes hollering, don't say I didn't warn ya."

Of course, you wouldn't think of covering for me, Wes thought. "Sure. Okay, gotta go," he said aloud.

★   ★   ★

The county courthouse was in nearby Calhoun. In the state of Georgia, there are something like 150 counties—almost one hundred more than in California. The reasoning behind that madness was to create a county system in which, back in the 1800s, each courthouse was within a day's travel via horseback. In today's world, all it did was confuse the stew out of travelers, because for just about every county, there was a town with the same name somewhere else in Georgia. The town of Jasper, for example, was a hundred miles from Jasper County.

Wes left his recorder in the car and grabbed a legal notebook from his bag, trying to pass himself off as a legal assistant or paralegal. He walked through the metal detector and took the elevator to the second floor. He strolled up to the clerk's desk and smiled a casual smile.

"Doing research for a case," Wes said. "Got anything on a Michael S. Gavin?"

The clerk disappeared. Wes waited. He knew it would take a few minutes. Everything from about 1990 on was on a computer system. That's where the clerk would go first, no doubt. He didn't immediately return, which signified that Michael hadn't broken any laws recently. The clerk probably trudged to the older archives. About ten minutes later he resurfaced. Wes met him at his desk.

"Nothing on record, just a sealed juvenile file," he said.

"Sealed?"

"Yeah, it's off-limits, thus the 'sealed' part," he said.

"Is there any way to look at court appearances around that time?" Wes asked.

"Zack!" a voice boomed from a side office.

"Hold on a sec," Zack the clerk told Wes. Zack took the file with him and walked into the office with his tail tucked firmly between his legs. A small man with bug eyes peeked his head out to get a look at Wes. He mumbled a few words to Zack, who returned with a bowed head.

"Sorry sir, like I said, the record is sealed."

"And what about information on court hearings way back when? What if I give you a couple days to work with?"

"I'm sorry sir, I can't help you."

"Yes you can," Wes said.

"No, I . . ."

"Buddy, withholding information like that is against the law, you know that? Ever heard of freedom of information?"

He glanced at the office window, but the bug-eyed man had disappeared.

Wes's phone vibrated. The number was from the *News*. Wes shot the clerk his most serious 'I'll get back to you in a minute' look, and walked over to a nearby seat.

"Watkins, what do you think you're doing?"

It was Starks.

"Checking on leads," Wes said.

"At the courthouse?"

"How did you know I was at the courthouse?"

"You're meddling in a buddy of mine's office, that's why," he said.

Wes looked up at the office manager, who was staring at him from the doorway of his office. Wes waved.

"That is a waste of time," Starks said. "Did it ever occur to you that while you're out digging for dirt on your current assignment, the community is watching you?"

"Does that really matter?" Wes said. "This is standard procedure. It's called 'Freedom of Information Act.'"

"It's called, 'You do what you're assigned to do,' Watkins, and I'm telling you to leave. There's nothing there for you to see anyways. Gavin's record is clean."

Wiped clean, Wes wanted to say.

"Got it," Wes said, and hung up.

Walking out, he felt the manager's cold stare boring into his back. Starks was right about at least one thing. Talking Creek was watching him as much as he was watching them.

Chapter 9

Good train wrecks were hard to find. But this one was sure to be delicious.

Wes called Lewis and gave him the rundown on Starks. Though he didn't receive the kind of supportive voice he was hoping for from his sports editor, he did get a juicy tip.

"I'm heading down to TCHS for the volleyball tournament," Lewis said. "Word is Coach Lawler has a surprise announcement. A lot of football boosters were notified and are going to be there."

"Think it has something to do with Gavin?"

"Probably," Lewis said. "He asked Lynn Gavin to be there."

So Wes did a U-turn on Main Street and headed over to the high school. Every space in the TCHS faculty parking lot adjacent to the gym was taken. Dozens of cars sported school flags and team magnets from various schools. Inside, the bleachers were crammed. Wes heard the screech of tennis shoes on the court as two teams competed in the district tournament. Although Talking Creek had a decent girls volleyball team, it in no way justified the size of the crowd decked out in Eagle colors.

Lewis, who was leaning against the gym wall next to the bleachers, walked over to meet Wes near the entrance. They stood parallel to the action to observe.

"Coach Lawler is gonna propose naming the stadium after Gavin," Lewis said quietly.

"Can he do that?"

"Nope," he said. "Not officially. He's gonna do it anyway. There's no way the school board would just squash it, either; not with the public outpouring for Gavin. Should be interesting."

"Should I be covering this?"

Lewis shook his head. "Scott's covering the tournament; he'll cover whatever happens." Indeed, there was Big Bird, sitting behind the scorer's table, fiddling with a handful of reporting tools, none of which he knew how to use effectively.

"I see Starks is here," Wes said, pinpointing his boss on the far left side of the bleachers.

"Of course, he's a big booster," Lewis said.

"Which he shouldn't be, as managing editor of the newspaper."

"Easy now," Lewis said.

The Talking Creek crowd roared in approval as the Lady Eagles finished off the visiting team with a perfect set-spike combo. As the players passed by each other for the customary handshake, all eyes were on the exit sign at the far end of the gym, which led to the football facilities. Coach Lawler was standing, arms crossed, waiting for a lull in the action.

The atmosphere in the room mimicked that of a football game at kickoff time, when everyone's breath is bated, waiting for the ball to hit the ground or a receiver's hands and the game to actually begin. The visiting teams' families looked around, confused, sensing that something important was about to happen. Even Wes was interested in seeing how Coach Lawler would do.

The coach strolled casually to the scorer's table, where a microphone sat. Wes and Lewis watched in amusement as Big Bird Friedman scuttled over to his briefcase against the wall, and then rushed back toward Coach Lawler. He made such an awkward dash that it caught Lawler off guard. He must have thought that Scott was trying to head him off, because he nearly body-blocked him from the side of the table. Big Bird changed direction at the last moment and placed a bulky tape recorder nearby. When Lawler realized Scott's intentions, he tried to conceal a grin of approval.

"Ladies and gentlemen," Lawler began, "please give me a minute of your time before the next match. I come to you today with a heart that's heavy. It's a hurtin' heart, folks, because we've lost one of our own. Michael Gavin left us Monday morning, and we're sure going to miss him. You can't replace a man like that. It's like a punch to the gut, losing him, and I'm sure I speak for all of us in sending our deepest sympathies to the family."

He paused for reflection. If he'd been talking to his football team, this was the point where he would toss off his hat and raise his voice to a bullhorn level to get everyone's attention. To his credit, he didn't. Whatever the audience, it seemed Lawler knew how to present his opinion effectively.

"But we've got to pick ourselves up," Lawler said, "together. We've got to slap the dust off our pants, bring it in, take a knee, and figure out what we're going to do next."

Wes almost groaned at the clichés.

"I say we win one for Gavin. I'm putting all my chips in, and the boys are too, for Friday's game against Calhoun. We plan on making this town, and most importantly, Michael, proud of the Talking Creek Eagles."

The crowd applauded politely and a few raucous shouts echoed from the top rows of the bleachers.

"But we can do more," Lawler continued, " and we should do it right here and now. Michael Gavin put more memories in our football stadium than a genie in a bottle. Each time we suit up, we ought to remember that, or else his memory will be about as meaningless as a tie in a championship game. We ought to remember Michael and win a few for the man. So I'm saying it here and now. I say we dedicate the stadium in Michael Gavin's name."

"Here comes the good part," Lewis said as Coach Lawler let the crowd digest his request. "Coach Lawler knows full well how the school board is going to react when they hear this. Ned Grady's one of them, and he's in the stands; and it's his family that the stadium's named after already. His father's construction business built it in the sixties."

As if on cue, Ned Grady, a bear of a man, rose from the stands. "Well come on now, Coach Lawler," he said in a high-pitched voice. "Coach, I agree wholeheartedly with you about Michael Gavin and all of us doing something for him, but this is not the time or the place."

"Well, when is, Ned?" The question came from the crowd. A man in TCHS blue stood and pointed. "You saying Michael Gavin ain't worth it?"

"That's Roy McCray," Lewis informed Wes, "another big football booster."

"Lawler planted his own sounding board in the audience?" Wes said. Lewis offered an amused smile.

"Did those words come out of my mouth, Roy?" Ned shot back. "Don't you go putting words into my mouth. There are a lot of factors to consider, and I don't think we should go off half-cocked renaming buildings and stadiums after a man who we haven't even buried yet. Let's have his funeral and then discuss it."

"That dog won't hunt," Lawler said.

Scott shifted his recorder, trying to capture Coach Lawler and the voices from the stands. Wes spotted sweat stains seeping through Big Bird's light blue polo shirt.

"Ten bucks says Scott loses it," Wes said, nudging Lewis, who tried not to chuckle.

"There are no dogs hunting anything, Coach," Ned said. "I think we've got plenty of ways we can honor Michael without making drastic changes to mainstays in our community."

"Stop lying!" It was Roy McCray again. "All you want to do is keep your family name on the press box, and you know it!"

"Shut yer trap, Roy," someone in the crowd said.

"Come over here and make me, big boy!" Roy said, rolling up his sleeves.

Roy's accusations set off a firestorm of debate in the stands. Half the audience rose to their feet, pointing fingers and hurling accusations. Members of the visiting crowd tried to inch their way out of the bleachers and to the concession stand, hoping whatever it was that was going on would be resolved before the next match. The two teams scheduled to compete eyed the court warily; their warm-up time was being cut into. Scott wasn't holding up well under the pressure. He waved his recorder every which way, like he was trying to catch raindrops in a canteen.

Wes relished every minute of this. In fact, he was a bit jealous that Scott was getting to cover the meeting. Wes made a mental note to write this one up on the blog.

"Man, this is better than watching *Fight Club*," Wes said to Lewis. "And look at Scott. All I'd have to do is pull the fire alarm and you'd have one less sports writer, by reason of a heart attack."

"Hey now," Lewis said. "Don't do it. I need a live body for Friday's game. This is the most action that poor fella has had in a while. He's gonna be talking about covering this meeting for the rest of his life."

"Won't be a long life if he has any more assignments like this one. And look at Lawler. He's just sitting back watching his handiwork."

"Looks like our boss is about to enter the fray," Lewis said.

Sure enough, during the confusion, Starks had quietly positioned himself between Coach Lawler and the audience.

"I thought he didn't want us to be a part of a story?" Wes said.

"Do as he says, not as he does," Lewis said.

"All right, all right," Starks said in a booming voice. It had the desired effect. "I think there is merit to what both parties are saying. Coach, I think the support in this town to do something special in Michael's honor is justified. Ned, your prudence is always an asset to this town. If this were up to a vote, like anything else, I think we should consider due process. Sit on it for a few days. Coach, it won't get any cooler next week or next month, but it'll allow us to pause, reflect, and come to a consensus. An open forum is the best answer. In fact, the *News* is planning on putting out a special section on Michael this Sunday, and we'd be happy to include an op-ed section for folks to respond to this proposal. How does that sound?"

"Did he just sell out our editorial?" Wes muttered under his breath. Lewis didn't answer.

Coach Lawler was silent for a moment, unsure of Starks's intentions.

He'd just had his platform taken away, but it hadn't completely squashed his idea.

"Well I guess that's something we'll have to think about then," Coach Lawler said. "But before we do that, why don't we hear from Michael's family? Lynn, would you mind coming down here and saying a few words, if that's all right?"

A hundred heads turned to one spot in the bleachers, and it was then that Wes spotted Lynn Gavin in the crowd. She was dressed in a blue blouse and yellow sweater, looking the part of an Eagles mom. All eyes followed her descent to the scorer's table, where she smiled weakly at Coach Lawler as he handed her the microphone.

Why had Coach Lawler called her? And what was she doing here? Judging from her facial expression, she hadn't been prepared to speak. She held the microphone down at her side and bit her lip. Then she closed her eyes, and for a few seconds at least, it looked as if she was saying a prayer right there in front of everybody. The display quieted the crowd, which only moments before had been in a shouting contest. Now you could hear a pin drop. Everyone was trying to hear the words that Lynn mumbled to herself. Then, just as quickly as she had gone into prayer, she seemed poised and ready to address the crowd.

"Hey everybody," she said in a warm voice, as if each person in the audience were a family friend. "I'm sorry, but I may not be the most coherent person here. It's been a rough couple of days, I think you know. I really believe that the Lord has been with us, comforting us, and been working through all of you, and we're very thankful for that. We appreciate the love and support you've shown Michael over the past few months. I think we all loved him in our own unique ways, and how we want to remember him is how we're reacting now. I'd rather not comment on what I think would be the best way to honor him as a community. I think that's really all up to you. I'm just thankful to have all of you to call on if we need it. So thank you."

She hesitated, as if she wanted to say more, but instead she nodded, set the microphone back on the scorer's table, and walked away. Coach

Lawler judiciously followed suit, allowing the volleyball teams to again take the court.

A large portion of the Talking Creek crowd spilled out of the stands to go home, their reason for attending now gone. A handful of well-wishers surrounded Lynn near the exit, offering hugs and handshakes. From across the gym, Wes couldn't hear what they were saying, but he guessed it included little stories about their encounters with Michael. Lynn appeared gracious to them, but as Wes walked closer to the group, he saw the signs of a worn woman. Despite a dab of makeup, her eyes were swollen and her face tired. Probably from back-to-back sleepless nights. Wes was walking over to the thinned-out crowd to talk to Lynn when he felt a tap on his shoulder. It was Scott.

"I covered for you here, you know," Scott said.

"Good for you," Wes replied.

"And I barely made it here in time. But Starks just now promised me a front page story. This is going to be a big deal for tomorrow's paper. Going to have to struggle to make deadline, but I'll do my best."

"You might want to get to it then," Lewis said, having caught up with Wes. As Scott scurried over to the scorer's table for the next match, Keith Starks trudged toward Wes and Lewis.

"Oh man, I really don't want to talk to him," Wes said.

"Go interview Lynn Gavin then," Lewis offered.

"But I already have," Wes said.

"Follow up," he said. "I'll talk to Starks. Be prepared for a meeting though; he *loves* those."

Wes nodded and took off.

Lynn was outside the gym now, minus the mob but still dealing with a few well-wishers. She was listening to a woman's spirited speech, probably about Michael, nodding respectfully but also twitching her left ankle slightly. The woman ended her speech by giving Lynn a bear hug. When they detached, Lynn took a huge breath to recoup the air in her lungs and started walking toward her car. After standing at a respectful distance, Wes saw his chance and closed the gap. Lynn turned around.

"Hello again."

"Wes, good to see you," Lynn said. She looked tired, like the weight of an entire community was on her shoulders.

"Did you know about the stadium dedication?"

"No," she said. "At least not before we talked this afternoon. Coach Lawler called us at the last minute and asked if I could attend, but he didn't say why."

Wes nodded. "So are you for it or against it?"

She smiled. "Yes."

"I'll take that as a 'no comment' then." It was a little harsh, not playing along with her joke, but Wes didn't want to cross the line from professional to overly personal. He still needed answers from her, and everybody else, and the questions in his mind weren't all of the pleasant sort.

"I'll have a comment for you later, Wes, just not tonight, okay?"

"Fair enough."

Wes put his pen in his pocket and watched Lynn as she got into her car. For the widowed wife of a town hero, she had the look of someone totally alone.

★   ★   ★

Wes fired up his laptop after making himself a ham sandwich. He checked his e-mail to see if any of his college friends had written. No new messages, other than the usual assortment of spam. It didn't surprise him, but he still held out hope each time he scanned through his in-box.

He took a big bite out of his ham sandwich, prodded on by his Accu-Check reading and insulin shot a few minutes earlier, and washed it down with a glass of water.

Back Words

I went to a volleyball game today, and a political stump
speech broke out. Seriously. It seems the legend of one man has

spilled onto every dinner table, every in-town diner, and every sporting event.

When does a legend begin? In Little League? What great play turns an ordinary player into an ideal? How many championships does it take?

In any high school graduating class, there might be future software engineers and business moguls; a young woman who will find a cure for a disease, or a young man who will invent an alternative fuel for cars. Yet the one we'll all remember is the star quarterback. Everyone else is an afterthought. I wish I had the time to interview my star subject's graduating class, to see who did what. This football star made his imprint on the town's psyche as a teenager and it has never diminished.

Therein lies the problem: He's just too GOOD. They're glossing over his weaknesses. Rarely do players admit weakness. If they get burned for five hundred yards, they have "things to work on." And when teammates talk about their stars, they exalt them to the point of absurdity. The first time I heard about an athlete who was competitive at everything from video games to pool to counting out-of-state license plates on road trips, I happily wrote it up as a description of the player's character. By the fiftieth time, however, it went in one ear and out the other. The problem with these interviews is that they're all about praise. I uncovered one juicy morsel with this person's friends, and the moment I looked interested in knowing more, they closed ranks like a Roman legion. If any of those guys were doing the eulogy, the subject would have no weaknesses. They want him to be forever squeaky clean. Is it my job to tell them otherwise?

He wasn't good at everything. At the next level, the local hero stumbled. Collegiate athletics is faster, more competitive. Many a small-town Hercules has crashed and burned on the bigger stage. I wonder how many towns ever come to terms with that? It must be like those crazy-eyed soccer moms who can't fathom their child's failure on the field. Blame the coach, blame the teammates, but whatever you do, don't blame the kid. Just give 'em another trophy and a pat on the head.

Things are going to get interesting around here. One former teammate is trying to raise support to honor the local hero in a way that's sure to rub some other people the wrong way. If I continue with the path I'm on and show this town that their golden boy had some major flaws, the eulogy won't just be divisive, it'll be a bombshell.

Chapter 10

Routines ruled the roost at the *North Georgia News*. Each press night at 10:30 p.m., Tucker Sweeney, the sixty-year-old production manager, stomped into the newsroom and cupped his hands. Although a casual conversation with someone across the newsroom was possible because of the confined space, Sweeney took no chances. If anyone's hearing was as bad as his, they might miss the message, and the message was his job.

"Half-hour till presses!"

Most reporters smiled at this point. They were done with their assignments. But Sweeney's last call sent chain-smoking copy editors scrambling back from the exit door to their seats to lay out the last few pages. They preferred pacing themselves, one page, one smoke, but Sweeney's call turned the process into a race. It was at this point in the night that the copy editors mumbled unpleasantries about editors or reporters getting their stories in late. If they had been on time, this rush wouldn't be necessary, they said to themselves, all nodding and bobbing their heads over their computer monitors. If it was really tight and they were in their seats longer than the nicotine buzz lasted, then there would be trouble.

Sweeney bent his rule for special occasions. Autumn Fridays, for instance. The Saturday morning paper was the second biggest seller behind the coupon-weighted Sunday paper. *News* subscribers and newsstand buyers wanted what no other paper could deliver: a blowout high school sports page. On Friday nights, every game from the region was staffed by a *News* writer. The full-time sports reporters staffed the big games. Road games or minor matchups meant freelance writers. Those ranged anywhere from retired teachers to car salesmen whose only experience with the written word was their high school yearbook committee. Still, Lewis had a knack for maintaining his motley crew during the season. He kept a lengthy list of potentials, and over the years groomed his part-time workforce into homers with a handful of workable leads. He kept the guys on the same beats, the same games, so the coaches would recognize their faces. Once trust was built, the reporters would gain access to the school stats, which was a much better record than trying to maintain stats while writing a story in your head during the game. On autumn Fridays, Sweeney grew a little patience. He slid a chair from an unoccupied cubicle, propped his legs up on the desk, read a day-old copy of the *News*, and occasionally glanced at Lewis, who would give him the thumbs-up when most of the stories were in. Still, the copy editors eyed Sweeney nervously, agonizing about when to take their last smoke break before the mad dash.

That was one *News* custom. Another routine stressed the newsroom staff even more, and it started in Starks's sunroom. Each morning, his wife would put on a fresh cup of coffee while Starks snapped his *News* copy from one page to another. On his ride to the office, he turned the radio to news, let it hum low, and pondered how his paper stacked up in national and local coverage. He didn't say hello to the secretaries operating the front desk. He didn't say hello to any of the accountants or salespeople. He walked into his office, shut the door, and grabbed his red pen.

By lunchtime, the damage was on display. Starks had bloodied the paper with editing marks. He found plenty to criticize. Misspell a name—and Starks knew names—and you'd get a huge, thick mark on your article. Widows and orphans—single lines that slid to the top of the next column and single words that fell to their own line—well, they got him fired up too. He critiqued headlines, decks, story placement, and word choices. All things that might have been avoided if he had decided to stay past 5 p.m. and work with the editors and reporters. But it was his prerogative to run the newsroom as he saw fit, and he saw fit to be home for dinner like clockwork. Occasionally, he marked an article with his green pen—a sign of approval, but the odds were about ten to one.

Wednesday was a bloody, bloody day. Wes was certain that had he written an article, it would be at the morgue. Not unlike his first few months at the paper, when it seemed as if every story he filed was a bloodbath in the making. He took Starks's critiques personally at first. Lewis had to explain that it was just how Starks broke in rookies. Wes thought it was a perfect way to run them off; but slowly through the months, Starks began to mark up other pages in the sports section, leaving his articles alone.

If only the readers had been so kind. When your byline is right there at the top of the article, it makes you vulnerable to the public at large. Which is fine. Wes didn't mind the occasional irate parent who'd send a snappy note of disapproval because junior's late game heroics weren't worked into the lead paragraph of a story. One reader in particular, once he discovered Wes's byline, would send him clips of his articles with notes of encouragement. He followed Wes's career closely enough that Wes felt his breath on the back of his neck. After Wes's first byline for a college football game, he received a cut-out copy of the story with an "I'm proud of you" note.

It was from his father.

He sent Wes more than notes. He sent bridges, attempts at reconciliation. Letters about himself and how he was trying to get his life back together. Trying, after a decade and a half of failure. What could he offer Wes? Why would he reach out to take more? What kind of a man does that?

Wes looked to his mom for guidance, but she said that he was an adult, and he could handle his relationships on his own. A part of Wes wanted to call his dad, sure. He had just as many questions as his father had excuses. What kept him from picking up the phone was his mom. All the work she had put into his childhood, the duct tape she had wrapped around the holes in his life left by a fatherless upbringing; it seemed like a betrayal to let him in now.

The letters were stuffed in a worn cardboard box and put on the top shelf of the closet. Then Wes buried it under clothes and hats and things.

Wes didn't want his father's praise any more than he wanted Starks's disapproval. There were types of critique he liked and types he didn't. Lewis, for instance, offered constructive suggestions. If Wes made a mistake on a story, like using the wrong rushing total for a running back, Lewis steered him in the direction of the school's scorekeeper to at least compare notes following a game. Lewis built Wes up instead of tearing him down. He went about editing as a craft and not as a process of covering your rear end. Which is more than could be said for a few others at the *News*.

"So what do you think about my front page story?"

It was Scott. He had snuck up behind Wes, and was now gazing dreamily at the walled newspaper.

"I haven't read it yet," Wes said. He didn't plan to either.

Scott frowned and pointed. "It's right in front of you."

"Well looky there." Sure enough, the lead story was about Coach Lawler and the field dedication pledge. Below Scott's byline were the words "Good Job!" in bright, thick, green pen.

"I made deadline by five minutes," Scott said, as if this were some monumental achievement. Wes didn't have it in him to congratulate mediocrity.

"What about the Talking Creek notebook?" Wes asked. "Did you talk to Coach Lawler yesterday about Calhoun?"

"I couldn't have possibly fit that in," Scott said. "I had too many assignments with the tournament, your beat and then *my* beat. Talking Creek's practice notes will just have to wait until Thursday."

Wes shrugged. "Well, he's going to be ticked, that's all," he said. "You better call him today and write a notebook."

"I don't understand why you can't do that," Scott said. "It's not like you've got more than one story on your plate."

Wes shrugged again, wishing the conversation was over. Fortunately, Starks opened his door and gestured for Wes to come in.

After the door closed behind Wes, Starks retreated to his desk and took a long sip from his coffee.

"Scott did a great job with the lead story, don't you think?"

"Sure," Wes said.

"I gave him an assignment, and he followed it perfectly. I like to see that in my reporters."

The undertone wasn't lost on Wes. He gripped the seat, waiting to be berated.

"You know, I've got a peculiar situation on my hands," Starks continued. "First, the biggest story in this town is Michael Gavin, and I've got a reporter with amazing access to the family, but I can't let him write about it until after the eulogy—almost a week from start to finish. That's an eternity in the news business. Competitors are crawling around my town like a bunch of salamanders. The *Constitution* sent a reporter up from Atlanta. The broadcast news stations are sniffing around. I heard that even one of the cable news stations is sending a correspondent to cover the funeral, and here I am, unable to tell my story the way I want to tell it. Instead of honoring someone, I've got a reporter digging around the courthouse for traces of a criminal record."

"If I didn't, then you know the Atlanta outlets would," Wes said.

"I already told you, he doesn't have a record," Starks said.

"You're right, he's got a sealed juvy record."

"Second," he said, ignoring Wes's interruption, "you are the only controversial part of this whole week, and don't think that people don't notice where you go. You had more business being at last night's tournament that you showed up late to, than you did in the courthouse looking for ghosts that aren't there. Period. Thankfully, Scott covered your butt."

"So you don't care at all that he has a sealed juvy record?"

"I hardly see the relevance," Starks huffed. "Sealed means it's in the past."

"But Michael asked me to do his eulogy. He himself told me to look for the truth. And I have. I even know when whatever is on his record happened. His senior year, middle of football season. Nothing in the police blotter, but you want to know the strangest thing? This morning I went through the archives. There's an article about a big community service day for folks with minor brushes with the law and how a judge wiped their record clean if they worked it all day. Michael is in the picture for that story, and a cutline includes his name in tiny print."

Wes handed Starks a note with a specific date. "Go check it out on the microfiche; see for yourself. How is it a coincidence that he disappears right before a big game, comes back a changed, humbler person, and then ends up the next weekend doing community service? Something happened."

Starks took the note, crumpled it, and threw it at a trash can across from his desk. It bounced off the side of the can and onto the floor.

"You have a list of names to call that Michael and his family provided, and I suggest you stick to the script. I didn't ask for anything else, and I don't want to see anything else. Consider this a warning. Do I make myself clear?"

"Yeah, sure, no problem," Wes said.

"Don't ruffle my feathers. I'm letting you off easy. We've got to run a tight ship this week. Consider your byline locked up until the weekend. I don't want to have to . . . discipline . . . a reporter on a big assignment, understand? Now, who are you talking to next?"

"Funny you should say 'locked up,'" Wes said, ignoring the not-so-veiled threat, "because I'm going to the police this afternoon."

Chapter 11

Been in a cop car before, buddy?" The police officer said in a husky voice.

"Uh, no sir, can't say that I have," Wes said.

A loud snicker.

"Well then, this must be an adventure for you, huh?"

"You could say that."

In the span of a couple hours, Wes had gone from Talking Creek to a police station in downtown Atlanta, to a squad car with Police Sergeant Rod Shackleford, who had been a platoon leader in Michael Gavin's company in the National Guard and had served with him in Iraq. In the civilian world, he was a police officer. He looked the part. Although he was short, five-foot-eight, maybe, he was solid. Built to explode. Exercise wasn't a hobby for this guy; it was a passion. His arms bulged out of his sleeves. His forearms had pulsating veins, and his wrists looked like they were made from nuts and bolts. It formed an odd contrast to his lower torso of chicken legs and a small waist. His face was clean-shaven but rough. His blue eyes had a lazy feel to them, more from not being impressed with his surroundings than from idleness.

Lynn had called ahead. She said that Shackleford would answer any questions Wes had concerning Michael's tour in Iraq. So, after the tongue-lashing from Starks, Wes informed him of his intentions to talk to Shackleford. Starks actually approved. Wes drove south for the interview, thinking it would be in the confines of police headquarters. That was scary enough; but instead, Shackleford had him sign the necessary paperwork to do a ride-along in a squad car on patrol.

"Well, what do we have here?" Shackleford pulled over to a roadside convenience store. A man in faded blue jeans and what was once a white shirt was outside, sagging on a bench, a brown paper bag in his hand. He had scraggly, unkempt hair.

"Man, it's not even close to happy hour," Shackleford said as he set the parking brake and radioed into base. "Give me just a sec," he said.

The drunk was in his own world until Shackleford came within two feet. Wes watched as the officer struck up a conversation.

"Whatcha got there?" Shackleford said.

"Nahthin, nahthin," the man slurred.

"Any of these cars yours?"

The man shook his head no.

"So what are you doing with that beer in your hand?"

"Weren't gonna drive, officer," the man said, leaning toward Shackleford, who put his hands on his hips.

"That's not the problem, sir. The problem is, you've got an open container of alcohol in public."

The man eyed his brown bag as if it had ambushed him. "Nah, nah . . ."

"Listen," Shackleford said. "Before you try to make up a stupid story and waste my time, why don't we try and resolve this problem."

The man nodded weakly.

"Okay, first, I want you to throw that beer away." The man reluctantly put it in the nearby trash bin. "Great, now I want you to check your pockets for change. How much do you have?" The man stuck out his pockets.

"I ain't got no change."

"That's fine, sir," Shackleford said. "The next question is, how far away do you live?"

"'Bout two miles."

"Along the bus route?"

The man looked puzzled.

"Uh, yeah, yeah."

"Okay then. I think we can both agree that you'd rather not be taken home in a squad car. I don't want to do the paperwork and you don't want the notoriety. So here's what we're going to do." Shackleford pulled out a transit coin. "I want you to go sit on that bus bench over there. When the bus on your route comes, get on it. Act like a perfect gentleman, because I'll be watching. Get yourself home, sober up, and don't come to this store again for beer, got me?"

The man nodded.

"All right then, sir, I'll be over here, watching." Shackleford returned to the car. He put his seat belt on and radioed in that all was well.

"Didn't smell like alcohol, which is the only reason I'm making him get on that bus and not in the back seat. If he moves from that seat except for the bus, I'm arresting him," Shackleford said. "You know, in Iraq, we'd sometimes have to shoot at drunks."

"What?"

He eyed Wes, gauging his reaction. Apparently it had the desired effect. "Yep, these guys would drive out to a checkpoint, liquored up. Factor in a language barrier, and automatic rifles, the threat of car bombs, and you've got trouble. If they didn't stop where they were supposed to stop, then we had to fire warning shots. Never had to actually shoot anybody, but we fired pretty close warning shots at a few of them to get their attention."

"Wow."

"Roger that," Shackleford agreed. "If a .50 cal over your windshield doesn't stop you in your tracks, then you must be hitting the bottle hard.

"So other than the warning shots, what was Iraq like?"

"Hot, dry, and boring," Shackleford said. "You want to know anything more specific than that?"

"Whatever you think I should know for talking about Michael Gavin," Wes said.

Shackleford tapped his fingers on the steering wheel. He monitored the man at the bus stop. Shackleford's eyes were like a leash, commanding the man to sit tight for the next bus. Then he looked at Wes again and pounded his chest.

"This Kevlar vest seems like a pain in the butt to wear to work, but really, it's nothing," he said. "Imagine being strapped with forty pounds of armor and almost as much gear, full dress from head to toe, a Kevlar helmet and sunglasses. Imagine dressing like that for seventeen hours a day and working in 110-degree heat. You're constantly drinking water, and the sweat just evaporates off of ya. And the sand storms—when was the last time you used a baby wipe?"

"Uh, I guess when I was a baby," Wes said.

Shackleford grinned. "Well I ain't no baby, but across the pond I was pulling wipes out of their carton like they were going out of style. You get sand in crevices you didn't even know you owned. If you weren't careful, you'd get windburn on your face and a scalpful of Babylon's finest. Showers don't come every day, and the smell outside the wire was awful. Mix dead animals, donkey dung, and bad body odor and you're getting close to the sniff. That's part of it. Then there's the danger. IEDs, snipers, mortars."

"IEDs?"

"Improvised explosive devices. The mortars came constantly. All you needed was a moron, a tube, and a POO. That's the point of origin they'd fire from. They'd set themselves up somewhere inside a town and fire a few rounds, then book it outta there. Our artillery guys tracked them pretty good, but we didn't have orders, nor wanted, to smoke a mosque. Rules of engagement. Fast movers and choppers can't exactly unleash payloads with enough precision to keep the building and civilians intact. We played by the rules; they didn't. Snipers didn't pose too much harm, because we zeroed in on them almost immediately after a shot was fired. The IEDs, though, now there's where you saw the creative side of an insurgent. It was a cat and mouse game. Anything, and I mean anything, could be a roadside bomb. Debris, old tires, brown paper bag with a rigged artillery shell, they'd even stuff a bomb into a dead dog or donkey. Sick stuff. The most dangerous part, though, was yourself."

"How's that?" Wes said.

"Boredom. You had to stay fresh and alert. An IED only has to be at a place in the road that you'll pass over—less than a second. That meant you had to stay sharp for every minute of a five-hour convoy. We knew the streets and alleys of our sector like our hometowns, because you never did a patrol the same way twice. We'd dogleg patrols all the time, make sharp turns and keep the bad guys guessing at our location. You watched the children, too. Most of the time, they'd come running to demand candy or toys. Captain Gavin had a policy of giving tons of toys and candy away, so they loved us in our sector; but occasionally, they'd run away, and that set us on high alert. Bombs and bad guys weren't far away. The mortars were the most frequent hassle; the snipers and IEDs actually only happened a handful of times."

"Including the incident where Gavin earned the Medal of Honor?"

"A whole 'nother ball of wax," Shackleford said. "Firefights like that, company or battalion-level engagements, come around once a tour, if that. Most of what we saw were patrol or platoon engagements."

"And Michael led a company, correct?"

"Roger," Shackleford said.

"What kind of a leader was he?"

"Out of our whole battalion, Captain Gavin had the best credentials of the commanders," Shackleford said. "Ranger trained, 82nd Airborne; just like me when I was in, 'cept we were in at different times. He had combat experience in Desert Storm. The 82nd got about as much of the firefight as there was in that one for grunts. 'Cept maybe the Marines."

"What was he like with the soldiers?"

"How do you mean?"

Wes frowned. He thought the question had been straightforward. "I mean, was he friends with them? Did they like him?"

"Wes, officers—the good ones, anyway—don't make friends with their soldiers."

"They don't?"

Shackleford shook his head. "There's a line. Has to be. Although we're granted some flexibility in the Guard, it's still a professional operation. You have your noncoms—NCOs, like sergeants—and then the grunts, and then you have your officers; and even they don't fraternize the way you would think. It's like that to keep the chain of command strong; keep things professional. If you had privates questioning LTs or higher ups, chaos would ensue. If a soldier had a beef, he brought it up with a sergeant. Captain Gavin's first sergeant took care of all that, and he was sharp as a tack. Now, the first sergeant's role is kind of lead administrator for the company. A lot of paperwork, and an easy excuse to pack on a few pounds around the midsection. You've got your good ones and your bad ones. The bad ones will mill about with the paperwork and not keep an eye on the other NCOs. They'll form little cliques to watch out for each other too. The good ones, well, if they see a platoon sergeant not carrying his load, they'll take care of it.

"Happened to me one time in the 82nd. The company first sergeant comes up to me and says 'LT, your platoon sergeant ain't pulling his weight. When there's a lull, just so ya know, I'm going to pull him aside and straighten him up. He'll be a brand new sarge, no questions asked.'"

Shackleford looked over to see if Wes was still following.

"Long story short, the question you're asking, whether Captain Gavin was friendly—it's irrelevant."

"Oh." Wes couldn't tell if Shackleford was being difficult or not.

"I know you want something deeper than that," he said, "but it wouldn't do him or our company any justice. You have to understand the chain of command and how it works. In my opinion, yeah, he was a good commander. He made sure we had the best equipment we could get, kept us sharp in the face of mundane missions, and the men did think highly of him. You can tell morale is good when the only time he'd put a man down was when someone challenged him to a run. Anyone ever tell you about that?"

"No," Wes said.

"Captain Gavin was a fitness fiend. Loved to run. He could be in his sleep and still belt out a morning jog. Well, he had a standing bet among the company that no soldier could beat him in a two-mile race. A bunch of guys tried. One kid who ran track in college gave the captain a run for his money; but even that guy couldn't beat him. Captain Gavin had horse lungs. With cocky grunts, he'd practically lap 'em, wait for 'em to make it to the finish line, then knock out fifty push-ups right there in front of 'em as they were sucking in air."

"Did you ever challenge him?"

"You kiddin' me? Wes, look at me," he said. He flexed a swollen bicep and grinned. "I bench, I don't run—and especially when I was over there. Hit my best max and squat in Iraq. Used to drive my wife nuts, I'd write her with my updates. Couldn't think of what else to write about. Thankfully they had a weight room at our FOB though. I woulda gone crazy being away from my wife and family if I couldn't pound some iron."

"What was it like being away from home so long? You were there a year, right?"

"Little bit more than a year, yeah," Shackleford said. "It's a little different from being on active duty, like the 82nd, or 101st, or 3rd ID guys. National Guard, that's civilian folks doing soldier duty a few times a year until they're activated. If there's not a war going on, then we're usually involved in relief help for disasters, that sort of thing; but we all have regular Joe lives to leave, jobs to depart, when we're deployed. Then, when we get in the field, the active-duty guys are busting our chops. They use the fancy equipment and state-of-the-art rides and scoff at us Guard soldiers getting by on Vietnam-era body armor. That eventually changed and we got better Kevlar, but there was a constant respect thing to earn from the active-duty soldiers. Course, you get in a firefight or two, all of that false bravado gets thrown out the window. Same team."

There was a lull in the conversation. Shackleford watched a bus pull up to the stop. The man glanced wearily over at the squad car, then jumped up from the bench and practically leaped into the bus, hand outstretched and the coin on display. Shackleford chuckled at his small victory. Wes took a breath, and used the opportunity to push into the main reason he had driven down to meet him.

"Officer Shackleford, I've read the citation on the incident that led to the Medal of Honor, but I wasn't sure on a couple of things."

"It's pretty straightforward, I bet," he said.

"On the citation, yes, but—" Wes paused. He wanted to phrase this the right way. "Was he reluctant to receive it? I asked his family, and they said you'd be a better person to talk to. All I know is that the medal is missing."

"Is that your angle?" Shackleford said sharply.

"Just a question I have," Wes said, shrinking a little bit into his seat. "Did he follow an order he thought was wrong? I can't help but think it was something along those lines. Why else would he want me to be doing this? And why is the medal missing? I was hoping you could shed some light on what happened, beyond the words on the citation."

"Right," Shackleford said. "That'd sure make for a good story, wouldn't it? 'Soldier throws away Medal of Honor,' or some song like that?"

"I don't mean any disrespect," Wes said.

"He may not have wanted the fuss that comes with having it. Did you ever think of that?"

"I wanted to see what other people thought. People who served with him."

Shackleford chewed on Wes's pitch—although, judging from his rigid jaw, he didn't like it. He leaned back in his seat, arms folded. "All right, I'll give this a shot. Did you play sports as a kid, Wes?"

"Yeah, tennis and basketball," Wes said.

"Wouldn't have been my choice. Don't get to hit anybody. But okay, did you ever get hurt in a game?"

"Yeah, I guess so."

"Your parents at that game?"

Wes nodded.

"So let's say it was a lot worse. Let's say you broke your leg or got knocked out, but your team won. Now, everybody in that stadium is celebrating the win, and they should be, including you and your parents. But how do you think your folks feel?"

"I don't know, probably sad or something."

"Exactly," Shackleford said. "The report said it all. Bad things happened that day. Terrible things. Stuff I wish I could forget, and I know the captain never did. But Captain Gavin wasn't upset at the Guard, or a soldier, or anything like that. No way. You're looking at this all wrong. He was upset with himself. The Medal of Honor and the fame that came with it meant squat to him. Before our deployment, he told the NCOs and platoon leaders that he had one goal, and only one goal in Iraq . . . and he failed."

Chapter 12

Cheaters.

Lieutenant Rod Shackleford of the Georgia National Guard despised them. He'd punched a kid in sixth grade who fibbed on a pickup basketball game score. On his high school football team, he was a vicious middle linebacker, who didn't take kindly to chop blocks. He would dole out punishment in a dog pile for late hits, cheap shots, and gang tackles. As an Atlanta police officer, he had no qualms about pulling over highbrow SUV owners who thought it was their God-given right to drive solo in the High Occupancy Vehicle lane. He was born with an inflated sense of fairness, of right and wrong, and he held to it in any endeavor he pursued. It had served him well in life, and, he concluded, it would serve him well in war.

But there was no such thing as "fair" in Iraq. Captain Michael Gavin, his commanding officer, trained the company with that core understanding. There would be no fair fights, no cessation of hostilities to remove the injured, whether they be combatants or civilians. They were fighting with hands tied behind their backs against an enemy tied only to its violent self-righteousness. The enemy employed no code of conduct, fought for no territory. Every splotch of land was a potential battleground. There was no front line, no rear, just inside or outside the wire. Fear, horror, terror, they were all weapons employed by the enemy.

The insurgents carried tangible weapons, too. They used AK-47s because AK-47s fired a lot of ammunition without a lot of maintenance. They fired from around corners, on rooftops, from behind children, and in crowds. They fired from windowsills and trenches. They fired without much precision and even less care. They fired on anyone and anything. It reminded Shackleford of drive-by shootings, how the participants had no regard for the neighborhoods and shopping centers they included in their bloodbaths.

The U.S. troops were armed with M16s. The M16 could fire thirty rounds per magazine. There were strict codes of conduct in using the M16. Soldiers lowered their rifles when talking with locals. A discharged weapon on patrol meant stern punishment from superiors unless there'd been a valid reason to fire. The Guard soldiers disassembled, cleaned, reassembled, and inspected their rifles with great care. They used them only as a last resort.

The insurgents fired mortars at American FOBs, the forward operating bases. There was no tactical reason for it. The insurgents didn't follow the shellings with an assault on the FOB. Most of the mortar attacks were poorly aimed, landing outside the wire. The insurgents fired from mosques, schools, and apartment buildings. They usually fired one or two shots before packing up and running to avoid the quick reaction force. The Americans could track the mortars and locate the source quickly. Had it been a fair fight, the American artillery would have wiped the floor with the insurgents; but because the insurgents fired from civilian areas, American guns were mostly silent. Michael ordered his men to wear body armor whenever outside the barracks. He would not have a casualty from the random shelling, if he could help it. That meant soldiers had to suit up in full battle rattle just to get a burger and fries. The order was met with reluctance, but everyone complied. Gavin's men and the rest of Camp McDonald took their lumps stoically, and they'd taken only two casualties, both minor, from mortars.

Shackleford hated the mortars. Not because of their danger, but because of the sheer cowardice in the act. Fire and flee. Where was the honor in that?

"It's a different kind of war," Captain Gavin told him during a conversation outside the mess hall. "First Gulf War, I was in the 82nd Ready

Brigade, on the tarmac all set to mount up and go and kick some butt; but then we were told to wait it out almost an entire day. You should have heard the rumors flying around about where we were headed. Africa. The Middle East. And what do they load us up in to get us to the theater of operations? Commercial jets. Airliners. We flew tourist class to war. I shouldn't complain, at least my rear wasn't sore like it would have been after a half-world jaunt in a C-141, but still, can you imagine being in full battle rattle, sipping on a soda and munching on pretzels before a gun-fight? Then we get there, and because the supply is all haywire, we end up eating burgers at a fast-food joint that was in the desert, connected to a foreign work project or something. Spent a pretty long time in the desert back then, with little action to show for it."

"Yes sir, but our enemy is right outside our doorstep," Shackleford said.

"Our enemies, and our friends, Lieutenant."

The two soldiers looked to the sky almost in unison as a hissing noise covered the FOB. On instinct, Shackleford crouched, prepared to duck for cover. Gavin casually traced the noise as it arced over the FOB and into the desert, exploding with a loud thud well outside the wire.

"Well sir, our 'friends' out there may not want to keep it that way," Shackleford said. "Bunch of cheaters."

"They don't fight fair, do they?" Michael mused.

The insurgents set off car bombs, if the opportunity presented itself. The FOB's border was dressed in razor wire, with a squared trench, a large con-crete barrier, and guard posts with soldiers who had little patience for Iraqi drivers who ventured too close. Two car bombs had been detonated close to the entrance by insurgents playing at a casual drive-by before sending themselves and their scrap metal into oblivion. The guards fired warning shots at suspicious cars to deter any more attempts. The car bombs pro-gressed to IEDs.

For the insurgency, the Internet was a propaganda tool. For Americans, it was a way to communicate with wives and children, brothers, sisters, and friends. The hub of Camp McDonald was a converted factory with bullet holes and crumbled concrete in parts that had sustained damage from the invasion. It served as HQ for a brigade of Guard soldiers, antennas poking out of the roof and wires connecting countless communication devices. Inside were cots and workstations. A side building needed to be cleaned out; Iraqi soldiers had used it as a makeshift outhouse during the war and had neglected to clean up after themselves. Lined around the factory building were tents for the grunts, a PX, a small weight room, a row of porta-johns that soldiers didn't dare use in the heat of the day, and the prize of Camp McDonald: a basketball court.

There wasn't much in the way of external communications. Captain Gavin had pestered the brigade command for a month to upgrade from the three computers and two phone lines in the converted factory that served as the only direct way to phone home. His efforts eventually paid off. He got an air-conditioned trailer full of computers and satellite pay phone lines. The computers were old, and one of the keyboards had the letters IRAQ plucked out as a joke, but the lines were shortened and correspondence increased.

The insurgents didn't care about the lives they took. American, Iraqi, their own; they were all the same, as long as blood was spilled. They kidnapped reporters, foreign workers, and Iraqis who supported the Americans. They threatened Iraqis trying to make the most of the new opportunities presented to them. Family members of interpreters were killed or beaten. Shops were bombed. The insurgents tortured and beheaded. There was no rhyme or reason to it, no tactical advantage gained, no town seized, no people freed.

Before their deployment, Captain Gavin had gathered his officers and noncoms. He wasn't one for speeches, in training or even at the deployment ceremony, so everyone listened attentively.

"I've got one goal," Michael said, "and I want it to sink in. Everyone is coming back alive. Follow orders, complete missions, and come home safe. Is that understood?"

Shackleford didn't consider Michael a coward. Michael had combat experience, a Ranger tab, and Airborne wings from his service in the Army. It wasn't a directive to avoid a firefight. Just a reminder to stay safe and not to let the temptations of a war zone take root among the soldiers.

"We're going to give out more Beanie Babies than we do bullets on this deployment," Gavin had told his officers. Boxes and boxes of toys arrived each week from Guard family members, and the company handed them out while on patrol. Gavin was very particular on this. Before each mission briefing, he would instruct his platoon leaders to supply toys to squad leaders. "Hearts and minds," he constantly reminded them.

The soldiers gave away stuffed animals, mini soccer balls, and an assortment of toys. When they ran out of toys, they handed out chem lights or pencils; and when they were out of those, they shook hands, patted backs, and drank tea.

And they rebuilt. Gavin's Guard company ranks included firefighters, policemen, welders, contractors, and retail store managers. They lived and breathed the word *community*. The Guard engineers turned an abandoned building into a schoolhouse. They rewired and rerouted electricity. Commerce went from a trickle to a steady stream. With American patrols increasing, town merchants had less to fear from the foreign fighters that made up the vast majority of the insurgency. Once a week, the medics ran a free clinic for the Iraqis, treating everything from burn victims to broken bones. They treated civilians caught in the crossfire. They bandaged what the insurgents had tried to burn, remade what the insurgents tried to destroy.

Then one day, the insurgents figured out a way to use the American's goodwill against them.

The first attack came as a salvo of mortar shells raining down on Camp McDonald. Unlike previous attacks, these were well placed. Three soldiers earned their Purple Hearts while playing a pickup game of basketball, when several shells landed on the court and injured them. And the shelling didn't stop with the first salvo. It continued far longer than what the soldiers had become accustomed to. American artillery located the source almost immediately—a nearby mosque. Captain Gavin radioed Lieutenant Shackleford, whose men were deployed outside the wire.

"Send in the quick reaction force," he ordered. He ordered the rest of the company to mount up, and put the brigade on alert. Something was going down, and he sensed he'd need all the firepower he could get.

Six miles south of the FOB, Shackleford's quick reaction force received the order to close on the mosque, secure the perimeter, and wait for backup. They'd have much rather kicked down the doors and cleaned house, but judging from the firepower coming from the mosque, this was going to be larger than a patrol engagement.

Shackleford had two choices in his route: the main road into town, or a zigzag through the side streets. Although they had rarely met resistance on the main road, the Americans still considered it a potential chokepoint, so they often avoided it. Two-story buildings enclosed it on both sides, with kicked-out windows and rooftops that were choice sniper beds should the insurgents wise up. Shackleford surmised that the rest of the company would take the main road in force, so he opted for an alternative. It might throw any would-be snipers off track to hear the rumble of his Humvees speeding away from the main route.

When his Humvees arrived at the mosque, Shackleford scanned the building, and spotted shadows scattering up top.

"Do you have a shot?" he said over the radio. Corporal Rich Tilley, an excellent marksman, was three Humvees down and looking for a target.

"Negative sir," he said. "They booked it down the other side."

"Secure the perimeter!" Shackleford boomed. His men spread out around the mosque at angles to support themselves should a firefight break out.

"What's the ETA on reinforcements?" Shackleford asked his radio operator.

"Five minutes."

His orders complete, all that was left to do was wait. Later on, Shackleford would wish he had those five minutes back.

An explosion erupted in the distance. The crackle of M16 and AK-47 rifle fire intermixed. Lots of it. More sounds of thunder, probably RPGs. Shackleford's eyes traced the mosque's frame for enemies. Nothing. He had no doubt that the insurgents who had been firing off mortar rounds from the rooftop were still there, but his ears and his instincts told him the real fight wasn't at the mosque anymore.

"Change of plans," he said. He ordered his driver to turn around. The other platoon vehicles did likewise. "Hit the streets that run parallel to the main road."

Shackleford had prepared his platoon for this maneuver with countless foot patrols through the town. They knew alleyways and shortcuts, and knew how to dog tail through their patrols so the insurgents couldn't get ahead of them. Today they'd use their knowledge to make a beeline straight to the attack on American soldiers.

On the radio, he could hear the sounds of chaos. The company radioman hadn't checked in. A second platoon leader, Jerry Stovall, speculated that Captain Gavin's Humvee had been hit. Up ahead, above the buildings, Shackleford could see plumes of black smoke.

Shackleford scanned the street for any sign of IEDs, a dead animal with a bloated stomach, piled trash in the center of the road, anything. He was sure they were heading into a trap, but there wasn't time to stop. Like before, he had two options.

Shackleford's men spilled out of their Humvees, kneeling or lying in firing positions, guns at the ready. For the first few seconds of the firefight, they did not have the advantage, however. Six insurgents covered the alleyway from concealed positions and waited for the opportune moment. Shackleford clung to the Humvee door as a shield, frantically trying to pinpoint targets, his men doing the same.

"I'm hit!" Private Doug Sims shouted, his leg a bloody mess. Another soldier dragged him into the back seat of a Humvee.

Once the firing positions were located, the Humvee .50 caliber machine guns came to life, obliterating the windows and alleyway hiding spots and the bodies behind them. Once the insurgents had been eliminated, the platoon's medic rushed to Private Sims.

"First Squad, on me!" Shackleford's men could hear rockets being fired from the rooftop of the building they were about to clear, gunshots from the side facing the road. They didn't know it, but they all sensed that men had died, and more were in danger of it. They had to move fast.

"Tell Stovall to keep the guys up top occupied until we're in position," he shouted to his radioman. "We're going in."

Sergeant Bill Darby, nicknamed "The Bear" for his thick Southern drawl and husky frame, kicked open the door. Two soldiers rushed in, rifles at the ready. Shackleford and the rest of the men weren't far behind.

One shot rang out to Shackleford's right. It was answered by a shot from an M16.

"Clear!" Darby said.

The squad cleared each room, cautious enough to do it textbook, but with a sense of urgency. The soldiers cleared the building to the top floor. Shackleford waved down to his radioman, who informed the pinned soldiers to cease firing on the roof.

Darby kicked open the door to the roof. Shackleford's adrenaline raced through his veins as he stormed through. He spotted an insurgent reloading an RPG, dropped to his knee and fired a three-round burst, pinning the insurgent to the roof wall. In the five-second span it took to eliminate his target, three members of his squad had rushed the rooftop, finding and dropping one more insurgent. The roof was now clear.

The battle by then was over. Four buildings, including Shackleford's, were scorched and bullet-ridden. Below, Shackleford was able to survey the damage. One Humvee had been obliterated. A second Humvee's engine block was in flames, blood surrounding the vehicles. One American's body lay slumped to the side. Another man was being treated. With the battle zone clear, soldiers rushed to the surrounding buildings to check for possible gunmen.

Shackleford put his hands to his knees. The adrenaline was working its way out of his system.

"Sir, we found Captain Gavin," Darby said.

The adjacent building had housed more than a dozen insurgents. They were all dead. As Shackleford walked through the war-torn structure, he paused at one of the dead bodies. He recognized the face, but couldn't quite place it. He'd later learn that it was Al-Sahim, the top-ranking terrorist in Iraq. Captain Gavin had shot him. Apparently, Gavin had shot all of them.

The stairwell was riddled with bullets and smeared with blood at the top. Another bad guy down. Shackleford could hear the shuffle of men upstairs. He climbed the stairs and entered the room where the last insurgent had made his stand. The room stank of sulfur.

Gavin was hunched by the window, a medic pressing a bandage to his right shoulder. His pistol lay by his left hand, a dead man across from him. Shackleford would never forget the look on Gavin's face, because it was such a contrast to his usual collected demeanor. There was distress and pain, and not stemming from the wound in his shoulder. Shackleford leaned down and patted his commander's leg.

"What happened here?" he asked the medic.

"Captain Gavin's Humvee was hit by an RPG," the medic said, still focused on treating the wound. "The lead vehicle got hit by an IED, then they railed into us. Both sides. We took a lot of casualties. Brigade is sending reinforcements. We'd have a lot more body bags though, if it wasn't for the captain. He rushed the house after his Humvee was hit. Only man that made it inside. Two from his truck were killed. He rushed this place and killed every insurgent in here, including Al-Sahim."

Shackleford digested that bit of news. "I saw him downstairs," he said.

"Dangdest thing I ever saw," the medic said, smiling at the captain as he tore open the top of his uniform to get to the wound. "You got 'em all, sir."

Gavin didn't respond. He just stared weakly at his adversary, who was slumped over, head resting on the floor, eyes looking back in a frozen glaze. Gavin seemed lost in those eyes, as if the two were still fighting to the death, only somewhere else, in another world.

"Get that guy out of here," Shackleford commanded. Darby came from behind and dragged the dead insurgent away.

"I didn't . . ." Gavin said.

"What was that, sir?"

Gavin met Shackleford's eyes, then looked away. It was the only time the lieutenant saw any semblance of shame in his superior. The captain gazed out the window, at his men picking up the pieces, regrouping as a unit. At some of them being taken away as casualties. Some in body bags.

"I didn't keep my promise."

Chapter 13

The doorbell ring produced the pitter-patter of a six-year-old's frantic steps. Addy Grace Gavin flung the door open with all her might, and set her hands on her hips.

"Yes?" she said.

"Hello, Addy," Wes said. "Is your mom home?"

"No, for your information station, she is not, mister reporter," she said. "But you have a ton of other big people over here. Take your pick."

"How about your grandmother or grandfather?" Wes asked.

"Sure," she said. "You can come in, just take off your shoes, and skip."

"Why skip?"

"Because if you don't skip, you're going to mess up the floor. Everyone is always cleaning up the floor for some reason. They're being very weird."

So Wes skipped inside with Addy Grace. A few of the Gavin relatives were in the living room, including Betty, who was holding court with grandchildren sitting cross-legged on the floor. Addy took a seat in the semicircle.

"Hello again, Wes," Betty said in her pleasant Southern drawl.

"I guess I'll be bugging you for a few more days," Wes said.

"Oh, not at all, we enjoy having you here," she said. "So, what can we help you with?"

Wes told her about meeting with Shackleford, and how he was trying to finalize the portion of research pertaining to Michael's military service. Betty bookmarked whatever she was reading to the kids.

"We've got one more officer in the house I bet you'd like to speak to," she said. "The major. He's taking a nap, but I'll go get him for you. Why don't you go sit on the porch and rest a second."

Betty departed upstairs and Wes made his way out to the porch and sat down in a rocking chair. Betty had warned him that it would take a few minutes to stir her husband. "He can be cranky, so give him a minute, and you can get some fresh air while you chat."

Sooner than Wes expected, Paul Gavin opened the screen door, stepped outside, and offered his hand. His grip was firm but not overbearing.

Wes took in the measure of the man. The major had a long forehead with cavernous lines that appeared poised to shift the earth on a frown. His bushy eyebrows curled at the tips and shaded his eyes like a pitcher's ball cap. His eyes, though, were razor sharp, with no hint of decline, despite his age. He looked the part of a man who kept his mind and body busy.

"Mr. Gavin," Wes began, "I'm Wes Watkins. I'm a reporter for the *News*. Sorry to wake you."

Paul disarmed Wes with his smile, which was good, because his voice still hinted at military authority. "Well, you weren't the one tugging at my sleeve a moment ago. You are the one giving Michael's eulogy, correct?"

"Yes."

"Please sit," Paul said, pointing to a rocker.

Betty stormed out with two lemonades, fresh from the kitchen. Then she was gone.

"Mr. Gavin, can I be up-front?"

He furled his massive eyebrows in a mock scowl, and then let up just as quickly. "Of course, of course."

"Why did Michael pick me to do his eulogy?"

Paul waited for the right words to surface. "A number of reasons, I think, Wes," he said. "The simple answer is, he wanted a thorough look at his life, as a last wish. And he wanted process; for someone to ask questions and do the digging without knowing anything up front, so that whatever they . . . you . . . found, would be genuine. And I appreciate the fact you're willing to humor him with the task. Plus, he liked your prose."

"He liked my writing in the *News*?"

Paul smiled. "He did."

Wes decided to get straight to the punch. "Maybe you can help me with a question I have about his medals," he said. "I was in Michael's study looking around with Betty and Lynn yesterday, and there were awards and citations from his military service, both in the Army and the National Guard, but Lynn said that he didn't display his medals for personal service, including the Medal of Honor. Why would he do that?"

"Wes, soldiers aren't all cut from the same cloth," he said. "We never spoke about what he did with the medal, so I can't answer that. Medals have a symbolic meaning for real-life sacrifices, so we each honor that in our own way. I've heard of soldiers mailing their Purple Hearts to civilians who wrote them heartfelt letters of encouragement. You've no doubt seen stories of decorated soldiers who throw away their medals in protest. Others may give them to a family member as an heirloom, that sort of thing. It's a federal crime, however, to sell them."

"So he gave it away? That just seems odd. Was he protesting something?"

Paul seemed ready for the question. "I don't think he gave it away. Perhaps someone on his list knows where it is. Michael was proud of his service. He was prouder, though, of the men who served under him. A leader worth his salt will care more about getting his men home safely than any medals or awards, and I think that was the point he was, or is, trying to make. The Medal of Honor is the highest award anyone can receive in the armed forces. I think only one or two other people received it for actions in Iraq. With the medal, though, came a lot of hoopla. He was somewhat embarrassed about all of the hype. He felt it took away from what his soldiers accomplished as a unit. If anyone asked Michael about the actions leading to the medal and if they asked to see the medal, he wanted to show the citation his unit received for their tour instead. Not having the medal in his possession made it easier."

Wes caught up on his note taking as Paul paused. The recorder now in his lap would help.

"Have you read the citation, for the medal?" Paul asked.

"A little bit, yeah," Wes said, wanting to continue the train of thought. "I hope you won't find any of the questions I have offensive, but, was the medal a burden to Michael?"

Paul paused, took a sip of lemonade, and looked at Wes thoughtfully. "I wouldn't say that. The memories that came with it, maybe. He lost men. Losing men is a tough pill for a leader to take, especially with a field command. It's a fact of war, but hard to accept sometimes."

"Why did he join the Army?"

"What was that?" Paul cupped his ear. "Sorry, Wes, I'm an old man, need things repeated occasionally. You seem to have switched topics. What was the question?"

Wes cleared his throat. "Why did Michael join the Army? I mean, he didn't seem to have a need to join. From what I understand, he had a legitimate shot of signing as a free agent with an NFL team, maybe even being drafted."

"You don't think the military was the right move?"

"I'm just curious. He had a chance to earn good money in a professional sport, even for a little while, if he's just on the scout team or whatever, and he had his college degree. A college football player can make money easily in the business world with the connections they make. So why go into the military?"

"What you seem to be inferring, Wes, is that the military was not a good career move for him." Paul leveled a professorial gaze, neither cold nor warm. It was blank, as if he were waiting for Wes to come out with his line of thinking.

Wes backtracked. "Oh, no, I wasn't trying to say that, not really. I didn't mean for the question to be offensive."

"It wasn't," Paul leaned back in his chair, "but would you care to elaborate? You have a theory, no doubt."

"It just doesn't seem like guys with business degrees graduate college and join the military. I heard of some people doing that after 9/11, but not a lot. And Michael joined the Army right before the First Gulf War."

Paul studied Wes. He seemed to know that Wes had an angle to his investigation. Wes tried to think of ways to ask why someone would want to be a soldier, without offending a soldier.

"Michael joined because he thought it was the best option out of college for him and what he wanted to do with his life," Paul finally said. "There are benefits to a military career, both seen and unseen. As you're probably aware, there are tangible and financial benefits to serving, as in college education, bonuses, a leniency in home loans, that sort of thing. There's also an education within the military, and in this case the Army, for leadership training. You learn how to lead under the most intense pressure. Life and death pressure. Life hangs in your hands, and the decisions you make affect those around you. Plus the discipline that comes with the Army. You don't question the hours you put in, or wonder if you're going to get a pay raise. It's actually a blissful kind of order that sometimes I wish we could practice in the ivory tower I work in at Tributary U. You simply do your duty."

"You never question anything?"

"Not in the sense that you might be thinking. You have a mission and you carry it out. You have a commander, and you might hate his guts, but you still carry out his orders."

"Man, I don't know if I could do that," Wes said, almost to himself.

Paul was silent. Wes felt as if he needed to explain.

"I mean, less money, crazy hours, life or death situations . . ."

"Tell me, Wes, why did you want to be a reporter? There's more money in being an Army officer right out of college than in being a reporter."

Wes shrugged. "Well, I love a good story, enjoy writing, and I want to uncover the truth."

"There you have it," Paul said, "An ideal instead of a fatter paycheck. That's commendable, wouldn't you say?"

"I guess so," Wes said, "but it's different."

"And how is that?"

"You don't get a say in the military. If I'm assigned a story based on one piece of evidence and I find the conclusion to be different, I can change the angle. A soldier doesn't get to choose who he fights, from what I understand. He's ordered to go, and he goes, right? But what if he doesn't agree with the war?"

"Any war in particular you're referring to?"

Wes opened his mouth to speak, then caught himself. He wasn't inferring anymore.

"I'd rather not get into political opinions," Wes said. "It wouldn't be fair to the assignment."

"It wouldn't?"

Wes shook his head, hoping to close this detour in the conversation. Paul grinned.

"Personally, Wes, I think supporting our soldiers and supporting a war can be two totally different things. Some may disagree—and you may be one of them, from what I gather. Correct me if I'm wrong. I'd be happy to explain to you why I believe what I believe, but you've brought up an interesting point. We've skirted the issue of soldiers fighting in a war they may not wholeheartedly believe in. What about reporters? How can they cover a topic they feel strongly about? Doesn't the story get blurred?"

"I'm sorry, Mr. Gavin, I got sidetracked. How about we go back to Michael's—"

"Good grief, man"—Paul slapped his thigh—"we can't turn back now!"

At this sudden outburt, Wes jumped in his seat, rocking the recorder. Wes fumbled to steady it as Paul continued.

"Let's dig a little deeper here, because I think you'll find the answer that you're looking for. Michael's service in the military really isn't that far removed from your noble venture into journalism, and we can answer this sense of duty you're wondering about too. The question remains on the table. Should a reporter, say a political reporter, cover an issue that he has strong feelings about?"

"Okay, I'll bite. In a perfect world, no," Wes admitted, "but it's impossible to ask someone not to have an opinion about something. Sure, there may be a hint of preference, but a good reporter can put those reservations away and report based on the facts. The media aren't as biased as you think."

"I wasn't aware that I offered my feelings one way or the other on the media and a perceived bias," Paul said flatly.

"I didn't mean—"

Paul waved Wes off. "I apologize. I enjoy these kinds of frank discussions. I've yet to be offended by anything you've said, and I'm unlikely to be offended by anything you might say. I'm merely trying to challenge you on your own thoughts. An old professor up to his tricks. In the future, though, I wouldn't take a discussion like the one we're having as a perceived attack on your career. It's all in the process of finding an answer."

Wes nodded meekly.

"Perhaps we have gotten off subject," Paul said, "and that's my fault. Tangents lead me during a good debate, like discovering a deer trail on a hike and using that instead of the main trail; but let's complete the thought on at least this one subject. A reporter has opinions. A soldier has opinions. We do not live in a perfect world, and what a scary world it would be if a soldier did not have a conscience in his conduct of war, or a reporter his morals in delivering what is news to his audience. We've seen disastrous results of what can happen in both circumstances. What we hope, then, is that an individual exercises good faith toward his objective in his career.

"In a soldier's case, very true, he does not have the luxury of exercising his opinion on a war—at least not legally. Once you sign up, you are duty bound to do what your superiors tell you. You may end up fighting in a war that, if you sat down and thought about it, you'd have your reservations about. Our current conflict is very much open to debate, and I'm glad that we've been having the debate. That's what makes America what it is. It's just that, for soldiers, there's a time and a place for all of that, and it's not in the field. I certainly had my reservations about Vietnam, a war I fought in, Wes."

"I didn't know that," Wes said.

"Of course you didn't. Why would you? I don't go parading around my military service and campaigns. An old warhorse like me is more pleased with eating the grass than snorting out old snotty remembrances, but let's

lay the groundwork for a soldier and his conscience and his reasons for joining. War is a horrible thing. I can attest to that, and it would be my wish
that it never be revisited on this earth again; but it will, and we can never
rid ourselves of the tendencies. You can only hope that, when the time
comes, your country is fighting a war in the interests of its own defense.
What strategy that defense means, though, is interpreted in many ways,
and I think that has something to do with the public discourse today.

"As a soldier, you must trust that, despite the imperfections your government or society may have, your commitment to fighting for your country is being matched by the leaders; that they are truly calling their soldiers
to arms for the right reasons. You hope that you have a citizenry that elects
responsible leaders, and that you can trust their judgment as well. It's the
same hope that a journalist should have; that once they uncover a scandal
or hidden truth, the public will act appropriately on the revelation. But in
the military, you make this decision before you join, and then you apply
it, almost as a principle. Because once you're in the military and engaged
in a conflict, the only thing you have time to think about is the mission.
At that point, the soldiers under your command, their lives, and yours,
are all that matter.

"That's why I believe 'supporting a war' and 'supporting the troops'
are separate decisions. One is often politically motivated, and the other is
affected by politics, but hopefully not motivated by them. For instance, a
mother who opposes a war still loves and supports her son who is deployed,
correct? A family may have reservations about a conflict that their son or
daughter is being deployed to, but that doesn't mean they opt not to send
care packages.

"And let's keep in mind that these are grown men and women we're
talking about. The notion that children are going off to war to fight our
battles is preposterous. A nineteen-year-old grunt has more maturity and
discipline than most college seniors I see at Tributary. Does a friend dis-
own another friend because of the profession they choose? A lack of support for our soldiers is often because we mix support for the action and the
leaders in Washington who enforce the action as one entity."

"I see," Wes said.

Paul slapped both hands on the armrest of the rocking chair. "I'm digressing again, Wes. Let me finish things up. People join the military for reasons that you can't really put on paper. I can throw the words out, but I'm not sure you'd understand them, no more than I could comprehend the principles that you seek when it comes to journalism. Michael, in my opinion, joined the military for the challenge, for the sacrifice, as a call to duty—but most of all, as a test. A test of leadership and of himself. And that, my friend, is the end of my ranting. If any of that helped, then great. I doubt much of it did. There are plenty of other people better suited to tell you things about my son on the list he provided you. Officer Shackleford, I'm sure, was a fine example. Have you taken the time to call anyone else on the list?"

Wes hedged. "Sort of."

Paul looked as if he wanted to say more, but didn't.

"Honestly, it feels like going through a phone book, Mr. Gavin," Wes said. "Can you give me an indication as to why I should call everyone? A lead?"

Paul scratched the bottom of his chin in thought. "I'm not trying to be difficult here, but I think those folks are as important to Michael's story as anything I'd ever tell you."

"Can you at least tell me about the week Michael missed at school his senior year?"

Paul studied Wes, which Wes took as affirmation that he was on to something. "I'll make a deal with you," Paul said, a slight grin on his face. "You call half those folks and get their story, and I'll tell you everything you want to know about the days I plucked Michael out of school."

Wes couldn't hide his surprise at that statement. He opened his mouth, but knew he wouldn't get more until he got on the phone.

"Okay, deal," he said. "Do you know where Lynn is? I had a couple more questions for her."

"She's at the funeral home," he said. "There's an honor guard there and she wanted to say thanks to the people standing vigil."

Chapter 14

The *News* office was three blocks from Talking Creek's funeral home. Heading into town from Atlanta, it was on the right on Main Street. The funeral home rarely registered on Wes's radar, except for maybe after he'd watched a scary movie, and then only to give him chills. Tonight, he turned into the parking lot, opting to try to meet with Lynn before heading into the office to sort through the mess his investigation had become. He'd ask for one name, one lead, to the person most likely to know the whereabouts of Michael's missing medal. That would be his story for Sunday: "Soldier mourns lost comrades, hides medal." It wasn't disgraceful or heroic. And people liked a good mystery. Wes was too frustrated to continue the wild goose chase. The Gavins were helpful, but that was just it. They weren't pointing him in any particular direction. They'd answer his questions, but offer little more. Lynn's call to Officer Shackleford had so far been the only lead they'd allowed. These weren't people with an agenda, but it was almost as nerve-racking dealing with them. With Starks breathing down his neck—even as he drove downtown, his cell phone vibrated and Starks's number glowed on the screen—the payoff wasn't worth the effort. Wes let the call go to voicemail. Talking Creek would get a pleasant mystery, Wes would get a decent but not spectacular clip, and everyone would call it a week.

Parked outside the funeral home were two squad cars out of a police department that owned maybe half a dozen. A twentysomething male getting out of his car beside two squad cars registered immediately to the cops. Wes held up his hands as one rolled down the window and the other cracked the passenger side door.

"Hey officers, I'm a reporter for the *News*."

Wes was almost surprised they didn't unholster their guns at that point. "I'm the guy doing Michael Gavin's eulogy. Are you guys part of the honor guard?"

The officer in the driver's side nodded.

"You have policemen standing beside the casket?"

"Two, as a matter of fact," he said. "We have two in rolling shifts. Calhoun's police department has sent over an extra squad car so we can stay at full staff."

"Was this something that the family requested?"

The officer frowned. "The family requested no visitation, but this is different. Are you doing some kind of article? Am I being quoted on this stuff?"

"No, I was just curious. I interviewed a police officer that served with him in the National Guard in Iraq, actually. Made me think of you guys and the job you do, that's all."

"Maybe you should talk with Lynn Gavin," he said. She's inside."

The officer in the passenger side hopped out and ushered Wes to the entrance. The funeral home consisted of a main hall and four or five rooms, all appointed with outdated carpet colors, paintings, and floral arrangements. The air was pleasant, not the hospital smell Wes had expected, and slightly chilly, and the place had a feeling of peace. The doors to all but one room were closed. The officer escorted Wes to the opening of the door, but didn't allow him to go in. Wes was fine with the discretion.

The casket was centered in the room. Two men in formal police dress flanked the casket, at attention. They did not make eye contact although they must have known that someone was in the doorway, and the officer with Wes did not attempt conversation. They all took this assignment seriously. Wes felt a lump in his throat.

One of the officers spoke to Lynn, who was sitting on a couch in the corner. She walked out of the room and nodded her head toward the door.

Wes happily obliged. He almost thought it would be worthwhile to go over and look at the man whose eulogy he would be giving, but he let the opportunity pass and walked outside with Lynn. A gentle breeze lifted otherwise idle leaves through the streets.

"Paul told me you were here," he said to Lynn. "I probably should be waiting until tomorrow or something to interview you, but I talked with Rod Shackleford this afternoon, and I'm not sure what to make of things."

"Have you called anyone else on the list?"

"A few." Besides Coach Lawler and Shackleford, he hadn't called anyone.

Lynn didn't nod, didn't frown. Her head didn't move at all, and Wes could tell that she knew he was telling a half-truth.

"You might want to call everybody on the list; it could help."

"Anyone in particular?"

"As far as the medal goes, no," she said. "I thought Rod might be able to help you. Honestly, if I knew, I'd tell you. Not having it in plain view is like having a piece of him hidden. I don't like that; not now. We had enough time to prepare and make his passing as neat and orderly as it could be, but as you can see, he left a few surprises for everyone. I didn't think to ask him about the medal in his last days because we were just trying to enjoy each other's company. I thought it would show up. Maybe it's part of the eulogy he wanted you to prepare; maybe it's not. I don't know. I don't like thinking I don't know my husband."

"Officer Shackleford had no idea about the medal's location, though he wasn't surprised when I told him it was missing."

"Men in uniform can be such a mystery sometimes," she said.

"No kidding," Wes offered. His legs felt a little wobbly and he propped himself up against the building. It occurred to him that he should probably get something to eat. "Too much of a mystery, I suppose. So what made you decide to come down here tonight?"

"Questions," she said, sighing. "I've got so many questions, Wes. What am I supposed to do after all of this? How am I supposed to manage the foster care retreat? How in the world am I supposed to tell our six-year-old daughter that her father isn't coming home? I don't have any of those answers. Michael always did. He thought through a question, made a decision, and was done with it. Everyone knew they could come to him for answers. They think because I'm his wife, it's the same with me. It's not. I'm not Michael Gavin."

"You're not keeping the foster care retreat?"

"I don't know," she said. "We planned things out financially, so Addy and I will be fine in one respect. But the foster retreat is just a lot of effort, and coordination. It was us, Michael and me; but is it also me, all alone? I can't tell what God wants for my life. It's all different now."

"It is a lot of land," Wes offered. "A lot to manage. How were ya'll able to acquire and grow it?"

It was one of his remaining questions, and probably the safest one. This wasn't the time to ask about Michael's sealed record, or any problems they may have had after he returned from the war. Wes wanted at least one answer out of her, though.

"Earl Bishop," she said.

"His college coach?"

She nodded.

"I thought they hated each other."

"A myth, and a bad one," she said. "The Bud Lawlers of the world might want it to be true, but it's not reality. Michael's learning to play a supporting role his senior year was a big deal. I think it changed both coach and player. Nobody ever reports on this, and it's probably not common knowledge, but Bishop helps out his players once they graduate. He's invested in their companies, given scholarship money for their children. With Michael, he helped him purchase the land for the ranch."

A simple answer. Wes wanted the rest of his questions to have the same result, but his energy to ask them was waning. He couldn't breathe for some reason, and his legs were getting shakier. He reached for the building again, but missed. Everything was off kilter. He stumbled inside to find a place to sit.

The last thing he saw was Lynn leaning over him, eyes wide, motioning toward the funeral home door with her arms.

Chapter 15

The world returned in dotted pictures. There was a dull light coming into focus. Wes's head swam—it felt unusually heavy, so he stayed on the ground and stared at the ceiling. The two police officers from the squad car were talking to each other beside the doorway, but he couldn't focus on what they were saying.

Thoughts returned, but nothing made sense. Footsteps all around, then someone plunked a bag down at his side. Finally, Wes realized that he had fainted, that medics had arrived, and that Lynn was standing a few feet away. The picture became clearer. Then he looked at the face of the medic bending over him, and it made no sense at all.

"What are you doing here?" Wes asked, shaking the cobwebs from his head. Wayne Griffin ignored the question and grabbed a few things from his bag. Wes recognized what Wayne was doing: checking his pulse, blood pressure, respiration, and temperature. Wes was all too familiar with the process, though not usually while lying prone on the floor of a funeral home, or being attended by a possible news source. He let his brain catch up to the world while Wayne and the other medic went about their business.

"We called the paramedics when you passed out," Lynn said from somewhere overhead. "Is he okay, Wayne?" Wayne focused on Wes and not the question. He spoke to Wes when he was finished.

"Your pulse is fast, you've got a 120 resting heart rate. Blood pressure is 90 over 60, pretty low. Respirations are 28 per minute, which is too rapid."

"Oh," Wes said. For the first time, he was aware of the shiny lights of the ambulance from a window.

"He's going to be fine," Wayne said.

"You put a scare in me, Wes," Lynn said. "Don't do that again, okay?"

It wasn't a rhetorical question, but Wes was in no mood to reply.

"Your temperature is 97.8," Wayne said. "You're diaphoretic, sweaty. We checked your vitals just to be careful, but your wristband saved us a few minutes of worry."

He pointed to the blue band that Wes wore for just such an occasion. If he landed in the hospital, the nurses and doctors could work out the problem a whole lot faster if they knew he had diabetes.

Wayne pulled an Accu-Chek from his bag. "Let's see what your blood sugar is." He stuck Wes's finger and showed him the reading. "Your blood sugar is 45 milligrams per decaliter. And your normal range . . ."

He waited for Wes to answer.

"Should be 80 to 120," Wes said.

Wayne nodded.

Wes tried to get up, but Wayne put his hand on his shoulder. "You should just relax for a few minutes."

"You're not taking me to the ER, are you?"

Wayne smiled. "We'll see. Right now you need some sugar in your system." He pulled some glucose jell from his bag and gave it to Wes, who sucked on it dutifully.

A few minutes later, Wes was sitting up and leaning against the wall. An officer had gotten some OJ for him. He drank the orange juice under Wayne's studious gaze.

"I knew they told us as kids that OJ was good for you, but I had no idea it cured people," Lynn said, eager for lightened conversation. Neither Wes nor Wayne responded.

"I had no idea that you were a paramedic," Wes said to Wayne.

"Surprise."

"Well, sorry you had to come down here," Wes said. "I feel like a moron."

"Sometimes it's good for us to get calls," Wayne said. "People not tak-ing care of themselves is rampant everywhere, not just in hospitals. Even reporters are prone to it." The barb was gentle, but it struck home. "And it's mostly folks neglecting their bodies. You've got your own blood sugar monitor and wristband, you already know the drill. So what happened?"

"I lost track," Wes admitted sheepishly. "I drove down to Atlanta to interview a man who served in the National Guard with Michael Gavin. I skipped a meal and intended to make it up on the way back. Except, I forgot."

"First time fainting?"

"No, but the last time was in college," Wes said. "I know what I need to do."

"Do you have a support group?"

"Diabetes Anonymous?" Wes said sarcastically. "Sure, we meet once a month at the grocery store."

"I meant family, friends, who can check on you."

"I'm fine," Wes said.

Wayne frowned. "I'd recommend a support group to help you monitor your blood sugar. It can be family, friends, or even coworkers."

Wes snorted. "My boss would be too busy trying to avoid a lawsuit from me passing out on the job, or making up for almost getting me fired for an assignment he gave me to do."

"Do you have any family that could help?" Lynn asked.

"Only child," Wes said. "My mom is down in Alpharetta. She's not going to be a happy camper when I tell her about this, but I can handle myself."

"What about your father?"

There was a tone in Lynn's voice that Wes didn't like. He couldn't pin-point what it was; just that she had no business asking him such a specific question when he'd already answered her.

"No," Wes said. "I haven't spoken to my father since high school. No intentions of starting now."

Wayne nodded. "Well, it's a free world, so take my recommendation however you like; but for the record, going it alone on anything health-related isn't always a sign of strength or independence. Wouldn't hurt to admit that."

As Wayne started putting his instruments in his bag, Wes thought of ways of turning the conversation around. Now that he was here, Wes thought back to the Nooners interview. He glanced down at his shoes. The left shoe laces were undone. He gazed at them, working through his thoughts about Wayne and Michael. Wayne's description of Michael asking for forgiveness came crashing back. Wes understood the story's gist, of how Michael had taped Wayne's sprained ankle in front of the team; how it was a weird moment, that their teammates looked at their friendship as the turning point to their football season; but he knew there was more to it than that. Perhaps Wayne hadn't told him everything, being in front of the Nooners.

"Mr. Griffin?" Wes said. Wayne raised his head. "This may be bad timing, but for Michael Gavin's eulogy, I did want to talk to you, if that's okay . . ."

Wayne finished packing as the request hung in the air. He looked down at the ground for a moment, and then slapped his hands on his thighs.

"Let's step into my office."

Wayne helped Wes to his feet. Wes's strength was returning. He grabbed a pen and notepad from his pockets. As they walked into the parking lot, all eyes were on Wes. He squirmed. Wayne patted Wes on the shoulder.

"He'll be fine," he said to the police officers. Lynn joined them at the ambulance.

Wayne's partner was in the driver's seat talking on his cell phone. Wayne signaled that they needed some privacy, so he hopped out. They sat down on opposite benches, and Lynn stood by the door. Wayne's demeanor was neither inviting nor cold, just noncommittal; similar to when Wes had met him at Reese's, but that was before he'd stuck Wes for a blood sample. Wes figured that gave him a tiny bit of an in; but, judging from his blank face, apparently not. He was just another patient at the end of a shift. Wayne waited for Wes to begin.

"So, how often do you hang out with the Nooners?"

"It depends on what shift I work. I may catch up with them once a week. I was off yesterday, otherwise I wouldn't have been there when you interviewed them."

"When everyone was talking, they said that you knew Michael Gavin best. What do you think about the things Coach Lawler was saying about Michael? Did you agree with what he was saying, disagree?"

"He said it about right," Wayne said. "Michael and I were close because we had a lot in common, once we got to know each other. He helped me with some things, and I tried to help him with some things."

"Like what?"

He looked at Lynn, who nodded.

"He moved back to Talking Creek at the right time," he said. "We had similar struggles growing up, I guess. He just had to face them sooner."

"Why was it that he asked you for forgiveness?" Wes asked, taking a chance on so personal a question.

"I think he felt bad for ridiculing me," Wayne offered.

"I see," Wes said.

Wayne frowned and looked at Lynn. She was looking somewhere else.

"Did something happen?"

Wayne stared at the floor. Then he looked up.

"Michael had an accident," he said. "A car accident. Nobody was hurt, just him."

Wes saw an almost pleading look come into Wayne's eyes, as if this were a door into the past he would just as soon leave closed. The reporter in Wes told him to probe, to ask the next question. But something in Wayne's demeanor caused him to wait. Perhaps this was something that Wayne and Michael had talked about and agreed to keep quiet. Now that Michael was gone, Wayne seemed to be coming to terms with it. His eyes were watery, his face resigned to the inevitable.

"You've got to understand something, before I go any further," he said. "You'll probably judge him, and judge me, but I want you to know this first. If he hadn't had that accident, we both probably would not be alive today."

"Mr. Griffin, what *happened*?"

Wayne took a long, deep breath before beginning.

"Three times a week, Michael and I went running. Well, okay, he went running; I played keep up. This was usually a good time for us to talk about things, work stuff out without the distractions of our jobs, families, etcetera. During one of these runs, we talked about the old days, and we got into the game where he asked me to forgive him. He told me about his accident."

Wayne needed prodding to continue.

"How?" Wes asked.

"He crashed into the woods," Wayne finally divulged. "After he dropped me off that night I'd had dinner at his house, he drove to a gas station, bought a six-pack of beer, and chugged them on the way home. Apparently this had become his way of dealing with stress, a way to get the edge off. He said he parked off to the side of the road and finished the whole pack, then put the truck in gear and headed for what he intended to be battle royal with his old man. He said he'd rehearsed a pretty good speech, but he never made it home. He drove off the side of the road and smashed into a tree. Someone saw his car and called 9-1-1, and the fire department came. Gene Woods, his neighbor, was there. Had he not been, and had he not called Mr. Gavin, Michael would have been arrested for DUI."

"So he got off because he played QB at Talking Creek?" Wes said, whistling. Lynn cringed.

"No, I wouldn't say he got off at all," Wayne said. "His dad took him on a pretty eye-opening trip that weekend. Showed him some things he needed to see and understand. And apparently, he did some unofficial community service, cleaning up people's yards during fall and winter. So, he didn't get off; they just handled it 'internally.'"

"What happened on that trip?"

"You need to call some people on the list in order to find that out, I think," Lynn said.

"So you won't tell me?"

"We're not the people who should, Wes," Lynn said.

"Right," Wes said, frustrated at another dead end. "So answer me this, Mr. Griffin. You said that Michael's accident saved his life and yours. How, exactly?"

"Michael got his intervention at an early age," Wayne said. "I didn't get mine until I had a wife, a kid, and a failed career. He told me that story, Wes, because he wanted me to know he was on the same level with me. I'm a lot like Michael, at least in one regard. I'm a recovering alcoholic."

Chapter 16

A medical dictionary is filled with thousands of definitions of body parts, diseases, injuries, procedures, and treatments. And then there's pain. Pain is the central reason why a medical dictionary exists; it's a compendium of the sources of pain. There's good pain, or pain that produces eventual happiness, like the pain a mother feels while delivering a child, or the pain from a workout. There's bad pain too. There are infinite examples of bad pain.

Wayne's pain announced itself with a buzz from the red blinking alarm clock on top of the dresser. He placed it there as motivation to get out of bed in the morning. By nature, Wayne was a night owl. He worked the 3:00 p.m. to 11:00 p.m. shift with EMS, and the only way he had a fighting chance of rising before the roosters was with an alarm clock clear across the room.

His wife, Cynthia, stirred, but didn't wake. She'd long since learned to sleep through the ten seconds of irritation. Wayne walked barefoot downstairs to the kitchen and its cold tile floor. A good pain to help wake up. He counteracted the cold by downing a cup of coffee. He shuffled to the far end of the counter, peeled a banana, and wolfed it down. In the laundry room was a pair of well-worn sneakers, a T-shirt, and sweatpants. He did a quick balancing act to slip into the outfit. Still groggy despite the caffeine flowing through his veins, he returned to his chair and put his thick arms behind his head.

"Any minute now," he said to himself. Sure enough, a knock on the door.

"You gonna keep up this time?" Michael said, jogging in place.

The two men beat a well-worn path down Wiley Road. They ran a three-mile circuit and the last quarter mile was always a dead sprint to see who would finish first. For Wayne, it produced three kinds of pain: an embarrassing pain of losing to Michael; a pestering pain from Michael's constant teasing; and a healthy pain of sucking wind at the end of the run to settle his pounding heart.

Wayne welcomed all of it. It replaced a pain he'd been saddled with since his early twenties. The disease, Wayne had concluded, was partly due to genetics, to a father who passed on his ingrained habits to his children and then died early. For Wayne, the pain didn't come until things were actually going well: a wife, a child, a budding career as a salesman. He used alcohol to deal with the job stress of making numbers, of keeping painful childhood memories under wraps, of boredom. At first, it only numbed him a little. Eventually, although he wouldn't say it to himself, it threatened to swallow him whole.

It started with happy hour after work, stopping to unwind on his way home. When Cynthia began to complain about how late he was getting home at night, he agreed to come straight home, and he brought happy hour with him. He'd always add BEER to the grocery list in bold letters, so Cynthia made sure to keep a six-pack in stock. His liquor cabinet grew to wholesale proportions. He was never without a drink in hand at social functions, and it occasionally dripped into his morning coffee, from a small bottle stashed away at home and at work. He was under control, and happy, and so was everyone else—or so he thought. But it took only a few small twists to turn the sweet life sour. Eventually, Wayne stopped making his numbers. Cynthia seemed needier at home, huffing about the lack of time Wayne spent with his daughter compared to his drinking buddies. By now, he was firmly attached to the bottle.

Michael diagnosed his problem almost immediately after returning to Talking Creek.

"You're an alcoholic," he said. "So am I."

Before Wayne could muster his outrage, Michael spilled the beans on his car accident, his reconciliation, his battle with drinking.

"You need to stop drinking," Michael concluded. "You need to stop, or you're going to kill yourself. You're already killing your family life."

Wayne's response was sarcastic, filled with a touch of venom, like anyone being called out on an addiction. But Michael could see through the words. He'd been there himself once.

"So, what do you propose I do about it, Captain America?" Wayne had said.

"You start," Michael responded, "by running."

★　★　★

The duo ran down gravel roads. They ran Wayne out of sales and back into school for a career in emergency services. They walked to AA meetings, celebrated the milestones together. They avoided the beer aisle at the grocery store without glancing, stayed out of sports bars. They replaced Wayne's beer buzz with a runner's buzz.

Then came the day when Wayne beat Michael on their daily run, and he knew there was something wrong. Wayne had stepped out the door that morning with no illusions of besting Michael. He'd worked a hard shift the night before and just wanted to survive the run. A marathon enthusiast, Michael rarely broke a sweat on these three-milers, but this time he was huffing, and as the duo doubled back for the quarter-mile dash, Wayne didn't quicken his pace. As the two men collected their breath outside Wayne's house, Michael uncharacteristically had both hands on his knees and was sucking air.

"You feeling okay?" Wayne said.

"Sure," Michael said, gasping before attempting another word. "Just a bit under the weather, that's all."

"Well, take some medicine and rest up," Wayne said. "'Cause there's no honor in winning like this."

Two days later, Michael couldn't finish the run, pulling up at the two-mile mark.

"I'm hurting all over," he admitted.

★ ★ ★

When a visit to the doctor and prescription drugs didn't help, Michael
went in for further tests. A few weeks later, Wayne walked into an oncol-
ogy ward and saw his friend resting in a chair with an IV line—chemo.
Lynn was by Michael's side. Wayne felt the blood drain from his face and
he steadied himself on the doorjamb. The word *cancer* felt like a nail being
driven into his chest, now that Michael was actually going through the
treatment process. Lymphoma was the hammer driving the nail deeper. A
familiar word, but well beyond his expertise. Wayne treated broken bones,
heart attacks, and shortness of breath. Lymphoma would take a special
kind of medicine he didn't possess.

Wayne knew the transformation Michael would have to make to fight
the cancer. It was like watching the worst part of a movie over and over,
knowing the outcome, but still having to sift through it to get to the end.
Michael's muscular frame shriveled. His eyes were bloodshot and weak,
his lips cracked despite massive amounts of lip balm. His mouth was often
stained with vomit, his fingertips unsure and skeletal, seeking support.

Michael fought his physical agony with drugs, diet, and rest. He was
determined to overcome this latest obstacle. Friends and family offered their
time. The women grasped his hand and hugged him, and the men squeezed
his shoulder and offered encouragement. Lynn and Michael shared the
ordeal with their Bible study class. It was fitting, in retrospect, that they were
studying the book of Job and his tortured lessons from God. The group's
focus shifted from scriptural study to real-life application. Everyone prayed
and offered Bible verses as if they would slice out the cancer. The pain of
knowing that a friend was in trouble had softened hearts and smoothed over
petty squabbles. For the members of the group, it was almost a good pain. It
reminded them of the beauty that pain could occasionally create. Michael,
too, seemed to recognize the redemptive nature of his suffering.

Lynn grew from a sweet wallflower into an oak of courage, for herself
and for Michael—especially when the pain knocked Michael's bravado
into a whisper of determination. Wayne's occasional procrastination and

loss of focus turned into a zealousness to offer his professional skills to Michael's recovery. He badgered doctors and nurses alike with questions and instructions on the proper care. Pain turned well-meaning people into well doers. Michael's pain changed people's mind-sets and long-standing attitudes. Its labors produced good fruit. It also produced an unexpected change in Michael and a new pain for Wayne.

★   ★   ★

"I watched Lynn cut the grass last weekend," Michael told Wayne on the way to one of his last trips to chemo. His voice was dry, his inflection altered because he didn't have the energy to put his personality into his tone anymore. "I pulled a chair over to the screen door because I couldn't stand in front of the kitchen window. I watched her hop on the riding lawnmower. It took her a good bit to figure out the controls. You know Lynn; she analyzes every lever before she even attempts to start the engine. Me, I threw the owner's manual away before the first mow. You should have seen her clutch the handles for dear life. I almost laughed. She missed a handful of spots the first run-through, but surveyed her work and finished the job."

Wayne didn't respond, kept his eyes on the road, waiting for more. Michael was quiet for a minute, and then spoke. "I'm not even man enough to mow my own lawn anymore, Wayne," he said. "I have to get my wife to do it for me. Do you have any idea what that feels like?"

Wayne bit his lip. "It's just mowing the lawn, bud."

"What kind of a man can't do even simple chores?" Michael continued. "What in the world does God want me to gain from this? I either lie on the couch or in bed while Lynn spends almost all of her free time cleaning, sweeping, cooking, and now mowing. You guys have been great, but you know that upkeep is a full-time job. I've pleaded with her to call a cleaning service, but she insists, says it's good for her to stay busy. I hate it. I'm this sloth on the couch that watches TV or tries to read with a puke bucket ready and waiting."

"Michael, you're sick."

"So what? Like that's an excuse? I had a broken foot the last week of Ranger training; did I ever tell you that? I had a freakin' broken foot, man. We were roughin' it through trails at Benning. Not the rotation in the mountains or the swamps. A simple march at Benning. We were so close to graduation we were coasting. I was getting lazy, though, and took a wrong step near a bunch of rocks, and rolled it in just a way that broke a bone. Didn't know it at the time. My buddies helped me, they dragged me through the march. It was too late to be recycled, I would have never survived another rotation. If they had kicked me out during the first week, fine; but not the last. So I ignored the pain. I sucked it up and finished training. This, though, this is something different."

What was Michael looking for? Wayne had never heard him this discouraged. He was always composed, sure of himself. But here he was wallowing in pity, a word Wayne never thought he'd associate with Michael Gavin.

"This isn't a broken foot, Michael," Wayne said, straining to find words of encouragement. "It's cancer. And like you said, you needed help to get through the training, so you need help to—"

"Spare me," Michael said.

"What do you want me to say?" Wayne said.

"I don't want you to say anything. I don't want to hear it from anybody anymore, okay? No more nice words. This isn't nice. It's death. I'm dying."

"But you can't say that."

"Why?" Michael asked. "Because no one wants to hear a dying man in agony? Where did that idea even come from? You ever read the Psalms? Job? God doesn't want motivational speeches in prayers. He wants our soul, our guts. All the mush and all the emotion. Everything."

"Yeah, but shouldn't you be giving this to him?" Wayne said. "Asking him to heal you?"

"Is that really faith?" Michael said. "I think he wants the real *us*. This is the real me. I'm hurting. Dying. He doesn't want a smiley face and a thumbs-up. He wants me tearing at my clothes and pleading. Well, fine, he's got it."

★　★　★

There was pain in knowing that Michael had failed to believe in the miracle of medicine to stave off his cancer. The final round of chemo put Michael's cancer into remission, but it didn't erase Wayne's pain of knowing that Michael had broken. And both men knew the likelihood that the cancer would come back. Wayne calculated how much his friend had already lost. Fifty pounds, bushels of hair, his confidence. His aura of invincibility was gone. Another battle and he was probably finished.

That's why Michael's recovery was so important. Wayne, and all of Michael's friends, needed him strong again. He was a great Bible study leader and a good sounding board on marriage and family issues, even on raising children in the years before Addy came on the scene. Michael and Lynn had practically raised a hundred kids at the retreat before their own little surprise package and blessing arrived a few short years before the cancer.

Wayne took it upon himself to lead the charge for Michael, reinitiating the hallowed morning runs that had rekindled a friendship. At first they walked, and then jogged, as Michael recovered his strength. New hair sprouted from his bald head. His color recovered and his trademark smile and laugh returned. Each day, Wayne marked their progress in a journal. The exercise was therapeutic for both of them. Wayne led the prayers on Sunday. He even made it a point to pray before and after their runs. He may not have been able to say the right words, but at least he was talking to God.

Michael came back quieter, more reserved than his Type A nature. There was no ribbing during the jogs. He took to the renewed exercise like it was the only thing on earth he needed to focus on. Their once spirited conversations on local politics and sports subsided. It wasn't that Michael was hollow. He was simply thinner, in body and spirit. He had flushed out the superfluous and only concerned himself with priorities; and that was fine.

Wayne didn't expect Michael to be the same guy he was before. Cancer survivors never were. Michael had been exposed to his own mortality by fighting for it every hour of every day. Sometimes Wayne would catch Michael glancing around the country road, basking in creation, surveying every branch of every tree before their route took them around a bend. When the sun would rise, Michael would heave his chest out and lift up his neck, as if the sun's rays were life's fuel. Wayne considered it Michael's new lease on life, getting in touch with the details. He enjoyed this change.

But Michael was missing his benchmark; the one trait that everyone identified with him. There was no denying it. He had won two state football titles and the admiration of an entire town with it. It had seen him through a war and its aftermath. But now his confidence—some would say cockiness—was, without a doubt, gone. Wayne was familiar with the loss. He had experienced it himself, in one degree, as a high school senior. Michael had been the culprit, stealing it with harsh criticism and ostracizing him from the football team. Then, in a moment, he had retrieved it for Wayne and destroyed the built-up hostility. All with just a few sincere words. Their friendship was born from those ashes, their lives altered from that quiet moment in the locker room that most who had witnessed it never fully understood. Wayne thought it proper that he would be the one to restore Michael's confidence, to return the favor.

"Do you remember what you said before your last chemo treatment?" Wayne asked during one of their runs.

"Yeah," Michael said. His endurance had increased to the point where they could carry on a short conversation now. Each stride was no longer such an effort.

"I don't want you to be like that again." Wayne said.

A pace ahead, Wayne heard Michael's footsteps stop. He turned.

"Why?" Michael asked.

"Because it freaked me out, that's why," Wayne said. "You're better than that."

"Better than what? Cancer?"

"You're better than giving up," Wayne said.

"I meant every word, Wayne," Michael said. "I know everyone is looking at this remission as great news; and I am too, but the fact is, I messed up. I was full of it, thumping my chest like I could take on the world and beat this thing, and I nearly died."

"Don't say that."

"Stop it, Wayne. You work in emergency services, for crying out loud. You want to hear me say I'm doing better, but what if I'm not? If I'm in pain, why should I lie? How does that help?"

Michael kicked up a cloud of dust. "You want to know what the worst part was? During my chemo treatments, I had poison inside of me. Poison. My hair fell out; I threw up so much I thought I'd hawk out a lung. It took all of my will power just to get out of bed, Wayne, and I hurt, man, I hurt like nothing I've felt before. Forget the gunshot wound in Iraq; this trumped it all."

"I'm sorry," Wayne said.

Michael shot him a look.

"I'm not asking you to be sorry," he said. "Just listen. I was hurting, okay? But all of that stuff I just described paled in comparison to this. With my family around me, with you and Cynthia there, I refused to be honest. I said I was fine when I wasn't. I said I'd make it when I really didn't know. I tried to tough it out, when all I wanted to do was break down. I wouldn't let myself do it, either, until the very end, and then only to Lynn. We'd all look at each other and come up with some brave, profound words, but that's not being strong. That's the opposite of 'strong.' You want to know what strong is? Crying. Laying your guts out on the floor. Holding your wife for dear life because you don't know how much life is left. Trying to explain to your daughter that there is a very good chance you won't be around her whole life."

Michael turned to face the road ahead of them.

"That's strength, Wayne. David did that. Jesus did that. Where did we lose that in our faith? That's peace. It's like, before those moments, I didn't want anyone to be afraid, or see me whipped, but I was terrified. There's this unspoken rule that when you're in pain you can't be real about it. I was in tremendous pain, and I tried to suck it up, but why? Isn't that a part of it? How am I supposed to ignore pain when it's bringing me to my knees? I was up so many nights crying, it hurt so bad, wondering if I could just hit my head on the nightstand and knock myself out. Death is part of the journey. Suffering too. So here it is. If I am going to suffer again, I'm not holding back, Wayne. It may look like I'm giving up to you, but it's really just acceptance. You can't take all of the good and none of the bad; you're cheating yourself out of something if you do. So don't tell me not to act a certain way because I'm dying. I'm giving it all to God. I think that's what he wants out of this. It's the only thing I have left."

There was the pain of having no answer. Wayne knew he had nothing to offer.

Chapter 17

For the second time in half an hour, Wes told a half-truth. Having passed the lucidity test, he promised Wayne he would go home. He would, but only after dropping by the office.

The phones at the *News* scream on Wednesday nights in the fall. One of the negatives of having such an in-depth prep section is having scores called in from area games. Wednesdays were usually softball, volleyball, and tennis. It was to Lewis's credit that the *News* got so many. Other newspapers might have an eager head coach call in a win, but Lewis had developed relationships with almost all the coaches in the area, enough so that even the most tight-lipped coaches called in a score, maybe even a loss. They trusted Lewis to write big headlines for wins and soft leads for losses. He delivered in that area, and somehow managed to balance the coverage so the area coaches felt that their teams weren't getting a raw deal. If they were missed in the coverage, Lewis suggested they call in scores as a guaranteed way of making the paper.

With so many calls to field, and Lewis the main man on the pagination, the sports section was usually a few minutes late on Wednesday, which typically drew Sweeney's ire. He'd only allow Friday nights as an exemption. If he was mad enough, and Lewis late enough, the conflict spilled over to Starks by way of an angry note left by the ornery production manager.

As such, if Wes covered a home volleyball or softball game for Talking Creek, he usually zipped back to the office, typed his story, and pitched in on the layouts. Not tonight. He had a lead to tie up.

This much Wes knew from what Lynn and Wayne had revealed. Michael Gavin had driven under the influence the weekend before his apology to Wayne. He crashed. He'd driven off the road and hit a tree. He was discovered by a family friend, who called Paul first instead of the authorities. The secret would have stayed hidden had Paul not called the authorities himself. Paul had done two things as a father that weekend that may have changed Michael's life. He'd brought him in front of a judge to confess what he had done, and promised that Michael would complete community service, which matched the old clip Wes had found of Michael at the community service project. So it hadn't all been handled "in-house," just under the community radar. Paul had then taken Michael on a road trip. Neither Wayne nor Lynn would tell Wes where or what. And Paul had agreed to talk about it only after Wes made a few more phone calls.

"Call the people on the list," they all had said.

Wes was skeptical about the validity of anything those sources would say, but he was short on options. There wasn't enough time to do a background check on all of them, and he wasn't even sure it was worth his time making the calls. If the main sources weren't giving him enough to connect the pieces, secondary sources weren't going to offer much. Still, he sensed he was on the cusp of all of Michael's secrets. He wanted to write the story now, but he needed a few more pieces. There were the feuds in football that ended bizarrely. Michael had asked Wayne for forgiveness, but it didn't mesh with his previous attitude toward him. Then, in college, he had lost a quarterback battle, almost transferred, and then opted to play at one of the least appreciated positions in any sport. He attained fame with a Medal of Honor, and promptly hid it. Michael's motives were puzzling. What would have made him apologize to a guy who had cost him a state championship? And why not transfer to another college after losing his starting spot?

Lynn and Wayne had also divulged a dirty little secret about the *News*. Wes pulled up the archives on a computer and typed in "Michael Gavin race." A May entry came up, and he read the story. It was a charity race that Michael had participated in right as the cancer returned. According to Wayne, Michael had tried to finish four laps of the relay, but couldn't. He'd collapsed halfway around his first lap. According to the *News* article, however, Michael had finished his laps.

Someone had lied. He doubted it was Wayne, considering the man had just revealed to him that he was a recovering alcoholic.

Wes knocked on Lewis's glass paneled door. He was busy laying out a page for the sports section. Lewis slid it open, but continued staring at his screen. Wes slid the door shut.

"Can I ask you a question?" Still feeling weak, he sat in a chair.

"Sure." Lewis said, not looking over.

"Late May, we ran a piece on a charity walk/run at the TC track. You gave it to me for research on Gavin. No byline though. Who wrote that?"

"How in the world would I remember?" Lewis said, somewhat irritably. That wasn't like him.

"Well, only a couple of options for a story like that not to have a byline. Either it was a call-in/PR note, or you wrote it."

"Why is that important?"

"Because the article was wrong on a key set of facts," Wes said. "I want to know why."

Lewis saved his layout and swiveled his chair to face Wes.

"Well, if it was a call-in, there's no way we'd have time to verify it before press. What was the mistake?"

Wes brought him up to speed on the charity relay and the discussion he'd had with Wayne and Lynn. His intent was for the update to help the story along, with suggestions from Lewis, who was usually good at grabbing random observations and making a solid lead out of the information. Tonight though, Lewis merely listened. Wes didn't think he had been the one to run the story. It was probably a newswriter that Starks had slung on the assignment, and he probably hadn't verified the relay's results.

When Wes finished, instead of advice, he received a sigh.

"I dunno know what to tell you on the charity piece; I really don't,"

Lewis said. "That was a few months ago. However, I really wish you'da been answering your phone this afternoon."

Busted. Wes flipped it open and saw three missed calls from Starks. He played it off like it was news to him. "You been calling?"

"No," Lewis said. His eyes were looking down, a bad sign. "Starks didn't like your prodding around the courthouse."

"Oh, that," Wes said. "Yeah, he told me as much earlier today. Said he didn't want to see my byline in the paper the rest of the week."

"He told me that too," Lewis said. "We had a long talk today, as a matter of fact."

"Well, whatever. I talked to the family today, even got an interview with a policeman who served with Michael in Iraq."

"We've still got a problem," he said. It sounded rehearsed. On his desk he had a file flipped open. In it was a single sheet of paper, with "Wes Watkins" written on it.

"What's that?"

"I had to write you up," he said. He still wouldn't look at Wes.

"You have got to be kidding."

Lewis shook his head. "Starks said he'd like you to understand the seriousness of the assignment you're doing."

The temperature in the room seemed to rise a few degrees. Wes cleared his throat. "I have been taking this assignment seriously."

"I need you to sign this." Lewis slid the paper closer.

"I am not signing anything," Wes said, standing up faster than he should have.

"Look, it's no big deal."

"Are you serious? Lewis, can't you see what he's doing? He's painting me into a corner. It's like he wants to edit my story before I've even turned it in."

Lewis didn't say anything, apparently waiting for Wes to get it out of his system. It made Wes angrier.

"Don't sit there and act like you didn't have anything to do with it. You threw me under the bus, and you know what? It's not the first time.

Whenever Starks comes around looking for a punching bag, you're all too willing to give him a warm body."

"Okay, that's enough," Lewis said with as much authority he could muster. By now the newsroom on the other side of the glass door was probably aware of the debate, but Wes didn't care. His head was now swimming, and he had to prop himself up by holding on to a nearby filing cabinet.

"You are such a hypocrite!" Wes said. "What kind of jerk are you? I didn't ask for the assignment. I didn't want it. I don't want it now. I'm practically done. I've found nothing but grief. And at this rate, the way you guys are stringing me along, I won't have a job by the end of the week. You say you're on my side, but you're not. You're out for whatever is convenient for you. Just like Starks trying to get some extra ad revenue from Michael Gavin's death, or Coach Lawler wanting a stadium named after Gavin. You want to stay in Starks's good graces, and it doesn't matter if one of your reporters gets axed. I'm the whipping boy for everyone else's agenda. Whatever, man."

For a guy whose career hinged on keeping doors open and communication lines clear, Wes had a knack for destruction. There went his last ally in the newsroom. There was a heck of a lot more than a speech and newspaper story going on here. Wes wobbled out of the room, paper unsigned, and headed for the door. Back in his car, he waited to catch his breath, and then drove into a dark, empty night.

Chapter 18

A cool afternoon breeze met Wes as he slipped out of the car. Under any other circumstances it would have been a welcome signal that autumn was gaining traction, that the football season was in full swing; but today, it only made him shiver.

He had found his scoop—Michael's dark secret. Yet it brought little solace and no direction. A week ago, maybe. A week ago, the story would have been: "Local football legend crashes car before game, cover up," "War hero hides medal, juvy record," "Local philanthropist attends recovery meetings with friend." All of those were angles, and they were true. They were headline grabbers, sure bets for making the AP wire. They just didn't tell the entire story.

Wes's theory was that if he presented the story as objectively as possible, then his job was done. It was up to the reader to decide. Wes now had doubts. If he stood at the pulpit and revealed Michael's faults to his supporters, would it register that those were what Michael had wanted them to see?

Chances were, they'd brush those aside and fixate their emotions on Wes, the culprit, for painting their hero in a negative light. It was a toss-up as to whether Starks would even let him write the story now, with all that he knew.

Surprisingly, that didn't concern Wes. Michael Gavin still didn't add up. He needed answers from Paul Gavin on where he took his son following the accident. His conversation with Lynn and Wayne changed things.

Wes knew now what they had tried to hide for so long. Would Paul continue to keep it from Wes, when all he had to go on was a covered up mistake? Wouldn't he want to shine light on the accident in a positive way? Between last night and this morning, he'd done his part by calling exactly half the names on the list. Wes knew it had been somewhat of a hurried, half-hearted effort on his part—half of those he had called didn't even answer, and he didn't leave a message—but time was short, and so was Wes's patience. Paul Gavin would have to talk. Surely he'd want to talk, Wes convinced himself.

The family had accepted his request to visit again. They did him one better, inviting him over for lunch. A tall, well-built man with eyes as intense as Paul's greeted Wes at the door. He introduced himself as Adam Gavin, Michael's eldest brother. They shook hands and walked silently into the kitchen. There were sounds of scurrying feet, pots clanging, but no conversations. Betty, ever aware of a new guest in the house, immediately introduced Wes to Susan, her daughter and Michael's sister, who looked almost exactly as Wes envisioned Betty would have looked twenty years ago. Betty also introduced Wes to Lynn's mother, Alice, and two mother-son combos who were foster families involved with the retreat.

Five seconds after introductions were completed, Wes had a mason jar full of unsweetened tea in his hand. He heard the clinking of silverware on the dining room table as the boys prepared for the meal. As if on cue, Betty, Alice, and Susan swooped out of the kitchen with dishes of mashed potatoes, a casserole, and fruit salad and placed them on the dining room table. Addy wasn't far behind with the napkins, and she took on the duty as if it were the most important job in the world. A small card table was set up on the side for the children. The women took their places around the table. Betty pointed to a chair for Wes, and then tapped on the windowpane to the back door. Not long after, Paul, Adam, and another man, probably Susan's husband, entered with steaming grilled chicken. Betty finished the olfactory assault with a basket of freshly baked dinner rolls. It was a perfectly choreographed family meal.

And it was the complete opposite of a Watkins family meal. Those had always been rushed, nuked in the microwave, and almost never this crowded. When Wes would ride with his mom to Tennessee to visit the grandparents and cousins during the holidays, it was never a very warm reception.

The Gavins stood beside their chairs. Wes waited acknowledgement that a reporter was in their midst, but they weren't treating him as such. This was an intimate moment for the family, and they were including him. He looked around the table. Paul gave him a slight nod. Did he know what Wes was going to ask him?

Lynn walked in from the front room, her arms wrapped around herself. She smiled weakly. Her skin was pale, and she looked exhausted. The guard she had put up at the volleyball match, and even during their first conversation at the ranch, was clearly gone. The melting process seemed to have begun at the funeral home. The family held each other's hands to say a prayer. Paul nodded to Betty, who took Wes's hand. Her fingers twitched a couple of times before she spoke, as if her body was trying to find the words.

"Heavenly Father," she began, "we offer you thanks for this food before us. May it nourish our bodies, as we do your will. We ask for your strength, for your mercy, as we struggle with this grief. We ask for your guidance, Lord, for your love. We ask these things in Jesus' name, amen."

The prayer was short. Addy and her cousins scrambled for the dinner rolls before retreating to their table. The adults each released their neighbors' hands and began to sit down—all except for Lynn. She held a tight grip on Betty's and her mother's hands. Her eyes were closed, scrunched. She bit her lip, winced, as if in pain. Alice and Betty gripped her hands tighter. Then Lynn prayed aloud.

"Lord, forgive me," she said. The kids looked at each other and then returned to the circle. Addy clung to her mom's jeans, unsure of this new prayer. Wes watched faces as each person stood up again and resumed a praying posture of closed eyes and bowed heads. He couldn't close his eyes.

Lynn let out a deep sigh, followed by a sob. Then another.

"Lord, forgive me for doubting. For not being strong enough. I know that Your will is being done here, but it hurts. I miss my husband, and I can't fathom how you're going to keep his mission here going, if I'm still supposed to do this, and, I'm just hurt, Lord. Please . . ."

Lynn crumbled to her knees. Betty and Alice tried to steady her collapse. Addy stepped back, horrified, as if her mom had been struck with a bullet. The men rushed around the table as Lynn's cries turned to wails. The women lay on the ground holding Lynn as she cried, and the men huddled around them as if to protect them in the act of mourning. Addy, hands at her side, quivered. The cousins quietly sat down, arms folded in their laps.

Wes had seen this before. Death wasn't the culprit as much as loneliness. During his junior year of high school, he had come home one Friday night from a football game. His mom, who spent most of her Friday nights wrapped in a warm blanket watching TV, was in the kitchen, her elbows propped on the kitchen table and a blank stare in her eyes. Wes had asked her what was wrong—he could remember it vividly, because it was one of the few times his mom had let her guard down, had shown her broken spirit.

"I'm so lonely," she'd said through tear-drenched eyes.

Wes absorbed her pain, but he couldn't fix it. So, instead, he blamed. He blamed his father for leaving. He blamed God for leaving. He blamed himself for anything and everything.

The Gavins, he now saw, channeled their emotions differently.

As Lynn cried, Wes didn't move. He didn't want to draw attention to himself, to have them see him seeing this, but he was two feet away from a grieving widow, unable to help in any way.

Betty looked up. "Can you take the kids into the living room?" she whispered.

Wes nodded. He crouched beside Addy, and offered his hand. Her tears were like little needles poking his heart. The boys walked with them into the living room on their best behavior. One of them flipped on the TV and turned it to the cartoon channel. They all stared at the screen.

Up until this point, the assignment had been all about uncovering the truth. Wes hadn't considered the repercussions of Michael's death. Now it swelled in his conscience. What would happen to this family and their foster care retreat? They were gracious and welcoming all week, but now he was seeing a different side. The reality. When the funeral ended and the mourning crowd departed, the Gavins would be left to pick up the pieces. Lynn would be a widow with a foster care retreat to run, if she even had the energy to do it. Betty and Paul would have lost a son they poured so much love and energy into. And the kids who came to this retreat, what would they lose?

This was the part Wes had left out of the story. A missing medal and a crashed car—not a family's tears of grief—would have been the lead. He didn't quite know what to make of the huddled humanity—the family united in sorrow—in the other room.

Addy rose from her seat. Wes watched her as she quietly walked to the corner of the room, where a basket sat beside a bookcase. She leaned down and picked up a black rock, exactly like the ones outside on the path. The boys did the same. It wasn't a scene for Wes's benefit. They didn't make eye contact with him, they just sat down and bowed their heads. At their age, faced with the same circumstances, Wes probably would have thrown the rock through a window.

These past few minutes would completely change Addy's life, Wes thought. Gone were the innocence and exuberance with which she had greeted him only days before. Reality catches up with childhood and shakes away the shelter for everyone. For some it's earlier than others. Addy witnessed her father's erosion, but was protected by the love and warmth of her family. Now, in their time of weakness, she'd have a memory of pain. Even if she didn't know yet that her father wasn't coming back, she knew that something was wrong, and that her mom needed comforting; that her mom was not, in fact, a superhero.

Still, she prayed. Wes watched as her lips moved. He could make out the words *Jesus, please, Mommy,* and *love.* He watched the force she was putting into her thoughts. She didn't weigh half as much as he did, but he felt very small compared to her right then.

The adults slowly filed into the room. Wes rose from the couch to let Lynn, flanked by her mom and sister-in-law, sit down. Paul and the men brought in chairs from the dining room, while Betty sat down on the floor next to the coffee table. They all sat for what must have been five minutes, no one saying a word, the meal apparently forgotten.

Betty reached to the coffee table and flipped open a large photo album. Inside were old family photos of the Gavins. They all watched as Betty digested each page and moved on to another memory. Every couple of pages, Betty would smile. Then Paul quietly chuckled when he saw a goofy photo of Michael and Adam clowning around at a fort. He pointed to the picture below it.

"Who would have thought we could fit Michael into a cannon at one point in his life?"

The picture was of a much younger Paul and his chiseled arms holding Michael parallel to the ground, acting as if he were about to stick his son into a Civil War cannon.

Adam got up from his seat and turned the album a few pages. "I'll show you what my favorite picture of Mike is . . ."

He pointed to a picture of Michael at a farm. He looked to be about ten. He was inside the railing of a large pen, with a massive pig behind him.

"Before . . ." Adam said, then poked the picture beneath it, "and after."

In the bottom photo, Michael was jumping the railing, one hand gripped on the top rail, the other holding his butt. The pig had bitten him.

Everyone laughed.

"I remember him running to me with tears in his eyes," Betty said. "We had to pull down his drawers and make sure that the bite hadn't punctured the skin. It hadn't, but he owned some piggy teeth marks for a day or so."

The family followed that pattern for the next twenty minutes, glancing at the photos and making funny comments about famed Gavin exploits. Addy became the display model, holding up the photos for everyone to see, coordinating when they took one out of a sleeve and passed it around.

It helped to ease the tension, to delight in the past instead of trapping all their grief inside. Wes looked at the album too, but his eyes also wandered around the room. He glanced at framed pictures of kids from the foster care retreat. Michael and Lynn were posing with the children, everyone all smiles, but to be in those pictures meant something had gone wrong in their lives. He wondered about those children . . . what kind of a person would leave their own child, or do something so stupid to get them taken out of their custody? He thought of his dad, of how his dad had wanted to reconcile and how he had refused his attempts.

Wes felt for the kids; he knew what it was like to have a parent wash out; to have the bubble burst early on, and to know that grown-ups were faulty and stupid and hurt those around them. He wondered at what point people started to go bad. Is it ingrained? It got him to thinking about the photos in Michael's album. There were some missing.

"You want to see my pictures?" Addy asked, tugging on Wes's shirt. "Want to see them? Daddy is in lots of them!"

"He is, isn't he?" Betty said. "Michael was absolutely terrified during the delivery. That big, strong man used to barking out orders was reduced to fetching ice chips."

"He cried a lot too," Lynn said, a glow on her face from the memory. "He bowed his head like a scolded dog whenever a nurse gave him new instructions, and whimpered whenever I squeezed his hand."

"I'll go get them," Addy said, scurrying away.

Lynn wiped a tear from her eye as Addy left the room. "We had tried for years to have a baby. We suffered through four miscarriages, looked at the possibilities of becoming pregnant with the help of science, and came very close to several adoptions. But we really felt the hand of God in our lives, leading us to the foster care retreat instead. So naturally, Addy came along right as Michael was getting ready to leave for deployment. Our timing was always a well-coordinated affair."

Addy stomped back into the room with a large photo album, and sat it right on Wes's knee. She flipped open the first page to a picture of Michael holding Addy. Wes could see the stubble on his chin and the wear around his eyes. It was the look of a lengthy ordeal, but there was joy there also. His head was craned in a way to almost shield Addy from any danger, his forehead touching her tiny forehead.

Addy flipped the page and pointed to a picture in which Michael was leaning toward her left cheek. "Daddy likes to talk to me very, very softly," she said.

"I wonder what he told you in that picture," Wes said.

Addy grinned with delight. "I know! He said that before God made heaven and earth, he knew who I was and gave me a name, and gave me Mommy and Daddy as my parents, and that they'd never stop loving me! He'd tell that to me after reading stories all the time."

Addy spent the next ten minutes flipping through her baby book. Wes tried to play the part of a diligent viewer, but kept his eye on Lynn's reactions to the pictures. Addy's baby book was like a release valve to the tension the mealtime prayer had created. The family comforted themselves with warm memories of Michael to scoot out the cold reality, if only for a few minutes. When Addy was finished, she shut the book with a large thump.

"Want to see some pictures of me at a petting zoo petting ponies and deers?"

The room filled with laughter. Wes chuckled too. "Sure, Addy, that'd be great."

She giggled as she ran out of the room to fetch another album. Wes used the break to ask a question that had been on his mind since looking at Michael's pictures.

"I'm curious, going through Michael's pictures—there were tons of Little League games and high school pics, but I didn't see any of his baby pictures," Wes said. "Was there a separate album?"

Betty shook her head no. "We don't have any pictures of Michael as a baby," she said. Her eyes stayed on Wes's, watching the questions swell. She saved him the time. "Michael was adopted."

Chapter 19

The closed door meant Do Not Enter for the men. It was nursing time, so only the women of the family were allowed in the nursery. As Lynn nursed Addy, Betty leaned back in a chair on the other side of the room and began knitting. It was a quiet moment amid the hectic rush of becoming a parent. Changing diapers, waking in the middle of the night to prepare to feed, coordinating schedules, all of that slowed to a crawl as Lynn nursed Addy. It was such a calming moment, sometimes it took an effort to stay awake.

"How has Michael adjusted to being a daddy?" Betty asked as she looped a thread in the blanket she was making for Addy.

"Tender," Lynn said. "I thought having a girl would be tough for him because he likes to roughhouse so much. But he's been extremely delicate with her, fawning over her, which I didn't expect. He's joked that this may have softened him up too much before his deployment next month."

Betty smiled. "He's come a long way from the poor little soul we adopted to the man he is now; it's a blessing."

Lynn stroked Addy's soft cheek as she remembered when Michael had told her he was adopted, following their first miscarriage, while they were stationed at Fort Bragg. They were sitting on the floor of their living room, both dejected and trying to work through the disappointment with words of encouragement. Michael had said he needed to tell her something; that he had wanted to wait until the baby was born, but now that that wasn't happening, he needed to tell her now. Lynn, already hurt and confused from the miscarriage, didn't know at the time what to think or how to feel.

"Why didn't you tell me this earlier?" she had asked. "Why did you keep something like that from me?"

Michael, so rarely vulnerable, had shrunk his shoulders when he told her. "My mother died when I was born, I didn't remember my father—he died young too. There were a lot of things Betty and Paul had to help me through as a kid, really painful things, that I just didn't want that following me everywhere. I mean, they're my family. When we moved to Talking Creek, I think only the school counselor knew, and Betty had a stern talking to with her about not disclosing that information. There was no reason to, though."

"But that's such a big part of your life, Michael," Lynn said. "A part of your story . . ."

"I don't want it to be," he said.

Lynn had taken his hand, cupping it with both of hers.

"God can take anything, anything, and make something better out of it." She lifted Michael's chin so he was looking into her eyes. "Even us losing this baby. Even you losing your birth parents."

"It is a blessing," Lynn said, looking up from her newborn daughter. "There was a plan in all of this—from you adopting him to us doing the foster retreat." She brushed the top of Addy's head. "To this little joy."

Addy whimpered and looked up at Lynn. "She's got her mother's eyes," Betty said.

"And occasionally her father's temperament," Lynn chuckled. "She can be a booger getting to nurse."

Betty groaned. "Oh, Michael was a terror as a little boy," she said. "Most of it he couldn't help, and we knew that before we officially adopted him. They told us that he'd likely have a disorder of some sort. We knew he had some issues to work through, we had braced for the worst, but hearing that was an adjustment. They said Michael had shown some of the worst traits a child can have. We weren't strangers to raising children. I felt quite comfortable with a noisy kitchen, swamped laundry room, and a house full of war-torn carpets, but Michael couldn't be expected to be a normal child, and we'd be asking more out of our own children with him in our home. He'd be something different, challenging, and possibly terrifying."

"Did he have a lot of counseling then?"

"Oh yes, of course," Betty said. "We'd researched the foster care system, asked foster parents about children with development issues. We knew how hard it was for these kids to develop healthy relationships. They go into the foster care system under tragic circumstances; and it's not fair to think everything's rosy once they've been introduced to their new family. We had nothing but the utmost respect for foster families and foster children. Had Michael not come around, the circumstances leading up to the reasons we wanted him as part of our home, maybe we would have chosen to be a foster family."

"Why did you choose adoption?"

"We'd had a miscarriage not long before. It felt like God's plan, the way it came together. He needed our love and affection. It seemed like Michael's problems probably began mere minutes after his birth, and never ceased to let up. His mother died giving birth to him. His dad had drug problems and was in and out of jail about as often as Michael had needed a diaper change. Michael entered foster care at two years old, and when he was three his father died. Michael's file was just disheartening. He was malnourished, showed physical signs of abuse, was not potty trained, and displayed frequent fits of rage. He didn't know how to take hugs and kisses, because he never received them in his first few years of life. He was raised without love, without the most blessed emotion in the human experience. But I was so sure that love, and a wonderful soul, were somewhere deep down in that poor little boy. And I was convinced God had called me to find it."

"Was he aggressive at all?" Lynn said. Michael had never shown any kind of aggression to her.

"You could tell something bad was coming by just looking in his eyes. It was, well, an evil look. It's like he became a different child. Then he'd get hysterical. Screaming, punching. He acted out at the daycare the foster care system put him in. The director had to call his foster parents to come and remove him six times in a two-month period. He was probably within a week of being kicked out. He was also dangerous in a car. I was driving him to a therapy session one time, and he unbuckled his carseat and started whaling on the windows, kicking and screaming. I had to stop the car multiple times to try to calm him down. Usually the only warning you got was that look he had. He needed a lot of attention. His growth socially was stunted. There was the possibility that he would never develop into what you or I deem 'normal.' He was, frankly, a nightmare of a child at that point, and it took therapy and constant supervision for a long time before we considered him safe to himself and our family."

Lynn thought of the way Michael held Addy; how he had whispered a prayer to his daughter during those first moments in the hospital. She had mistaken his tears for fear of being a father, but maybe it was all for joy. The joy of giving his daughter a gift his natural parents had not been able to give him—a childhood. It was the same kind of relief they gave children at the foster care retreat: a time to be kids, a shelter from the ravaged circumstances that locked them into the foster care system. Michael's life, his purpose, to that point had been about creating a refuge he had never had as a child.

"You changed his life," Lynn said to Betty.

"We did what God called us to do," Betty said.

"I can't imagine anything more important," Lynn said.

Chapter 20

For the first time in his tenure with the *News*, Wes raced to Starks's door. Michael's story had taken on a life of its own. It wasn't just about medals and football games anymore. His adoption helped connect the dots but raised even more questions, and Wes was running out of time. How had he missed it? It made Michael's connection to the foster care retreat solid and understandable. Wes had just never thought to ask.

Michael's adoption provided another twist. Perhaps enough to mend the growing rift between Wes and his *News* bosses. Michael's story was too important to gloss over. Wes needed to fill Starks in on the details and then regroup at a computer and write down all of his discoveries. As Wes opened the door to his office, Starks actually smiled. He gestured toward the chair.

"As of nine this morning, I was going to fire you," Starks said before Wes had a chance to sit. He said it with unconcealed joy.

Wes's mind raced to catch up in defense.

"Look, I'm really sorry about not answering yesterday," he said. "Totally forgot to put the phone back on ring tone after meeting with Shackleford."

Starks, his shirt pressed neatly today, clean-shaven, and clearly ready for a fight, slapped his right hand on a stack of paper. "Not that," he said.

"So you really want to write me up then."

"We've passed that. Take a look, Watkins."

Reading upside down from across the desk, Wes could see a familiar looking masthead: *Back Words*.

The blog. The pages were printouts from Wes's blog. He delicately thumbed through his own words as his face flushed and his heart beat wildly. He tried to calm himself, come up with a valid defense, but visions of a faltered career—just one year into it—flashed before his eyes.

"Is this yours?" questioned Starks, playing the obvious card. Starks wasn't getting to the bottom of something, he was slicing up another young reporter.

Although he was basically caught red-handed, Wes wasn't willing to give the man the benefit of a full confession. "I've read it," he said.

Starks fumbled. "You've *read* it?" he repeated. "Well, Watkins, so have I. Interesting parallels between this blogger's world and ours, don't you think?"

Wes didn't answer.

"Aren't you going to ask me how I found out about this?"

"Found out about . . . ?" Wes was not about to cave in now. He had to play it out, keep his options open.

"Funny thing happened this morning," Starks said, as if Wes had told him to continue. "I was at the breakfast table, sipping my coffee and reading this morning's *News*. It was a clean edition of the *News*, by the way; not too many red marks to show the staff. I put it down, looked out the window and thought about how beautiful of a day it was going to be. Then Coach Lawler called."

Wes struggled to prevent his horror from reaching his face. He was quite sure he was failing.

"Imagine my surprise," he continued, "when I answer the phone and on the other end is an irate Coach Lawler. Now we go way back, Coach Lawler and I. At the very least, I want us to be fair to him and his team, especially with the Calhoun game coming up. But Coach Lawler starts screaming about making a fuss to the publisher, who happens to be a big supporter of Talking Creek football, but more importantly, isn't cutting paychecks to writers who cross the line."

He thumbed through the stack of *Back Words* blogs and picked one from near the bottom. He read the words that Wes had written about Michael's Medal of Honor.

"None of that says anything about a 'Coach Lawler,'" Wes pointed out with only a slight tremor in his voice. "So what is he upset about?"

"Scott told him about a blog written by one of his colleagues about Talking Creek football," he said. Wes about wrenched the armrest off the chair.

"I see," Wes said, "and what made Scott do that?"

He already knew the answer. Big Bird was probably fumbling his way through an interview with Lawler when the coach pulled out his standard line for new guys: "The other guy sure was a heck of a lot better than you." He'd tried that trick on Wes a couple of times, but it had just rolled off his back. Friedman, though, would've considered it an attack on his credibility. So he'd offered the blog to save his hide.

"Wanting to be fair and balanced with a source," Starks said. "Unlike some of the reporters we have around here."

"You said you were 'going to' fire me around nine . . ."

"Correct," Starks said, "and I still might. You have violated just about every code of conduct at this newspaper by creating what amounts to your own opinion column and insulting the people you interview. Had I known about this earlier, you would have been gone. But after I did some research on this site, I called Lynn Gavin, and informed her of your breach of conduct. She was insistent, however, that you be retained to complete this job. She said it was Michael's explicit last wish that you, and only you, do his eulogy."

Wes wondered why Lynn hadn't told him about her conversation with Starks when he had stopped by, but then remembered the scene following the lunchtime prayer. Lynn had more important things to deal with than this.

"You've put me and the *News* in a real sticky situation," Starks barked. "Coach Lawler has no doubt told plenty of influential people in the community that we have a two-faced reporter on our staff. That could have a negative effect on our ad revenues and make it tough for us to go about our business—which, as I *thought* you knew, relies on a level of trust between reporters and the reading public. Your little 'side column' could end up

hurting a lot of people, Watkins. Not the least of which is my own reputation and the reputation of the *News*. We are at the forefront of honoring
perhaps the city's most respected citizen, and now we've got a controversy
in our own ranks. If I have to do an interview with the city paper or TV
station on this blog, you're going to wish you hadn't ever set foot in Talking Creek."

Wes sank in his chair, head spinning, wishing that Starks's rant was
over.

"Michael Gavin may have wanted you to do his eulogy, but as long as
you're on my payroll, you're going to do it the *News'* way, you got that?"

The *News'* way. What did the *News'* way have to do with Michael's final
wish? Starks seemed happy with his discipline. What he didn't notice was
Wes's hand reaching inside his bag next to the chair.

"So you better spill everything you have so far," Starks rambled on, "and
I'm going to tell you exactly how your article, and your speech, are going
to go, or you're finished here the second you walk out of that funeral."

Wes spilled the beans. How Michael had failed as a college quarterback. Starks wanted to let that one slide. Wes's theory on Michael's reluctance to accept the Medal of Honor. Starks told him to ignore that idea
altogether; that it was just a theory. Starks liked the stories Coach Lawler
and the Nooners had told, and Shackleford's report of the climactic battle.

"That'll be great stuff," he said. "People will want to hear that."

And then Wes hit him with the big stuff, feeling the rush that a scoop
always provided. "There are two big pieces to his story that haven't been
told yet. Michael got into a car accident in high school. He did some community service for it, and we've got an article that has him in the picture. Not only that, but the Gavins told me today that Michael had been
adopted. Can you believe that? I've got some calls to make," Wes said. "I
feel like I'm really close to something."

Wes was practically falling out of his chair, ready to race to the phones
to fill in the missing pieces.

"Too personal," Starks said. "I wouldn't mention any of what you just
told me."

"What?" Wes said, losing his cool. "This *is* the story. An adopted child turns his life around and starts a foster care retreat? An apparent alcohol problem leads him to help his best friend later in life?"

"No," Starks said. "Michael Gavin was a war hero and a fine football player and everyone said so. That's what's going in the Sunday paper. Anything else would be too confusing and hurtful—a funeral is not the place for it, nor is the local paper. You've already trashed and belittled Talking Creek residents on your blog. I'm not going to allow you to make a mockery of Michael Gavin in front of my town."

"It's not a mockery; it's what he wanted," Wes said.

"I think I've made myself clear on what I want for the eulogy and the paper."

"Yeah, a lie," Wes said. Their eyes locked. "Just like what you wrote about Michael after his collapse at the charity run."

"What are you—"

"You know exactly what I'm talking about," Wes said. "The man collapsed at a cancer event, but the unsigned article says that he finished it to the adulation of the crowd. Just like you now want a hero's ending to his eulogy and the big ad bucks for the special section. I just gave you Michael's story, and you tossed it aside, and you're sitting here accusing me of making a mockery of him?"

"You better realize who you're talking to," Starks said, his right hand crunching the handle of his coffee mug. "I can take out this pink slip and—"

"Fire me for not lying?" Wes said. He stood up from his seat and pulled the recorder from his bag. "Go ahead and do it, and I guarantee you you'll be talking to those city reporters about something tomorrow."

Chapter 21

The blog comments section wasn't pretty. Wes shut and locked the door to his one-room apartment, then turned his computer on to see the carnage apparently taking place on *Back Words*. Carnage indeed. He'd never needed to censor the comments box, but today it was filled with all sorts of unpleasantries. Wes scanned the posts while gritting his teeth. The tally was up to 125, a record by a hundred or more. After making one pass through, he locked the comments section and began a final response.

Back Words

For the next few days, Back Words will be on hiatus. There are loose ends to tie up on the investigation previously noted here. Judging from recent comments, the word is out on who I am and what I'm doing, so you can now get your information from the pages of my newspaper. Suffice to say, I'd rather not make any more comments to give my editors more to worry about. Thank you for your understanding.

Wes surveyed the names on Michael's list, about two dozen, and only a handful of which he'd talked to. Time was not on his side. It would have been nice to space interviews out over the week, but he'd squandered his margin with his early research tactics. Wes had the afternoon, and that was it. He hooked his digital recorder to his computer and uploaded Starks's comments. He clicked an open folder for the upcoming rounds of interviews.

With so many people still to call, background research was out. He opted for a standard list of questions to ask, just like a survey, and then he'd work into details as the conversations progressed. Some of the questions were generic, some were unorthodox. He'd almost missed Michael's adoption, and would have never thought to ask, so he scribbled a few questions regarding Michael's medal and childhood that might catch or fall short.

Five of the people on the list he'd already interviewed in person—Lynn, Paul, Wayne, Shackleford, and Coach Lawler. Two of the remaining names were familiar. One he'd known since college, and the other Lynn had disclosed after revealing Michael's adoption. He'd start, and end, with those.

★　★　★

"Wally, how are ya?"

Legendary Georgia coach Earl Bishop's throaty, Southern voice echoed from the other end of the line. Among his many accomplishments—an overall record of 207–82, four conference championships, and two national titles in twenty-plus years of coaching—Bishop also claimed a superior memory. Once he met someone, he said, he would store and remember their name forever. Wes had interviewed him three times for the student paper. Each time, the coach had called him by a different name. Today made four.

"Hey, Coach, thanks for taking my call," Wes said, ignoring the name reference. He caught the coach up to speed on why he was calling.

"A terrible thing," Bishop said. "I'll be there for the funeral, you know."

"Really?" Wes said, somewhat surprised.

"Of course, Wally," Bishop said. "I've tried to make it to as many weddings, graduations, and unfortunately, funerals, as happen in my former players' lives. Michael was a special man, a great team player. And I was happy to see his mission outside of football grow."

"I wanted to talk to you about that," Wes said. "His wife, Lynn, said that you helped fund the opening of the foster care retreat."

Bishop grunted. Wes thought he was probably rubbing his famous bald top like he had on the sidelines for all those years. "That's nothing special. Sold a few stocks and the Gavins made it grow. I help my players when I can. It's hurt my pocketbook occasionally, but then it's also led to having a huge stake in the largest BBQ chain in Georgia, a nice real estate development in Augusta, and all the used cars you'd want in Tifton. I always want to know what's going on with my boys. It's like one big family at Georgia. I can't tell you how proud I am when one of our players goes out into the real world and makes a name for himself. Outside of football, that is. Michael was one of the biggest, what with what he did in·the war, and his retreat up there in Talking Creek. His service there was an easy decision to support."

"So I suppose there weren't any hard feelings from his college days?"

Wes expected some ice to form in the interview, but was surprised to hear one of Bishop's signature bellowed laughs.

"Son, if me benching Michael as a quarterback only to see him shine as a blocker turned out to be my worst mistake, I'd be a lucky man."

"But you've no doubt heard the grumblings from Talking Creek?"

"I hear 'em from every corner of the state," he said. "I did a call-in show, win or lose, for twenty years, and got an earful from just about everybody on everything. I was blamed once for rain coming on Thanksgiving weekend because I chose all red jerseys and that was bad luck, can you believe that?"

"Do you still keep up with Brock Sellers then?"

"Relentless, aren't you?" he said in an amused tone. "Fine, got a pen and paper handy?"

"Yes."

"Then write this down. Michael Gavin was one of the best, most gifted quarterbacks I ever recruited to play at Georgia. He redshirted, and then was edged out by a senior his first year on the field. He got injured the next year, and Sellers took over."

"So Sellers comes in, but Michael was originally the starter?"

"Michael played decent during our season opener," Bishop said. "We used a pretty basic offense, didn't want to show anything to South Carolina the next week. Michael racked up some big numbers that game. Next week, I called a scramble right to roll him out of the pocket. He made the pass, but a linebacker got him, twisted his knee the wrong way. Sellers took over, and didn't do anything to lose the job."

"How did Michael deal with the injury?"

"About as bad as a player can." Bishop let those words sink in. "At least at first. In fact, he came into my office at one point and requested a transfer after he lost out in spring practice on the starting job."

"Really?"

"Got no reason to lie to ya," Bishop said. "My days of buttering up recruits and donors is over, son. Told him to think about it. Now, I was prepared for his transfer. You have to be ready for the worst if you're a coach. I pretty much expected it that next morning.

"But I'll tell you what struck me about Michael." Bishop had Wes's full attention. "There aren't many players at his age to come in and admit he's not *the man*. Now, you can take that a number of different ways. You can look at this kid and say, 'Well, he's a quitter.' He admitted he lost. But I saw something different. I saw a twenty-year-old young man who was willing to give it his all and lose, and know that he failed."

Wes downloaded Bishop's comments to his computer via the digital recorder, then divided the pages in a spiral notebook into categories, guesses on the subjects of the calls. One was for Michael's childhood. Another his football days. Then Army/National Guard, then his business, and then personal. He'd funnel each interview into the notebook and compare conversations later.

It's funny the things people remember, Wes thought as he worked through the interviews. A random conversation to one person can mean the world to another. Each story has multiple parts, at least two angles. Michael must have realized this, even better than Wes had. Michael must have thought long and hard about these names as his body and life faded. It was an honest appraisal. The good mixed in with the bad.

Michael did plenty of good, but he also hurt people. Did that make him evil? No, Wes thought, as he listened to stories of high school pranks or misdealings with foster parents at the retreat, or a wounded soldier's family talking about their ordeal. What might be classified as a mishap or misunderstanding by one person is called a travesty by someone else. Michael had those stories. That's why Wes couldn't fathom talking at the funeral about how wonderful and perfect he was, no matter how much people might want to hear it. Michael had hurt people; some directly, some indirectly. He was flawed. Even in his greatest moments, someone close to him was almost always hurt. Two names on the list were of women who had lost a son and a husband respectively in Iraq. They were killed during the incident that led to Michael's Medal of Honor. Shackleford had gone into detail about Michael's actions that day and his recovery afterward. Wes imagined Michael sitting in a hospital, replaying the horrific battle and his actions. Michael's body healed long before his soul did—if it ever did. Michael had made the promise to his men that he would bring them all back, and he had, just not all with a heartbeat.

The two women's emotions were opposite. Wes didn't blame either for feeling the way they did. Michael must not have either.

The mother of the son killed was gracious in her remarks.

"He took good care of my boy," she said. "You tell those people that he took care of my boy, and I don't fault him one bit for what happened. My son died serving his country."

The widow, on the other hand, had only cold words to offer. Just the name Michael Gavin thickened her throat and sent her on a wave of emotion. She said Michael had written her multiple letters while recovering from his wounds, and had visited her, begging for her forgiveness.

"How could he ask that of me?" she said. "I couldn't. I still can't. He took my husband away from me."

The conversations were leading Wes in all sorts of directions.

Wes found himself wanting to get into Michael's head. He wanted to know his motivations, his dreams, what his priorities were. He seemed like a man worth following. So why bother with this? Was he not happy with his life? And why bother with Wes?

Four of the names on the list had either a disconnected number or the call went straight to voicemail. Wes left messages, but suspected their answers wouldn't stray far from what he'd already gathered. He had talked to Michael's wife and college coach; four high school classmates, including Wayne, Coach Lawler, and an ex-girlfriend; two families of soldiers killed in Iraq; four soldiers who had served under Gavin, including Shackleford, a former soldier currently living in South Carolina, another soldier who had excelled, and one who had been dishonorably discharged; two foster parents, who had opposite experiences with the Gavin ranch; and one man who had attended a group called Celebrate Recovery with Michael and Wayne. There was no hidden truth in the interviews; just stories and relationships.

★   ★   ★

One name did not have a phone number to call, which Wes needed to ask Lynn about. So that just left Sally Gibbons, a social worker from Columbus who, according to Lynn, had helped the Gavins adopt Michael.

"Mrs. Gibbons?" Wes said.

"Yes," a soft motherly voice came over the line.

"Mrs. Gibbons, hello, my name is Wes Watkins. I'm writing an article for the *North Georgia News* about Michael Gavin. He passed away this week." Wes paused. "I'm writing a story about him, sort of, and I'm also going to be doing his eulogy."

"Did you know him?"

"No ma'am," Wes admitted. "I've been interviewing people who did."

"Oh, I see," she said. "It was such a long time ago, and as you probably know he ended up a lot different from the little boy we brought into care. But I remember his case. I couldn't forget it, or what the Gavins did."

"I understand," Wes said. "I talked with Betty and Lynn Gavin about his situation."

"I'd been on the job for about six months as a case worker when he . . . it happened," she said.

"You mean his father's death?"

"Yes," she said. "Michael was already in foster care but his father's death accelerated a lot of things. First we tried to see if any of his family would take custody. But neither his mother's or father's side wanted him. You'd be surprised how many children end up in foster care because an aunt, uncle, or grandparent won't take them in. And why are we surprised when they have attachment issues? Betty and Paul were very involved right from the start. They got all of the necessary training and paperwork done, and were very straightforward that they wanted Michael, and Michael alone."

"So they had monitored the foster care program and came upon Michael's case?"

There was a long pause over the phone. "You mean you don't know?"

"Don't know what?" Wes said.

"Betty and Paul weren't strangers to Michael. That's what made this all so amazing."

Chapter 22

Tributary University stood on a rolling hill overlooking Talking Creek. There were five main gates into the university, most just streets with a decorative iron arch and the word *Tributary* written on top. All the older buildings were on or near the crest of the hill, and all were built with red brick. The liberal arts buildings dominated the campus, with the English, history, and foreign language buildings in the center. Behind these buildings were the science, communications, and education buildings. On the opposite side of the hill were the student center and newly refurnished dormitories—two for the men and two for the women. Lying at the base of the hill on that side were also the soccer fields, a baseball stadium, and tennis courts. A hundred yards south, the terrain dropped off considerably down into the Etowah River, which acted as a border between Tributary U and the rural mountain farmlands surrounding the university.

Tributary's campus roads were a trademark. There was absolutely no pavement on campus. The roads and the sidewalks were all brick. A former chancellor insisted on keeping the design when automobile transportation became popular. Brick roads were the perfect antidote to fast drivers. They forced cars to a crawl, and as a result kept the pace of life on campus just where the founders had intended. Wes parked in one of the dorm lots and walked across the street to Reynolds Hall, the history building, named after some old professor from when the university was still a women's school. Next to Reynolds Hall was a small daycare house for the professors and staff of Tributary. That's where Paul and Betty had said Lynn would be.

The grounds crew at Tributary did a fabulous job. In the spring, the gardens gushed with tulips, roses, and other assorted flowers. The flower beds were always lined with a fresh batch of pine straw, the lawns smelled freshly cut half of the week. Tree limbs and leaves rarely lay on the ground anywhere on campus for more than an hour, but this week even the Herculean efforts of the lawn crew couldn't keep up with the autumn rush. The leaves had turned bright reds and yellows last week, and now they were barraging the brick streets. The wind used the invasion for a symphony of rustling throughout the campus.

★   ★   ★

Wes could have walked outside all day, breathing the fresh air and pontificating as if he were an academic fellow. There was something about open spaces and nature that made him take a step back and think. He went on campus at least once every other week with an iPod or a book just as a breather from the nitty-gritty of the real world. He imagined that was what had brought Lynn outside.

He was wrong. It was the playground.

A handful of children fluttered to and fro between the swing sets and jungle gyms. Wes recognized one of the kids as Addy. Lynn was seated on a bench, a coffee mug weighting a stack of papers by her side. She was reading a paper and tapping her mouth with a pen. When she spotted Wes, she waved him over. He sat down at a respectful distance on the bench as they watched Addy float about from a swing to a rocking horse, trying to decide which to ride.

"So am I officially a stalker?" Wes offered lightheartedly.

Lynn smiled. The broken woman from earlier had recovered, albeit slightly. "Michael sure did love his runs. I guess he's using you to do his running this week. And we're here because we needed fresh air. This was one of our favorite places to go. If it was a weekday, Michael would go observe one of his dad's lectures, while Addy and I played here. Sometimes Michael would jump in too. The swings were their favorites,

Addy and him. He'd push her swing so high she'd scream in terror, and delight."

"What are those?" Wes asked, pointing at the papers.

"Admissions forms," she said. "I took the GRE this summer. Michael insisted I do it to keep my mind off his cancer. Well, I passed. I'd always thought of being a school social worker or counselor, but never went back to school to get my master's. Now, I think I want to do this. I don't know if it's right, and I'm sure some people will think I'm letting Michael down if I choose this instead of the foster care retreat. But that was a two-person job. I'm a single mom now."

There was a pause. Lynn clutched the papers, almost needfully, crumpling the edges as her palms shook slightly. Her lower lip quivered. Today was a rough day for the Gavins all around. She didn't look at Wes, though. She was waiting for him to speak.

Instead, Wes set two things on the bench—his notebook and recorder.

"I came here because I might owe you an apology," he said.

"You don't owe me anything," she said.

"Well, here's the deal. I know that you know about my blog—Mr. Gavin and you and your whole family; and yeah, there's a breach in journalistic integrity, sort of. Beat writers use blogs all the time; it's just that it'll be another decade before someone at the *News* even considers the idea. But, in hindsight, maybe I shouldn't have posted my reports about Michael until afterward."

"Wes . . ."

He didn't break from the lines he'd rehearsed on the car ride over. "So there's the blog, which I partly feel guilty about, but in a way, I don't. I'm wrong in the sense that my employer thinks it's a violation, without ever having instituted a rule against it. Now he's got a rule, and I haven't violated it. I looked at my recent entries, and . . . perhaps . . . I crossed the line, but really, it was never about you and your family. Just the perceptions going on around here—and I thought this assignment was for me to set the record straight. Maybe it's not an apology I need to give you, but a handshake, for talking with Starks. You saved my job."

Lynn smiled weakly, as Addy chose the swing, and began a weak push by pedaling her legs when they hit the sand beneath her.

"I don't know about that," she said. "I'd like to think I saved Starks from making a fool of himself. It's not the first time he's taken a local story by the throat and refused to let go. Paul told me there was a professor here a while back that, in the middle of a semester, decided he wanted to retire, for medical reasons. This was at a time when the majority of the faculty was rather lukewarm to the university president, and the president was getting feelers from a bigger university in the Midwest, apparently. Starks and the paper surmised that the professor was ousted, because he had been one of the more vocal opponents of the administration, so they pursued that story. They didn't let the facts get in the way. They coined it as a battle between a professor and a president who had his foot out the door. Except that wasn't what was really happening, according to Paul. The professor, who was in his seventies, was having health issues and realized halfway through the semester he couldn't continue. He had hoped to retire quietly, and everything had been worked out. Then the *News* comes crashing through the doors. The president was pretty thick skinned and let the stories, and editorials, and more stories slide. It was the professor who nearly took a torch to the *News*. It wasn't until he threatened a lawsuit that the *News* backed down."

"That's odd that he pursued a story," Wes said. "I'm coming to the realization that Starks likes suppressing them too. Like the charity walk at the beginning of this past summer."

Lynn nodded.

"We had more serious things to worry about than a back-page sports article after the race," she said. "You know, Starks isn't a bad man. He wants what's best for his community. Just like everyone else, though, our intentions often get in the way of common sense."

"You may disagree after you hear this," Wes said. He pressed the play button on the recorder and let Lynn listen to his argument with Starks.

"He's got you in quite a pickle," Lynn said, "and now you've got him in one too."

"I could get him fired, or at the very least, make him the laughingstock of the Georgia Press Association."

"You could."

"He'd deserve it."

Lynn tapped the notebook. "Did you want to tell me something about this?"

"Oh," Wes said. "Yeah . . . I guess this is where my apology might need to come from."

He flipped open the pages, and let her see the notes next to each name.

"I cold-called all of these people this afternoon. The remaining folks . . . I wish I had done it earlier. I would have, if only you would have told me why I should have called them."

Lynn traced her finger on the page, her late husband's handwriting, scrolling down to the bottom, where it stopped on one particular name. "You talked to her?"

"Yes."

"Good," was all she said.

"Why didn't you tell me all about Michael's adoption earlier? Or this woman?"

"Well, for starters, you didn't ask," she said. "What would you have done differently in your reporting if you had known Michael had been adopted from the start?"

Wes shrugged. "I wouldn't have wasted my time with football stories."

"But those are part of it as well. Michael did lay it all out for you," she said. "He gave you that list. Access to just about every person you would want to talk to for the eulogy. Access to both the good and bad. You didn't trust the list though, the people, and that's understandable. He was a stranger to you, after all, and the circumstances dictated caution. What did you initially think when you received his letter and package?"

"That Michael had some deep, dark demons in the closet and wanted to reveal them through me."

"It never crossed your mind that perhaps there was another message besides that in these 'secrets'?"

"I didn't know what I would find. I didn't think it would be . . ."

"Complicated?" Lynn said, smiling.

"Yeah."

"It isn't. You could have done your interviews in one of two ways. Thinking the worst about people, or the best. I understand that part of your training is to leave no stone unturned, and that usually means uncovering things that people don't want you to see. So that leads to skepticism. I think Michael understood that about you. He also knew that if you really did your research, you'd get to the bottom of everything, and perhaps, seeing the good with the bad, come to a different conclusion than Michael being some kind of fraud, or not the hero everyone makes him out to be. Actually, I'm quite encouraged by the reporting you did. There was one theme that he thought ran through his life, and you are very close to discovering it."

"And that is?" Wes asked. He was tired of playing this carrot-and-stick game.

Lynn didn't answer, at least not directly. "Michael wanted you to know something. He wanted an objective eulogy, and he wanted one other thing. Wes, it may be that I'm the one that owes you an apology, not the other way around." Her tone sounded regretful.

"Michael didn't choose you because you were a stranger. He knew who you were—and not just from the paper. He picked up on your blog a few months after you joined the *News* staff."

"So *everybody* knows about my blog?"

"As of a few weeks ago, no. Michael liked his Internet reading. A handful of members of his unit in Iraq started their own blogs, which got him interested in the blogosphere. When he returned from Iraq, he stumbled upon yours. Well, I wouldn't say stumbled. Someone else had tipped him off to it. This was about the same time he was diagnosed with cancer, I think. He was a big news junkie. He read the *News* every day. It didn't take him long to figure out who the author was."

"Oh," was all Wes could say.

"Once he pieced together who you were, he enjoyed the blog even more.

He liked your anecdotes about Lawler, said they were right on the money, and he pitied you for suffering in your working environment. Lawler is an earful off the field—as a teenager and now as a football coach. I read your blog too, you know, and I kind of liked it. Kind of."

"So he chose me because of the blog? He wanted his eulogy done by a guy who hates this place?"

Lynn shook her head. "No. The blog was just a small part. Michael wanted you to go through all of those names and dig into his life because it might offer you a fresh perspective into your own. The real reason he chose you was because of a family connection. He knew your father, Wes."

"No."

She nodded.

"This is all about my deadbeat biological father? I haven't spoken to him since high school."

Lynn didn't say anything. She let Wes work himself into a frenzy. He tried to keep his voice down, to not disturb the playing kids and their parents, but he was off balance now and grasping for equilibrium.

"You've got to be kidding. This is some kind of joke, right? What does my dad have to do with a eulogy? He doesn't even live here."

"So you know where he lives?"

"Atlanta," Wes said. His stomach clenched. "I'm guessing he knows about the blog because I told my grandmother about it. My mistake. He writes me letters every once in a while. I don't open them—I either trash them or throw them in a drawer, but I don't want to talk to him, and I don't want anybody telling me they think I should, so your husband conjured up this whole idea for nothing."

Lynn took a deep breath. "Talking to your dad is your own choice," she said. "And whether you resent me or Michael now because of the eulogy is also your choice; but do you at least want to know how Michael and your dad met, where this all came from?"

"Might as well," Wes said, as much as he now wished the whole story would just go away.

"When I'm finished, you'll have another choice to make. You can take your notebook and recorder home with you, but you'll only be able to use one for the eulogy. Best or worst, that's the choice. Reveal the truth and take the heat, or exact revenge on Starks. It's free will, Wes, and I hope you'll use yours responsibly."

Chapter 23

The weeds made a late push.

Sprouting from the backyard garden leading away from the porch were a few intrepid stalks and some straggly crabgrass. Their erratic locations in the garden were evidence that they were stunned to be taking root in an area that for years had been off-limits. Michael had spent hours in the yard, picking up sticks, pulling weeds, mowing the lawn, and raking leaves in the fall. He loved the outdoors and the work involved in making the yard beautiful. When his waning strength meant that he could no longer hold a shovel, much less cut the grass, Lynn didn't have the heart to hire a lawn service yet, but she'd need to soon.

Financially, Lynn and Addy would be fine. As a military family most of their lives, the Gavins were familiar with insurance policies, and Michael's life insurance check would mean that Lynn wouldn't have to work for a long time if she didn't want to. That fact didn't provide her much comfort, though. She refused to make plans without Michael as a part of her life, despite her husband's pleas that she look ahead with some foresight. When the time came, she'd have a heart-to-heart with God on her purpose; just not now.

Michael sat on the back porch in a rocking chair, a blanket covering him from the shoulders down despite the warm September air. Autumn was knocking. Lynn still had a hard time dealing with the fact that this would probably be his last fall.

"Do you see the tall pine tree at the edge of the lawn?" Michael said, pointing to the far right corner of the yard. Lynn nodded. "The one hit by lightning a few weeks back? It's got to be one of the strongest trees on our property. That sucker coughs up more pine cones than a cat does hairballs. I'd kick 'em back into the wooded area and think I was good to go, and then it would spew out another half dozen when I mowed around there. Its branches stick out at just the right height and angle to be a constant pain in the butt for yard work. All the other trees do as they're supposed to and dump their debris in the woods. I would have cut it down years ago if it weren't the biggest tree on the property. Couldn't do that to the strongest of the strong, you know?

"When the lightning strike sheared off part of the trunk, the side you can't see from here, I thought about going out there and putting it out of its misery, except I can't even lift a chainsaw anymore without passing out from exhaustion. Probably a good thing. I've been thinking a lot about that tree lately. I like having it out here. That tree and I have a lot in common."

Lynn took stock of her husband. His complexion was winter pale, not the warm bronze he typically wore from hours in the outdoors. His hair had grown back from the chemo, but in a slightly different tone, matching the landscape the autumn leaves would paint in a few weeks. The biggest red flag, though, was his posture. The Army had drilled slouching and slumping out of him years ago. Today, however, he sagged.

"I wonder if I'll outlast that tree."

"Michael," Lynn said softly. "Please."

"I need to say this," he said, breathing deeply before letting out an anguished sigh. "It comes to us all, you know? It's just a matter of how— fast or slow. That attack in Iraq, one of my soldiers in the Humvee with me died instantly. Another had a chest wound that might have been treated in time had we taken out that building full of insurgents quicker."

"You did what you could do."

"I know," Michael said. "What I was going to say is, out of all of that hell, I did see one man die the way he wanted. I shot him. He was the last insurgent in the building I cleared. Top floor. Probably the guy whose

RPG started the whole ambush. If anyone needed a bullet in the head, it was him. All the other ones, I don't remember the action of firing. I can remember taking them out, but it was automatic; I wasn't conscious of squeezing the trigger. Even the big, bad terrorist we bagged. They probably gave me the medal for eliminating him, but he was nothing. Misfired his weapon, blew a hole in his foot, and I just finished him off. The last insurgent, though, I knew he was the last, and you could tell he'd been waiting a long time for a moment like that."

Lynn cringed. She knew the dangers Michael had faced, but hearing it in detail, no wife wanted that. The emotional wound was deep for Michael, though, and his time was short. He needed to purge himself of whatever was still in him.

"He masked his face, but there was something in his eyes. Evil. Like revenge had consumed his body and soul and all he wanted at that moment was to exact it on me. He had me. Perfect firing position and the perfect angle. He drilled me in the right shoulder. Had it been the left, I probably wouldn't have been able to get my pistol around, but he hit my right side. Had he shot me again as I hit the floor, I would have been dead. But I think he was so into the experience that he freaked out. His gun fired into the ceiling, and I hit him three times in the chest and one in his firing shoulder. He wouldn't be lifting his weapon again.

"We sat there with our wounds. I was ready to finish him off if he so much as twitched. They carried grenades everywhere. Made it some afterlife salute to leave a surprise on their dead bodies when we searched them for weapons. He wouldn't be doing that with me. I was losing blood, but I knew he'd die first. He'd know that I killed him. His mask was off now, so I could see his facial expressions. And you know what? He was happy. He had this sadistic expression, like he had won, despite the four bullet holes in his body, because he had shot me in the shoulder. This was the type of death he wanted, so he died happy. And how many of us die happy, on our own terms, like that? So I watched him attain his pleasing death. When my men stormed through the doors a minute later, I was furious at myself. I was mad I had given him what he wanted. I couldn't shake that thought after the war. I had nightmares, seeing his smirk. An 'honorable' death fighting the American devil, or whatever it is they called us. It wasn't until recently that I did a one-eighty on that day."

"By thinking of the tree?"

"No, that's later," he said. "I was throwing up, actually. Great time for an epiphany, on the floor in the bathroom reeling from chemo. That's when they come though, right? No dramatic music in the background, no panoramic sunrise, just a porcelain tube holding last night's Jell-O. I puked myself silly and I thought about Mr. Insurgent and how happy he was and how unfair my plight was. Then I stopped. Not the throwing up, but the self-defeating wallow. I zeroed in on his eyes from my memory, and right there on the floor, I actually started to feel sorry for him. I mean, how pathetic is it to live a life for that? To live for one shot at one soldier and that's it? We were over there fighting for ideals, for people, and he's fighting for himself and for one pitiful moment when a stranger comes in and lights him up. I wondered about his family and friends, and how selfish it was of him to choose to die like that. He could have been building a school or watching the neighborhood kids. But he chose to ambush American soldiers. That was his big accomplishment. What a loser. And it got me to thinking . . . I can't be like him. I don't want to choose how I go out. That's part of the dance, right? But I can choose what I'm thinking about, what's important. Me and that tree didn't ask to get lit up by lightning, or cancer, but that's how it is. That's how we'll go. Fine. But I'm not going like the insurgent. I'm not going to be thumping my chest about what I did when I could be praising God for what he did with me despite myself."

Lynn and Michael were silent for a few minutes. Michael needed to collect his strength after talking for so long. Lynn was at a loss for words. The wind whipped the leaves in the nearby woods, even on the dying pine. A couple of pine cones rustled below its branches.

"Lynn, I want to change something at my funeral. I want a stranger to give my eulogy."

Startled, Lynn leaned in and studied the sincerity of Michael's eyes. Then she studied their lucidity. "Michael, why would you want that?"

"There's a reporter at the *News* that I've been reading up on, and I think he's a good fit for the job. He'd give the best eulogy."

"A reporter? Why? I'm not following you on this."

Michael covered his mouth in anticipation of a coughing spell. He waited for the urge to subside. "I know this kid's father. Wayne and I met him at a recovery seminar in Atlanta. He's shaky, but real remorseful. I think he needs grace, Lynn; grace more than anything. Both of them, actually. I need a way to make my life mean something, one more time; maybe this will lead the two together."

"How? That's a tall order. Are you going to reunite them?"

He shook his head. "They'll have to do it on their own. It probably won't even happen, but who knows? I just think that, with what happened to me, maybe it'll resonate with this reporter, make him think about his life differently."

"So why don't you just go tell him now?" Lynn said.

"Because I want him to have never met me before giving my eulogy. Clean slate. I want honesty. Reporters go for facts, right? He would look at things critically, he wouldn't gloss over details. I think this is how I want it."

"Okay," Lynn offered, trying to follow Michael's errant direction. "Why would you want someone to be critical in your eulogy?"

"Because I don't want lies," he said.

"No one is going to lie when they say things about you."

"No, but they will sugarcoat it."

"That's how funerals go. We remember the best in people."

"But what if we can find the greatest value in the worst that they went through? I want it all to be out there. One or two friends may be extremely helpful in painting a portrait, but they cannot be the only source of record if you want to be accurate. We all know that people lie, scheme, digress, and wash over the messy parts of their lives. That's where relationships come in. Do you think you can have an accurate portrayal of someone by just interviewing their family and friends?"

"I see where you're going with this," Lynn said. "But your eulogy isn't some magazine article or scoop for a newspaper. This is what people do; this is how they honor the people they love."

"I know," Michael said. "But I can't have it that way with mine. I'm not trying to hurt anyone. I just keep picturing what it's going to be like, and it makes me sick. Even sicker than I already am. I don't want people, whether it's you, or some guy that knew me in the Army, standing up and shouting hallelujahs in my name. I wasn't perfect. Life isn't perfect, and a funeral shouldn't hide that fact."

"So you want us to go up there and talk about all the bad things you did?"

"No."

"Then why are you doing this?"

Michael sighed. "Here it is: I have a theory. I think our lives reflect in the people who are around us; but they, or I, can't see it, because we don't have a mirror for that. I affect you, but I can't see it. And vice versa. Well, if my life, if it meant something, then I think it will reflect to a total stranger. It may even, God willing, change the course of someone's life when they face a similar situation. If what I thought was important was truly important, someone should be able to see that, even if it's not spelled out, even if it's just a whisper or blurry or whatever. Even if they're not looking for it at first."

Chapter 24

One name remained on the list. JeMarcus Wynn. No phone number. No e-mail address. No home address. Wes had mentioned this to Lynn before he left her and Addy at the university, and she had said to stop by her place on Friday morning, with clothes he wouldn't mind getting dirty. He arrived at 10:00 a.m. and parked along the fence, because the driveway was crammed.

After Lynn had explained Michael's connection with his father, Wes went home to collect himself. He was a mess. His job was on the line. He could have already been fired by Starks and not known it, because he wasn't answering his messages. He was an emotional wreck, which was a first. The past connected to the future. He couldn't get through the eulogy without thinking of his family, and his father. This assignment was personal. He couldn't give his thoughts about Michael and his life without making a decision on his own. Wes didn't know if he hated Michael for that, or if it was something else. He just wanted the weight off his shoulders.

Wes shifted one strap of a day pack onto his right shoulder. He'd brought his notes, his father's letters, the recorder with Starks's ridiculous demands, and Michael's list. He didn't know which of those he'd use today. He didn't know what to think about this final interview. He didn't even know the subject or his relation to Michael.

Lynn was beside the children's cabin, flapping the dust off a mat. Some of the kids for the foster retreat showed up early, she had warned, so Wes had better arrive before lunchtime. There were already a dozen volunteers, judging by the cars and synchronized T-shirts on the property, doing various chores to get ready for the influx. Wes wondered if any of them was Wynn. A handful of kids had already arrived too.

Lynn dusted her hands off when she saw him and they shook hands. "I'd like you to meet somebody."

He followed Lynn into one of the cabins, where Lynn introduced a group of men and women—but none was JeMarcus Wynn.

"These folks are from an adoption agency in Atlanta," she said. "I worked with Annie here at the county for a few years. They're looking into helping out with the place. I got a call from them last night."

"I've read your blog, Wes," Annie said, winking. "Cute."

"So people in Atlanta know about it?"

"Oh yes," Annie said. "You're quite a hit at our office. In a roundabout way it led to a half dozen folks volunteering for the weekend. We'll supervise here on Saturday. We wouldn't have gotten nearly the response if you hadn't allowed me to tell all the silly gossip about this town. So thanks!"

Wes smiled weakly.

"JeMarcus is over by the pond," Lynn said as she disappeared into a closet. When she returned, she held a paddle and two life vests. "You'll need these."

"Okay . . ."

Lynn walked with Wes over to the pond and introduced him to JeMarcus, a ten-year-old boy pacing the shore of the pond. "Where he been, Mrs. Gavin?"

"I told him to get here before noon, JeMarcus," she said.

JeMarcus eyeballed Wes in an unapproving evaluation. He pointed to the paddle. "Bring that with you," he said. "We got us some work to do."

The work involved shoving off the shoreline and paddling to the middle of the one-acre pond so JeMarcus could cast his miniature fishing reel.

"So, how do you know Michael?" Wes asked.

JeMarcus wasn't much for small talk. "He took me out fishing all the time," he said. "And he didn't mess with me while I was doing it, so you best try and be like him."

Wes made a lip-zipping gesture and leaned back in his seat. JeMarcus spent the next half hour casting and spinning, catching nothing, his eyes intent on the water beneath the canoe.

"Got us a big fish in here we gotta catch," he said. "All the little fish already caught. The dumb ones, too; they get caught quick. Mr. Gavin always talked about this one big fish in here that it would take a pro to catch. I've been fishing this pond for a long while now, and I'm gonna catch it."

Another half hour later, still nothing. Volunteers rounding the shore-line waved occasionally as they sat and watched the fishing line soak in the water. Wes sheepishly waved back. JeMarcus sat still, a scowl on his face, trying to will the line to jerk.

All of a sudden he said, "Okay, this isn't working, and I'm hungry. Let's go." They paddled to shore and broke for a lunch of peanut butter and jelly sandwiches. JeMarcus was playing around, but Wes decided to fire off some questions anyway.

"Why'd Michael want you to talk to me?" Wes said. "He had you on a list I was given, did you know that?"

JeMarcus bit off a large chunk of his sandwich and chewed. "He said you'd ask me a lot of questions if you showed up."

"If?"

"He said it wasn't a for-sure thing. You might bail, not get here, what-ever. Might not be smart enough to ask everybody Mr. Gavin wanted you to talk to."

"I see," Wes said. "So do you think you know why he wanted me to ask *you* questions?"

"Looking for something, aren't you?" He grinned mischievously.

"Sure," Wes said. "Lots of things. But what are you supposed to tell me? Like, what was the reason behind going fishing?"

"No reason," he said. "I'm ten years old, for crying out loud. You think they let me just paddle out there on my own?"

"Okay, so you just wanted me to paddle," Wes said.

He rolled his eyes. "Man, you're gonna annoy the heck out of me if you keep this up. Okay, here it is—we're looking for a bookmark," he said. "But we gotta search for it. I don't remember where it went."

"What kind of bookmark are we talking about here?"

"*Michael's* bookmark," he said.

Wes continued peppering him with questions. None of the Gavin-related questions landed. JeMarcus was more than happy to talk about his life, though. His biological parents lost custody of him and five other siblings five years ago. He saw them occasionally, but was adopted by a single dad who worked construction in Ellijay.

"That gazebo thing you see near the pond, that's him," he said. "He makes all kinds of stuff; you see it everywhere in our town. I've only got one thing from my real dad, though."

He pulled out a silver watch, fiddled with it before tossing it to Wes. It was one of those fake watches made to look fancy that sold for twenty bucks at the mall.

"Why did your dad give you that?"

"'Cause he felt bad, I guess," he said. "Gave it to me the last visit before the social workers said he and my mom didn't do what they needed to do to keep us. So he stopped trying."

"I'm sorry," Wes said. "I know what it's like for a dad to stop trying."

Wes pulled out the letters. "My real dad sent these to me."

"Like a few days ago?"

"Recently."

"Sounds like he's trying to me, man."

"I guess," Wes said. He put them back in his backpack.

"You write him back?"

"No. He didn't do the things he needed to do either."

"Well, I still see my dad and write to him. Michael always said forgiving's the best medicine out there, so I figured I should forgive him. You forgive your dad?"

Wes looked down. "Hadn't even thought about it, to be honest."

JeMarcus frowned. "Well, we've got work to do. I think I know where the bookmark may be."

He took Wes on the trail that looped around the property. They walked it twice. JeMarcus stopped every fifty yards or so, tapping a tree with his palm, looking under a rock.

"We used to race on this trail; might have left it under a rock or something."

He was obviously leading Wes on. JeMarcus overplayed his hand, talking to himself as much as to Wes as they looked for the mysterious bookmark. He must know where the 'bookmark' was, but enjoyed his power trip over an adult. They circled the pond twice, went around the trail twice, dug through a sandbox once, played a game of Horse in basketball. JeMarcus said the letters helped him remember better.

Wes played along. He had no choice, and frankly, he was starting to enjoy himself, despite his deadline-driven, pushy journalist instincts. JeMarcus and his land of make-believe kept Wes from sulking in a coffee shop, worrying about his imminent demise behind the pulpit on Saturday morning. It helped to loosen his muscles, clear his head, and smile. JeMarcus would lead him to whatever he was supposed to soon. He had a ten-year-old's attention span, so Wes wasn't worried.

Eventually, they made their way to the steps of the gazebo to sit in the shade. JeMarcus wiped his brow in mock exhaustion, and poked a hole in a juice box he had grabbed from the refrigerator. Wes did likewise with his grape juice. They sipped.

"I think I know where it is," JeMarcus said, frowning.

"Oh?"

"Yep. Gotta be in the house. Probably in the study, if you ask me."

"Well, I'm asking."

"Yep, gonna be the study."

Five minutes later, after crawling under the porch for no apparent reason, they entered the study. Wes watched JeMarcus's eyes, which immediately went to the desk, before he caught himself and pretended to be interested in the bookshelf. Wes followed his quest to the encyclopedias, as he opened up the A's. He thumbed through the A's, then picked up the B's. Meanwhile, Wes sat in the chair beside the desk, feigning nonchalance, as JeMarcus continued the act.

"Why don't I look in the desk?" Wes said.

JeMarcus pondered whether to give up or try and keep his routine going. He shrugged. "Sure."

Wes opened the bottom drawer. Inside were a few papers, and Michael's Bible, a bookmark's ends splaying out the side. Wes treaded lightly. He had entered Michael's house, his family, his work and personal life, but this was different. Michael hadn't struck Wes as a particularly religious person. Clearly he was a Christian. He just hadn't led him anywhere near a church building. The investigation ended here, however, as Wes opened the pages and saw what he had been looking for.

"Well?" JeMarcus said, tapping his foot. "What are you gonna do now?"

"That's a good question," Wes said.

Chapter 25

Cymbals crashed. Drumrolls echoed off buildings. Trumpets spilled into nearby neighborhoods. It was a fall Friday in the South, and the Talking Creek Screaming Eagle Band marched in unison toward the stadium.

Whatever grievances Wes harbored about football coaches, managing editors, and small-town trivialities, they all went out the window on Friday nights. There was something about the aroma of the concession stand, the buzz of the crowd, the energy of the teams warming up out on the field, that brought everything into a fresh focus. He enjoyed being the storyteller, the guy everyone read the morning after a game. That was why he'd signed up for this gig. He didn't mind the stage; he just wanted it bigger.

By now, most of the town had heard about the blog. Although he locked out the comments section, he checked the site before coming to the game and it was still getting a tremendous number of hits. Luckily, very few people could match the face to the byline, and the ones who knew Wes personally were up in the press box, the last place he'd be tonight.

The crowd for the Talking Creek–Calhoun game was huge—much bigger than usual—because of the rivalry with Calhoun and for Michael's tribute. Wes spotted the town's mayor escorting a number of men around, one of whom he recognized as the governor, who was waving to the crowd of potential voters. Sitting in the stands were military types, men with close-cropped hair and solid bodies, none of whom were slouching or making fools of themselves, which was completely opposite to the hundreds of teenagers milling around the track, who used football games as a social event.

Wes walked halfway around the track, dodging teenage couples holding hands and parents running after seven-year-olds in Talking Creek jerseys. He waited with Scott Friedman outside the fieldhouse. Wes didn't use the opportunity to scold Big Bird for leaking the blog to Coach Lawler and starting the firestorm. Wes had done the writing, after all. This was on him.

They heard Coach Lawler, just inside the doors to the fieldhouse, waxing poetic with a string of clichés, slapping shoulder pads, convincing his kids it was them against the world in the biggest home game of the year. The echoes were charged with enough emotion to stir a little fight in Wes. Tonight, just about everyone in Talking Creek wanted to suit up for Coach Lawler.

"He's pretty upset with you," Scott said.

"Ya think?"

"Just saying. Might want to skip interviewing him tonight, if you were thinking about it. Although it would have been nice to get a little help on this assignment. Lewis has me doing the game story *and* a sidebar."

"We all do game stories and sidebars on Friday nights, Scott," he said. "I'm not interviewing anyone."

"Figures," Scott said, snorting. "You realize this isn't my beat."

"It is tonight," Lewis Banner said. He had snuck up behind them. Scott's neck retreated slightly into the collar of his polo shirt. "Where ya been, Wes?"

"Looking for a story," Wes said. "Am I still on the payroll?"

"Are you kidding?" Lewis said. "You've single-handedly doubled the paper's Web site traffic—for the *year*, with a link Starks put up to your blog. Have you even checked your page today?"

"No. Comments are off but I'm probably getting lots of e-mails. Haven't checked my inbox."

"And I'm guessing you didn't answer those critics, either. Once you finish this eulogy business, you really are going to have to start answering your phone again. An opinions editor would kill for the kind of running commentary you created. But no, long answer short, Starks ain't pulling the plug on you. He said one of the Gavin family already asked for you to continue and okayed the blog. He said that was the last conversation he had with you. Was pretty short about it, like he was leaving something out."

So, Lewis had managed to cool the newsroom. Even after Wes had blown up at him, he had managed to temper Starks and settle everyone else down. He probably even got into Starks's head to make him think it was his idea to link to the blog.

Wes opened his mouth to form an apology, but was saved by the football team. The Eagle captains blasted the doors open, and the team spilled out of the fieldhouse. Once the stampede reached the turf, the assistant coaches trotted out, followed by Coach Lawler. His ball cap was low, but not low enough to hide his fiery eyes. He looked angry at the world, hands to his hips, begging for a fight. He found a worthwhile opponent when he spotted Wes.

"You got a lot of nerve," he said, shaking his finger. He marched toward the three newspapermen. "I always knew your coverage was shoddy, Watkins, but then you go and talk behind everyone's back instead of just reporting the news. You talked about the wrong people on the wrong week, boy. If it weren't for the Gavins saving your hide, I'da run you out of town myself."

"You're right," Wes said. "I owe you an apology."

Coach Lawler's scowl turned into puzzlement. He had been prepared for an argument, not an apology.

"What did you say?"

Wes sighed. "You're right, Coach. I shouldn't have said those things."

"Well I—" he said, then paused. His scowl returned. "That's the second time you've surprised me today, Watkins. I've got a football game to win, and you're just wasting my time."

He stormed off to supervise the pregame warm-ups.

"The second time?" Lewis asked.

"I called him earlier, but I didn't apologize," Wes said. "I think that speech was for everyone else to hear."

"You called him about what?"

"About naming the stadium. He needed to know a few things about Michael and Lynn before he did that, and no one was going to tell him. So I did."

Lewis frowned. "We need to work on our editor–reporter communication thing."

Wes smiled. "Yeah. I need to work on a lot of things. Including a eulogy."

Scott scratched his neck and looked at his watch. "Well, guys, I'm gonna head to the press box before they give my seat away. I need to get started on that sidebar so I'm not juggling a double deadline later."

That left Lewis and Wes alone at the fence line next to the football field.

"You've made quite a mess," Lewis said.

"Thanks for covering for me," Wes said. "This whole deal has kinda gotten out of hand."

"Just a typical Friday night in small-town America," Lewis mused.

Wes looked at him and almost laughed. Here was a guy whom, not that long ago—beginning of the week, in fact—he'd actually looked down upon. Wes had thought that Lewis didn't have the stomach to be a big city editor or reporter. Yet, Wes was the moron journalist who had injected himself into a story, a cardinal media sin. He was beginning to think that Lewis knew more about telling a story than he'd ever understand. When Wes called someone for a story, he'd get the quote, the facts, or confirm the source; but once the light on the recorder went off, so would his connection with the source. He had created a wall—he thought he was just being professional—but it didn't need to be there. Lewis, on the other hand, was a guy who would sit down to dinner at a person's house, play with their kids, and offer words of comfort to them as they held each other in grief. He would have contributed to the Gavins this week, whereas Wes had only looked for a way to take advantage of the situation. Sometimes rules and distance were good, but strangely, Wes didn't want that anymore. At least not this weekend.

"Do you know what you're going to say tomorrow?" Lewis asked.

Wes looked him squarely in the eye. "I think I do, yeah."

"Well, good luck. I'll look forward to hearing you," Lewis said. "I'm going to catch the first quarter in the press box, to settle Scott down, and then hightail it back to the newsroom."

They shook hands, and Lewis trotted off. Around the track, kids chased each other and tossed mini footballs the cheerleaders had thrown out to the fans. Wes walked halfway around and found the Gavins inside the fence near the Talking Creek sidelines. Paul, Betty, Lynn, and Addy were busy hugging friends and well-wishers. No one was guarding the entrance, so Wes let himself onto the field, and motioned to Lynn during a reprieve. Addy broke off from her mother's grip and darted toward him. She was wearing a blue outfit to match school colors.

"Hello, Mr. Watkins, I've got my game outfit on," she said.

"I can see that. You look stunning," Wes said. Addy beamed from cheek to cheek.

"So did JeMarcus wear you out?" Lynn asked, stepping away from her in-laws to greet Wes.

Wes smiled. "You have no idea. He completely immersed himself in whatever he did. Pretty impressive."

"Boys are not impressive," Addy said.

"Well, thanks for hanging out with him," Lynn said. "He and Michael were two peas in a pod for almost six months, until Michael got sick. It means more than you know for JeMarcus to have a big brother, even for a day."

Wes nodded. "There's something I wanted to talk to you about. When we were in the study rummaging around the bookshelves, I found something. Well, not in the bookshelves. I have to confess, I opened a desk drawer and found Michael's Bible. And I found this."

Wes dug into his pocket, and displayed a small white sheet. He unwrapped a corner, enough for Lynn—but no one else—to see what it was.

"Michael's Medal of Honor," she said, putting a hand to her mouth. He put it in her hands.

"Way to go, JeMarcus!" Addy shouted.

Lynn and Wes looked at her, puzzled. "Addy, did you know about this?" Lynn asked.

"Mmm-hmm," she said. "Daddy used to read to us all the time. He put his medal in the Bible for places he wanted to read later on."

"So why didn't you tell me when we were looking for it?"

"Daddy wanted me and JeMarcus to keep it a secret," she said. "He said it was JeMarcus's job to help Mr. Watkins find it, and I had to be a good secret keeper."

"Well, you certainly did a good job of that," Lynn said. "So would you have told me if Mr. Watkins hadn't found it?"

Addy shrugged.

"I guess it's fitting I found it when I did," Wes said, confounded at how even a six-year-old could put one over on him. "I'm done with my so-called investigation. Just wanted you to have that."

Wes was about to walk away, but Lynn touched his shoulder.

"You should have it, for the eulogy," she said.

Wes took it back with the greatest of care, unsure of what to say.

"I'll give it back then, after the eulogy."

Lynn nodded. There were tears in her eyes, but they weren't from grief. It looked more like relief.

A man with a microphone approached the family. "Thank you, Wes," she said, then turned and walked to midfield with Paul and Betty, holding Addy's hand.

The announcer asked for a moment of silence, and the capacity crowd hushed itself. Even the Calhoun contingent was quiet. This was bigger than a game, bigger than a town. And certainly bigger than one reporter.

A woman from the stands stood up and shouted.

"We love you, Gavin family!" She was joined by the people in the stands and on the track, who set down their bags of popcorn and cups of hot chocolate and clapped, cheered, and shouted words of encouragement. What

Wes might have mistaken for hokey or sappy a week ago, he didn't mistake tonight. It was love. This town loved the Gavin family. Wes felt very small for how he had regarded these people. He was the smallest fish in this pond.

The Calhoun contingent was on their feet now, as well. The bright lights of the television cameras centered on the Gavins. Three helicopters from the Atlanta stations were parked outside the stadium—underscoring the importance of the game. Only a top matchup *and* a newsworthy tribute would merit fly-ins from the big city anchor crews. This was the most important venue of the night.

Wes thought about how all the reporters and anchors would want the access he had to the Gavins and this story, and just how badly he had botched everything. Would anyone even listen to him, or was he already a parlor joke?

Coach Lawler was beside the family now, microphone in hand.

"We lost one of our own this week," he began. "But it's more than that. Michael Gavin was bigger than a high school, or a town, or a state. He was a national hero. What he did in Iraq won't soon be forgotten, and what he did for the kids in our community will live on for a long, long time, as well. We'd like for his name to live on, so we're doing two things tonight: one, we're naming the field Gavin Field at Grady Stadium." The crowd erupted in cheers, and the coach paused for a moment to allow the applause to die down.

"Second . . . now this is just the beginning, but you know Michael and Lynn worked real hard on that retreat. A little birdy told me this afternoon not to forget about that retreat and how important donations are to it when we're out here paying our respects. They'll need our support to keep on coming. So, a portion of the proceeds of tonight's concessions and admissions is going to the foster care retreat. And I'm chipping in myself, folks, so I expect y'all to pony up. Ain't nothing more important than how we raise our kids, now is there?"

The crowd cheered again as Coach Lawler handed the microphone to Lynn. She waited for the noise to die down, and then spoke in a clear, strong voice.

"Thank you, everyone, for all you've done. Your love and support has gotten us through some rough days lately, and it will lift us up in the rough days that are still ahead. The contributions you make to the foster care retreat would have meant so much to Michael, so thank you. All of those proceeds will go toward running the facility. I'd like to say at this time, though, that I will be stepping down from running the foster care retreat."

The response from the crowd was muffled confusion. Lynn held up a hand.

"I'm donating the land to an Atlanta agency that will find someone to run it full-time. There will be more children coming, and I will still have a supporting role, but it's become clear to me in the past few weeks that God is calling me to other things. My work with Michael will live on, but it will live on in other, capable hands. Thank you for your prayers and support."

The crowd didn't react at first—no one knew whether it was appropriate to applaud or not. Questions were whispered throughout the stands. Was giving up on the retreat the right thing to do? What would Lynn do now? Why wasn't she continuing Michael's mission? Finally, a smattering of applause rippled through the stands as Lynn handed the microphone to the president of the booster club.

Wes sensed the apprehension, the whispers swirling around the Gavins as they walked off the field. He met them at the field gate and opened it for them. For reasons unclear to him, he wrapped his arm around Lynn's shoulder and gave it a squeeze.

At first, Lynn looked up in surprise, but when she saw it was Wes, she smiled lightly and patted his arm.

"That was a brave thing you did," Wes said. "It takes a lot of guts to stand up in front of that many people and tell them something they may not want to hear."

Lynn surprised Wes by offering a smirk. "Well, I was just warming them up," she said. "You're next."

Chapter 26

Funerals are often draped in black. Michael Gavin's funeral was awash with red, white, blue, and yellow. Yellow ribbons lined fences, mailboxes, shop entrances, and town lights. And almost as many American flags were on display. Businesses were closed and peewee soccer games were canceled. No one complained.

The church parking lot was full. Cars parked on side streets and in driveways. The chapel seated only about two hundred, not nearly enough for the number attending. The pews were reserved for Michael's family, close friends, assorted teammates from high school and college, church members, and a large group of soldiers in dress blues. Wes saw those he had interviewed: Coach Lawler, Bruce Foster, and Par Stoddard; Earl Bishop, Wayne Griffin, and Rod Shackleford. A few pews were saved for dignitaries—a handful of generals, a U.S. senator, two congressmen, numerous Georgia legislators, and the governor.

The media, comprising four news vans and a dozen newspaper and magazine reporters, camped either at the front steps of the church, giving a respectful distance to the mourners, or inside the Talking Creek High School auditorium, where a few thousand had come to pay their respects. A broadcast team had assisted in equipping the church with a video camera for a live feed to the auditorium crowd.

Outside the church, a crowd of onlookers stood across the street and prayed. Wes sat in the front row with the Gavins, feeling wholly unworthy of being the voice for this tribute.

Keith Starks, in his best suit and black tie, pulled Wes aside before the funeral. His hand was soft on Wes's shoulder, partly because he may have thought Wes still had the recorder; partly because he may have wanted to avoid a scene; and partly because the controversy Wes had stirred had actually been good for business. The discovery of the blog had spiked newsstand sales around town the last few days, along with Web traffic. It made whatever Wes said today and whatever he wrote for tomorrow pure circulation gold. Still, Starks couldn't pass up one last chance to try to dictate the course of the story.

"I think you realize the magnitude of your speech," he said.

Wes nodded.

"Good." Starks patted Wes on the back. "Then I know you'll say the right things. It's been a hard assignment, Wes; nobody understands that more than I do. We'll go over specifics on what you can write for the Sunday edition this afternoon. We'll go for a burger or something afterward, okay?"

Wes nodded again, even though he knew that'd never happen. Starks had never taken a staff member out to a meal that Wes knew of—and he sure wouldn't be the first.

At 11:00 a.m., the church bells rang, and the pastor walked to the pulpit and opened his Bible. Michael had given no formal instructions for his funeral, aside from designating Wes to give the eulogy, so Lynn had composed a suitable ceremony. The pastor recited a few verses, and the audience sang two hymns. Wes's heart pumped rapidly during those hymns. He took short breaths, opened and closed his fists, did anything to keep his mind off the speech.

But all bad things must come to a beginning. As the final hymn ended, Wes looked over at Lynn. He admired her. She had steadied herself from two days ago, when he had seen her collapse on the floor in tears; that was obvious from how she had handled herself at the football game. With a stadium's worth of eyeballs on her, she had accepted their well wishes and exuded a strength that Wes didn't think she could physically possess at that point.

Maybe it wasn't physical at all.

Wes didn't consider her resolve today to be a front—and he wouldn't later, after he heard how she had spent her time before and after the funeral. In the morning, she had sat on her daughter's bed as Addy primped and fussed about what to wear. She had asked Addy to sit beside her as she explained what the day was about. She told Addy that Michael was no longer in pain, and that he wasn't on a trip. He was with Jesus and wouldn't be coming back. Addy had simply nodded and said, "Okay, Mommy." She'd never known someone who didn't show up the next day. Lynn told Wes later that she was sure the pain would come, just not in those moments, and she'd have to explain things to Addy all over again. But she'd done it before, and she could do it again.

Wes sensed a greater calling for Lynn today. She was in this church, the same church in which she'd been married, to complete the final chapter of her marriage with Michael; and though she hadn't picked the ending, it was how it would be done nonetheless, and she had accepted it. She had accepted Wes. She returned his gaze, smiled, offered a nod of encouragement.

The congregation was seated and Wes rose to make his way to the platform. He brought his bag, full of notes and a few surprises, to the pulpit. He hadn't composed a speech, per se. He had notes for what he could say, and what he wanted to say. He knew that the next several minutes would be some of the most important in his life. They held bearing as to his job status—and, more importantly, to his conscience. Even as he faced the community of Talking Creek, he still hadn't decided which consideration carried the greater weight.

He placed his notes on the wooden pulpit and adjusted the microphone to his level. He cleared his throat, took a deep breath, and looked out into the crowd. "Hello, I'm Wes Watkins," he began.

He gripped the pulpit to counter a wave of nausea. He'd eaten properly before he came, so he knew it wasn't on account of his diabetes. Standing in the pulpit of a church, he felt more than a little sacrilegious: an unholy man in a holy place leading a holy ritual.

"For those of you who don't know me, I'm a reporter for the *North Georgia News*. But based on my actions this past week, I'm guessing there's probably only one or two of you who hasn't heard my name."

Wes noticed a slight smile on Paul Gavin's face. He spotted Wayne Griffin, seated in the fourth or fifth row, and the former receiver and current EMT gave him a slight nod of acknowledgment.

"The only place I can think of to start my thoughts on Michael Gavin is where it began for me. I'd like to read for you the letter Michael wrote to me." Wes pulled out the letter and read it aloud, then set it on the pulpit.

"Most of you are probably thinking I'm the last person who should be up here, and I agree. Michael Gavin deserves better, frankly. He deserves a better eulogy than I can give. He deserves a better speaker. He deserves a better send-off, but this is what he wanted.

"Before Monday, I knew nothing of Michael. I'd never talked to him or been in the same room with him. That probably shows you how connected I am with this town. As a reporter, I covered my beat and that was it. I didn't feel as if I needed to know anyone outside the beat, so I didn't. In hindsight, that was a mistake, and I guess it took this assignment to steer me toward that conclusion.

"But I know you're not here to listen to my story. I'm supposed to talk about Michael Gavin, and I will. You heard what he wrote in his letter to me. He also gave me a list of friends and acquaintances. I called every one of them and talked to most. I collected press clippings from the *News* and interviewed his inner and outer circle. My guess is that Michael in some way wanted an objective account of his life, and I'll try to provide that in a story format, as if I were writing this for the paper."

Wes presented the story. The safe version. The version they wanted to hear and probably expected. Interview by interview, he walked them through Michael's life. He listed Michael's high school football statistics and where they ranked in state lore. This went over well, of course. He retold Michael's Talking Creek legends and spotted an approving Coach Lawler, who perked up even more when Wes mentioned him a few times.

Surprisingly, Coach Lawler was the one that gave Wes hope. His team had defeated Calhoun 20–17 on a last-minute drive, the kind of storybook heroics that Michael had created years ago for his championship teams. Scott had even had the nerve to use "Calling the ghosts of Talking Creek football" in his lead for the game story.

Wes used the accumulated goodwill from reliving Michael's glory days for the next topic. Considering what Wes was holding back, what he'd tell them in the next few minutes wouldn't hurt. Maybe just sting.

"Michael graduated from Talking Creek and went on to play for the University of Georgia. By his senior year, he had moved from quarterback to fullback and became an all-conference player. Coach Earl Bishop considered Michael to be a key component to their conference championship his senior year.

"I'm aware of a rumor that Michael was not given a fair shot at quarterback and thus moved to fullback. I investigated this, and Coach Bishop was kind enough to provide me with some answers."

Coach Lawler shifted in his chair, and Wes swore he heard a gasp from the coach's side of the church when he told them that Michael had requested to transfer. They settled down when he read Bishop's remarks on Michael's adjustment.

"It is never easy for a superstar to yield his role to another player. This happens all the time, though, in college and the pros. People used to being the center of attention are no longer capable enough to hold that rank. It's not a sign of weakness, though I'm sure Michael struggled with it; his wife, Lynn, said as much. But those lessons probably prepared him better for what was to come than the same type of notoriety he had enjoyed in high school would have. I'm sure if Michael were here today he'd be the first to tell you that he was not the best quarterback on those college teams. Fullback though—maybe."

The crowd's mood lightened with the fullback remark. Wes transitioned into Michael's military career. He read off the names of all the units in which Michael had served, the awards and medals he'd won. He recited word for word his Medal of Honor citation, and mentioned Rod

Shackleford's admiration for his commanding officer. Wes painted clear blue skies and a rainbow for the town.

"The list that Michael provided was excruciatingly fair," Wes said. "There were just as many people who had a less-than-favorable opinion of him or his actions as there were people who loved him. With no direction as to which questions to ask, I don't know if I gleaned everything I was supposed to from those talks. I tried. And what I told you already is everything on Michael Gavin that I could write for tomorrow's paper."

He stopped and looked out over the assembled gathering. Then he collected his notes and stuffed them in his bag.

A gentle murmur rustled through the audience. People looked at one another with puzzled expressions, as if to say, "That's it?" Starks looked relieved. Coach Lawler grinned. Paul, Betty, and Lynn waited patiently.

Then Wes took a sip of water from a bottle underneath the pulpit, cleared his throat again, and continued. "What I'm about to say, you can consider off-the-record."

Starks looked at Wes with a mixture of horror and disbelief. Wes looked directly at him as he spoke. "What I am about to say was not approved by my editor. This eulogy draws a fine line between objectivity and opinions, but I've already crossed that threshold, as many of you know. I thought about stopping with only what I've already told you, but the last two days have convinced me that Michael wanted me to give his eulogy for another reason. This goes beyond my responsibilities as a news reporter. I feel that I owe it to Michael to tell you the *whole* story."

Wes paused to let the audience take a collective breath. If he'd offended Starks to the point of being fired, he figured he'd hear something from the man now. But Starks sat stone-faced, unmoving. It seemed the crowd would have the final say as to whether or not Wes would be fired.

"I'm going to rewind to Michael's high school football days. Before the second game of his senior season, Michael disappeared. Not just for the weekend, but for a couple of school days also. He returned at the last possible hour that he could have and still participate in that week's game. He returned with a bruised body . . . and a humbled heart. Everyone I talked to about that weekend said that he was changed somehow. He acted funny before the game, befriending a teammate who had been an outcast. I think their friendship is important to Michael's story overall, for a number of reasons, but I'll start with the weekend. You should know what happened to Michael. I think he wanted all of you to know. I'm going to tell you the story that his father told me."

★   ★   ★

The road was familiar. Paul had driven it so many times that his car tires had practically made their own ruts in the pavement. His passenger was familiar with it too. Michael was silent, encased in muted rage. Paul had seen the look before. Most teenage boys displayed some sort of rebellion at his age. Michael was an extreme example, because he had been in a quiet rebellion for years. His personality, and the experiences of his early childhood, made him a powder keg. Paul and Betty had hoped his success in high school, both athletically and socially, would quell his chances for an outburst, but there would be no quelling now.

Paul had many ways to play the scenario, to administer the needed discipline. Michael had crashed a car into a ditch. Thank God it was a fairly shallow ditch and not a tree or another car. But the fact that he had been intoxicated was the culmination of a long-held fear for Paul and Betty. They'd known that Michael's biological father had abused alcohol—had killed with it. They had sworn, when they adopted Michael, that they'd do anything in their power to prevent the trait being passed from father to son. That was why Paul didn't play the silent game with Michael now. This drive was too important.

"Do you know where we're going?" Paul asked.

"No."

"Michael, are you concerned at all about what you did? The severity of your driving drunk?"

"So punish me."

"This is a big deal, Michael. We've talked to you before about how important it is to make good decisions. What you did, you were taking your life, and possibly someone else's, into your hands."

"Like I said, punish me. That's all you do anyway."

"Is that what you want?"

"Since when have you cared about what I want? Rules and regulations . . . yes sir, Major Gavin! You've always had me on a short leash. So fine, I screwed up, whatever. Take away football like you've taken away everything else."

"We give you rules because we love you."

"Whatever."

"I should have done this earlier," Paul said, more to himself than to Michael. Michael didn't respond. "So, do you want to know where we're going?"

Again, no response.

"We're going to see your biological father, Michael."

Weeds covered the grave. As much love and care had been put into Derek's final resting place as he had put into his life. Paul had done his research on the man before adopting Michael. Derek's criminal record was lengthy, but mainly involved DUIs, drugs, and petty theft. Michael had been put in foster care because no other family member wanted him. The two aunts on his father's side were drug addicts, and the one uncle on his mother's side wanted no part of the boy's life. Only one grandparent was still alive, but he was in no condition, physically or mentally, to care for a child. It amazed Paul that a boy who had brought so much joy into his life had been rejected by so many.

Paul bent down and cleared the twigs and weeds covering Derek's name.

"How did you know where this was?" Michael said. He had said he would wait in the car, but then had followed behind Paul.

"I knew a lot about your father."

Michael huffed. "You knew what? That he was a drug dealer? Alcoholic? Deadbeat? So what? Does that make you feel better? Are you more of a man now that you took in his son? I bet you're only half the man and father he could have been."

The words seared, but weren't unexpected. Adopted children, especially those going through the foster care system, often hold their biological parents to a different standard. There was probably still a part of Michael that thought his dad could do no wrong, despite their horrible relationship and that he had been too young to remember or understand what type of man Derek was. Paul refused to respond in anger, although he had every right to be angry. Michael was like an injured animal, attacking anything near him in order to gain space, to escape. Paul would let him rant and rave and cuss all he wanted, but Michael would hear the truth, too.

"I brought you here so you could see what happens when we make bad decisions, horrible decisions; but I also brought you here to show you that you have the power to conquer them. That if something horrible happens to you, you may not have the ability to change it, but you can decide how you feel about it, how it affects you . . . and move on."

"Got it," Michael said. "'Don't do like Daddy did.' Don't want me to end up like him, huh? A trailer park trash nobody?"

"We've never been ashamed of you, Michael, or where you came from," Paul said. "We're very proud of the man you're becoming, and we don't want to see you go down the wrong path."

"Fine," Michael said. "Are we done?"

"No, we're not. There's something else you need to know."

Paul waited a moment before speaking again. He touched the tombstone delicately as he gathered his thoughts.

"Your father was driving thirty miles over the speed limit when he hit us," Paul said. "He passed out in the car. I could see him slumping in his seat, even from the other side of the road, before his vehicle swerved into the median. I tried to avoid him when he came over on the wrong side of the road, but I couldn't. It was too sudden, too fast. His vehicle hit us pretty much head-on. It knocked me out and broke a few of my ribs, and it hurt Betty pretty badly. Your father was dead at the scene.

"Betty was four months pregnant when it happened . . . and we lost the baby later that night."

★ ★ ★

Wes cleared his throat. "Betty and Paul Gavin adopted the only son of the man who killed their unborn child. There it is, right there. Ugly, unfathomably tragic events, and a response completely above what I thought human beings were capable of."

Wes paused, and soaked in the silence from the crowd. They were just as stunned as he had been when he'd heard the story. Sally Gibbons, the retired social worker from Columbus who had helped the Gavins adopt Michael after the accident was the one who had told him. Only then did Paul tell him his side of the story and fill in the details.

"I almost missed that story. You can certainly fault me for not being as in-depth as I might otherwise with all the interviews, because I didn't get to some of them until the last minute. The most important part of this man's life—of Michael Gavin's life—was right there, close to the surface. I went looking for medals and trophies and stats. Instead, I learned about friendships, sacrifice, and a strong marriage. I looked for heartaches and mistakes; but when I found them, I had to ask myself, 'Why was I looking for them?'

"I began my research hoping to find actions, headlines. They were there. Then I searched for a motive. What made Michael tick? Why did he put the people on the list that he did? If you put all those voices together, nothing synced. There was no overarching theme in the list of names— until I talked to Sally Gibbons. Then you could see Michael's intent. In everything he did, even the people I talked to who were hurt by him, there was a humbleness, an attempt to right what was wrong, even if he didn't have the power to do it—to bring back a son or husband from a war, to help a struggling child. And sure, he struggled with life—losing in competition, losing soldiers under his command, losing to cancer. But I don't think any of it would have clicked if I hadn't seen where it started. Lynn told me yesterday that Michael thought that what Paul and Betty had done would reflect in the lives of the people around him. He was right— and wrong. It did reflect; but for me, I had to have a starting point.

"There's a word for that starting point. I couldn't quite place it, but once the pieces started to fit, I had to know. I spent yesterday at Michael's house, walking the trails around the property and thumbing through books in his study. I had to know what the word was. I knew that it was the key to the reason why I'm up here; the reason why those medals and trophies and fame didn't faze Michael or define him. If you want to know the truth, I believe he was a great man, flaws and all. Actually, *because* of his flaws. We all have them. He wasn't afraid that they'd smudge what really defined him. Let me show you."

Wes reached into the bag, and pulled out Michael's Bible.

"I found this in the bottom drawer of Michael's desk in his study. Not visible for everybody to see once they entered the room, but easily accessible for Michael when he wanted to read it. Two days ago, I wouldn't have even thought to look inside. But a lot has happened since then. One page was bookmarked; a ribbon to one of his medals was peeking out of the Bible."

He showed it to the crowd and opened to the page.

"Ephesians 2:8–9. 'For it is by grace you have been saved, through faith—and this not from yourselves, it is the gift of God—not by works, so that no one can boast.'"

Then Wes showed them the bookmark. It was the Medal of Honor.

"In those words, I think Michael found the meaning of his life. He forgave himself for his wrongs and didn't measure himself by his deeds . . . but I think the most important word there is something he couldn't possibly earn or deserve. None of us can.

"It's *grace*. Michael wanted us to know that his life was defined by grace."

As Wes left the platform and returned to his seat in the front row, the church was silent. Not even the usual coughing and fidgeting noises you'd expect in a crowd that size. Wes expected the preacher to return to the pulpit, or for one of the Gavins to stand and offer some final words. But that had been Wes's responsibility. The two hundred people assembled in the church, hushed to their own thoughts, gave no visible or audible reaction to the eulogy.

Sometimes the greatest tribute one could pay was just to listen . . . and wait.

★ ★ ★

What happened next was something Wes would carry with him for a long time.

A man seated next to Shackleford, dressed in full military blues, rose from his seat. He was tall and broad, a poster cutout of a military man. His name was Bill Darby, and he had been the first soldier to rush into the room where Michael had killed his final enemy in Iraq. Darby had witnessed the haze in Michael's eyes, the first pangs of guilt over losing men in combat that had taken months—maybe even the rest of Michael's life—to work through.

Darby had been an Airborne trooper, just like Michael and Shackleford. After the Medal of Honor incident, he had been wounded by an IED during a routine patrol in the city. They'd shipped him to Germany to repair his body, but he, too, desperately wanted to be with his men. He wouldn't get that chance, at least not in Iraq. After a grueling rehabilitation, Darby had rejoined his unit for a homecoming parade in Canton, Georgia. He'd marched in the front of the column, with a limp, and with a new prosthetic leg.

As all eyes turned to look at him, Darby swelled his chest, and then began to sing in a wistful, gentle voice.

"Put on your boots, boots, boots and parachutes, chutes, chutes, we're going up, up, up and coming down, down, down . . ."

Then Shackleford stood and joined him. "We're All American and proud to be, for we're the soldiers of liberty . . ."

The military ensemble then joined the duo, those who weren't paratroopers instead singing the Army's anthem.

When the soldiers were done with their songs, a former Georgia football player rose and began to sing in a well-modulated tenor: "Mine eyes have seen the glory of the coming of the Lord; He is trampling out the vintage where the grapes of wrath are stored; He hath loosed the fateful lightning of His terrible swift sword; His truth is marching on."

Next, on the family side, one of the foster parents, Isabel, stood and began to sing "Amazing Grace." By the end of the first line, the rest of the congregation was on its feet and joining in.

Four songs. A life can't be defined by one song, but those songs—so different, yet each so perfectly appropriate—were a unifying symphony. As the congregation sang the final stanza, their voices grew louder and people throughout the sanctuary began hugging each other, shaking hands, and clapping shoulders.

Wes was among a handful of people who were not singing. It wasn't just that he didn't know the words to any of the songs—though that was true; but he was too shell-shocked by the events and overwhelmed with a new feeling.

Grace, he was coming to understand, does that.

Epilogue

On the one-year anniversary of Michael Gavin's funeral, Wes still had some regrets. He didn't, however, regret what he had said in the eulogy. He'd meant every word, and he still relished every word; it was as if what he'd said had released a lifetime of frustration. Paul Gavin had been right. There was something liberating about the truth. It wasn't safe, but it was freeing.

Despite the wounds he had inflicted on some of the people of Talking Creek during the week leading up to Michael's funeral, he found that they had truly forgiven him. It was as if they realized that his coming into contact with Michael, however indirectly, had changed him.

In the end, Starks had allowed him to write his thoughts about the eulogy, and the Sunday edition of the *News* had sold out in record time across North Georgia. But it had been Wes's final byline.

Starks had accepted his resignation, and though he had insisted it was reluctantly, Wes knew the truth. Too much had been said and done to repair the damage he had caused. At first, parting ways with the *News* was one of his regrets, but he soon came to realize it was the right decision. He couldn't afford to live on a small-town reporter's salary anyway. It had taken him a few months to find something new, but eventually he'd landed a job as a copy editor at a magazine in Atlanta, which turned out to be a better fit at a less stressful workplace.

The Gavins had been gracious with him after the funeral and thanked him for what he had said about Michael. When someone dies, people put their best face on and look for words and deep thoughts to explain the tragedy—as if it were an obstacle to overcome that, if conquered, would lead to a higher plateau. But that's wrong. With love comes loss, and Michael was much loved. So the Gavins grieved.

After Coach Lawler's speech at the football game, the community had chipped in enough money to keep the doors of the foster care retreat open for another six months. By then, Lynn had arranged to sell the property to the Atlanta-based agency that planned to turn the grounds into a full-time retreat for foster kids and families. Lynn and Addy moved into a townhome close to the Tributary campus, and Lynn found a teaching job at Talking Creek Elementary School.

If anyone in town should have held a grudge against Wes, it was Wayne Griffin, whom Wes had exposed as a recovering alcoholic when writing about his morning runs with Michael in the Sunday paper. But Wayne had used the revelation as an opportunity to start a recovery group at his church. The last time Wes had talked to Wayne, the group had grown to at least a dozen regulars.

Over the past twelve months, Wes had received several more letters from his father, but he hadn't seen him or talked to him. He had mustered the courage—once—to actually write back, but the experience made him realize he still needed more time to sort through his thoughts and feelings.

First, Wes had to grapple with the implications of grace. It wasn't exactly something he embraced with open arms. He had lived with his bitterness, anger, and grief for so long—had been fueled by it in many ways—that he wasn't certain he was ready to give it up, even though the more he studied about grace, the more he realized that his anger and resentment were empty and in vain.

Between the time of the funeral and when Wes moved back to Atlanta, he met Paul Gavin for coffee several times, and they had talked about the underlying cause of the changes in Michael's life. Wes had understood—and even agreed with—much of what Paul had said about God; but when he took the magazine job and moved to the city, he eventually lost contact with Paul.

The real issue, though, was that Wes understood that he would have to be willing to forgive before he could fully embrace God's forgiveness. His own sense of integrity and honesty demanded it. After all, he had often disdained professing Christians that he deemed to be self-righteous and hypocritical, and he didn't want to be like that himself. But he also realized that in order to move in the direction of wholeness and grace, he needed to address the pain in his life. And that meant coming to grips with his relationship with his father.

He could think of only one place to start.

The retreat center was quiet when he parked his car along the fence line and walked down the driveway toward the house. It was a Wednesday, and he had taken the day off from work. As he rounded the house and made his way toward Michael's stalwart pine tree, he paused at the corner of the back deck and selected a smooth, black stone from a pile on the ground.

When he reached the line of trees along the back edge of the property, he set the prayer rock at the base of the pine and looked up into its branches. It seemed like it was waiting for one more thing before it too departed this world. What he prayed for was complicated, but probably obvious. He prayed for forgiveness and for grace for what he was about to do.

His heart thumped in his chest, and he took a few deep breaths—but he knew it was the right thing. Grace had brought him this far, and grace was about to change everything. That's just what grace does.

Wes pulled out his cell phone and dialed the number he'd been given in a series of letters. It rang three times. Then he heard his father's voice for the first time in years.